WAYNE STINNETT

STEADY AS

SHE GOES

A JESSE MCDERMITT NOVEL

Caribbean Adventure Series
Volume 21

Copyright © 2021
Published by DOWN ISLAND PRESS, LLC, 2021
Beaufort, SC

Copyright © 2021 by Wayne Stinnett

Library of Congress cataloging-in-publication Data
    Stinnett, Wayne
    Steady As She Goes/Wayne Stinnett
    p. cm. - (A Jesse McDermitt novel)

ISBN: 978-1-7356231-1-5 (print)

Cover photograph by VaLife
Graphics by Aurora Publicity
Edited by Marsha Zinberg, The Write Touch
Final Proofreading by Donna Rich
Interior Design by Aurora Publicity

This is a work of fiction. Names, characters, and incidents are either the product of the
author's imagination or are used fictitiously. Any
resemblance to actual persons, living or dead, businesses, companies,
events, or locales is entirely coincidental. Many real people are used
fictitiously in this work, with their permission. Most of the locations
herein are also fictional or are used fictitiously. However, the author
takes great pains to depict the location and description of the many
well-known islands, locales, beaches, reefs, bars, and restaurants
throughout the Florida Keys and the Caribbean to the best of his ability.

If you'd like to receive my newsletter,
please sign up on my website.

WWW.WAYNESTINNETT.COM.

Once a month, I'll bring you insights into my private life and writing habits, with updates on what I'm working on, special deals I hear about, and new books by other authors that I'm reading.

The Charity Styles Caribbean Thriller Series

Merciless Charity

Ruthless Charity

Reckless Charity

Enduring Charity

Vigilant Charity

Lost Charity

The Jesse McDermitt Caribbean Adventure Series

Fallen Out

Fallen Palm

Fallen Hunter

Fallen Pride

Fallen Mangrove

Fallen King

Fallen Honor

Fallen Tide

Fallen Angel

Fallen Hero

Rising Storm

Rising Fury

Rising Force

Rising Charity

Rising Water

Rising Spirit

Rising Thunder

Rising Warrior

Rising Moon

Rising Tide

Steady As She Goes

All Ahead Full

THE GASPAR'S REVENGE SHIP'S STORE IS OPEN.

There, you can purchase all kinds of swag related to my books. You can find it at

WWW.GASPARS-REVENGE.COM

To the memory of Colonel Roy Shelton, who served our great nation from 1963 to 1993 as a Marine Corps officer. Colonel Shelton passed away suddenly on March 18, 2021, at the age of 79. It was also the day I began writing this novel.

He and I rode many missions together with Upstate South Carolina Patriot Guard Riders, honoring those service members and first responders who'd fallen before us. He was an easy man to talk to, always making other riders laugh with his sharp wit and sea stories. He always had a ready smile and words of advice or encouragement. He also was a quiet and kind man, and I'm certain he never told an untruth in his life.

The colonel was a big reason I started writing. In June of 2013, after a ride briefing, he and I were talking. The PGR is a hodge-podge mixture of civilian and veteran bikers. He and I were often the only two Marines in the group and Marines tend to gravitate toward one another. On that particular day, while talking about books we'd read, Roy told me I should write a novel.

He was a colonel. I was a corporal. The oaths we each swore decades earlier had no expiration date. Part of the oath I swore said, "I will obey the orders of the President of the United States and the orders of the officers appointed over me...."

So, I told him, "Aye aye, sir," and started writing my first novel the next day.

The colonel never ordered me to stop. Thanks for the kick in the pants, sir. Semper Fi, Brother!

"The highest form of evidence in English Common Law is the sworn word of a person of good repute. This tenet is also the basis of our legal system. In other words, just as one is considered innocent until proven guilty beyond a reasonable doubt, one is considered to be telling the truth, unless it can be proven otherwise, beyond a reasonable doubt."

—Colonel Roy H. Shelton, USMC (Retired)

MAPS

Jesse's island in the Content Keys

The Caribbean coast of South America

CHAPTER ONE

Friday, August 6, 2021

Osmin Mejia stood in the open doorway of his home. Behind him, on the other side of the dirt road, the Essequibo River flowed lazily past, oblivious to all but its steady march to the sea.

He and his oldest son had just returned from a night of fishing, having caught several hundred kilograms of shrimp—one of their best nights in months.

They'd met with a ship at dawn to deliver their catch. They did this to avoid the heavy taxes that were levied if the catch were brought to shore and sold at the docks in Parika or nearby Georgetown.

His house wasn't much; just three rooms and a roof, but Osmin had built it himself on land that had been left to him by his father. Land that would one day belong to his sons.

The door to the small house was hanging on one hinge. The room inside was in complete disarray. What little furniture there was had been overturned or pushed around in an obvious struggle.

His wife, two daughters, and youngest son weren't there to greet him.

"Dis is bad bad," muttered Augusto behind him.

In Guyana Creole, or Guyanese, as the locals would call it, there is no word for "very," and adjectives and adverbs are often repeated for emphasis.

Guyana was a poor poor country made infamous in 1978 by Jim Jones and his cult, the Peoples Temple Agricultural Project, when they all committed mass suicide by drinking poisoned Kool-Aid.

Osmin dropped to his knees in the doorway and began to sob.

His son pushed past him, looking around. He picked up a toy that belonged to his little brother—a handmade stuffed sheep, which little Franco slept with every night.

There was a sound outside and Augusto turned, dropping the toy to the bare wood floor.

A neighbor stood beyond the porch, the dark river behind him. He looked at the father and son with deep, sorrow-filled eyes. His name was David Clarke and he walked with the aid of a crude crutch. As a boy, he'd had his left leg mangled by a huge black caiman while netting fish in the Essequibo.

Osmin turned and saw David, who cast his eyes down at the ground beneath his feet. "Raiders came to de village," was all the crippled man could say.

Augusto helped his father to his feet, and they stepped down off the porch together.

"Raiders?" Augusto asked the man.

"They came in the middle of the night," David said. "They took my Mariam."

Fire flashed in young Augusto's eyes. Mariam was a year younger than him—the same age as the oldest of his two sisters.

"Who were they?" Osmin asked, his voice cracking.

"From across de border," David replied. "They came by boat."

Augusto took a step toward the man who was supposed to be his father-in-law one day. "How do you know they were Venezuelan?"

"They knocked me down, Augusto. As if I were just a nuisance to them. They spoke the Spanish."

"How long ago?"

David shook his head. "Late last night. They took a dozen others, including your brother, sisters, and mother. They are long gone and the authorities have yet to arrive."

"We must go after them," Augusto implored his father. "Our boat is the fastest on the Essequibo."

"Their boat is much faster," David said. "A big, open boat, with three motors on the back."

Augusto looked over at David. "Did nobody try to stop them?"

"Andres tried," David said. "The raiders had guns. Andres is dead."

"We must gather the people," Augusto declared. "Did anyone see or hear anything else?"

Though young—only seventeen—Augusto was a natural leader. All his peers looked up to him and his father was on the village council, so that gave the young Guyanese some say in the overall community. The older men admired his calm confidence and inner strength.

And he'd been abroad, working as a deckhand on a cargo ship for all of his sixteenth year. He'd traveled and seen much of the coast of South America and even up to the northern islands of the Caribbean—Puerto Rico, St. Croix, and St. Thomas—islands owned by the United States.

The crippled man nodded. "They were from Caracas. This was overheard as they took our people away."

Augusto thought for a moment. Caracas was a long way—almost a week in his father's boat. A fast boat like David had described couldn't possibly make the journey without many stops for petrol, and that was a rare commodity on the desolate coast. Plus, carrying a dozen captives in an open boat would draw suspicion wherever they stopped.

Augusto turned to his father. "The boat took them to a ship offshore."

Osmin looked up at his son. "But which one? Only last night, we saw four ships go by as we worked the nets. There must be many more out there every day."

"I must get to a telephone," Augusto said, already planning

what to do and say.

"You know there are none in the village, my son. And who would you call?"

"When I was in Puerto Rico," Augusto began, "I met an American. He used to be a soldier, but he lost a leg."

Osmin looked back at their home. "What good is a one-legged cripple?"

"He told me that he worked for a man who fixes things when the government cannot."

"What man is this?" David asked, stepping closer.

"He said he worked for a man named Jack Armstrong."

CHAPTER TWO

Monday, August 16, 2021

O ver the past few months, I'd gotten a feel for her—a deep connection and greater understanding of how she behaved in all kinds of situations. When you're together twenty-four hours a day, seven days a week, it'd be surprising not to. But the relationship was constantly changing, evolving, as we got to know one another more intimately.

During the first few weeks we were together, I studied every detail of her; how she moved and reacted, the sounds she made, the subtle nuances she would divulge to me alone.

Nils Hansen had explained what I should expect from her and what her limitations were. And more importantly, he showed me what she would *demand* from me at all times.

"She can be very insistent at times," he'd told me. "And you will become the only man she will completely trust and rely on."

It was a complicated relationship, exacerbated by the fact

that I could never completely understand everything about her. She would always keep something hidden from me, something in reserve. Nils had talked about her soul and how she felt right about doing what she was asked to do. He told me I needed to connect with her in an almost spiritual way.

For the past three months, ever since Nils had left, I'd set aside time for her, just the two of us. Early each morning before dawn. Not for deep meditation or lengthy dialogue, but a few minutes each morning, just for the two of us. Alone, we explored new facets of each other's innermost beings, and what each of us wanted and expected from the other.

I talked to her about my feelings, my expectations, even my fears. I told her about my wife and son, still asleep on the upper deck. Slowly, she opened up and showed herself to me and made her desires known.

Ambrosia was a complicated lady, of that there was no doubt.

On this particular morning, I was in the mechanical room. I'd asked one of the crewmen, a young Portuguese engineer by the name of Heitor Silva, to show me the water maker and all its parts and accessories.

Heitor was from Lisbon, the capital city of Portugal, on the Iberian Peninsula, a seafaring town that dated back to before the Phoenicians' arrival more than three thousand years ago. When we first met, he was quick to point out that though his name was pronounced similarly to Hector, it was spelled Heitor, and pronounced with a very subtle C sound.

He'd left Portugal at the age of eighteen, attended MIT, earned a master's in marine engineering, then worked for ten years at a shipyard in Fairhaven, Massachusetts, on Buzzards Bay. He'd married and had a son, but his wife and child were killed by a mugger who was never caught. Soon after that, he got a visit from Jack Armstrong.

Heitor told me that *Ambrosia* was capable of producing enough drinking water every day to sustain a small village. And with both her generators and main engines running, she could not only provide electricity for the entire ship, but also for a small hospital on shore.

During bad times, like a hurricane or earthquake, *Ambrosia* would be a fine lady to have around. A comfort to those in need. But humanitarian missions weren't what she'd been redesigned for.

Ambrosia was a wolf in sheep's clothing.

With her twin turbines spooled up, she was capable of sixty-five knots. She'd only reached that incredible speed once in her ten years of operation, and that was during her final sea trials in calm waters.

After being signed over to the Saudi prince who'd had her built, the prince had been less than enthused that she wasn't able to duplicate that speed in the open ocean. In even moderate seas, she was limited to no more than fifty-five knots. The prince quickly sold her to Jack Armstrong.

I'd witnessed *Ambrosia* going nearly full speed only once. It was when I was aboard my fishing boat, *Gaspar's Revenge,* along with several friends. We were on our way to meet Jack Armstrong for the first time. *Ambrosia* had passed us while the *Revenge* was making forty knots in open water. Witnessing a 199-foot yacht at that speed had left me, and everyone aboard the *Revenge*, slack-jawed and speechless.

As *Ambrosia's* captain for the past three months, the fastest I'd run her was forty knots, and that was only at fifty percent power from the turbines. The crew and I had done it twice during regularly scheduled run-up and maintenance checks. But it was very comforting to know more speed was there if we ever needed it. With just her diesel engines, she was able to reach twenty knots, which was still incredibly fast for a boat her size.

Once Heitor left me alone in the mechanical room, I did as I usually did, and found a seat where I could see most of the equipment. I allowed my eyes to roam over the hoses, gauges, and valves, sometimes talking out loud as I traced each or figured out what it did.

Nils had given me a basic outline of everything aboard and Heitor had provided a more in-depth tour of the mechanical suite, which took up most of the lowest part of the ship. But I liked to be hands-on and figure things out on my own.

"Ah," I whispered quietly, while studying a specific set of valves and hoses. "Backflush valves."

Heitor had told me that he'd personally installed a system whereby he could reverse the water flow, moving clean, potable water from the storage tanks back through the filters and strainers to the through-hull fitting, clearing it of any debris that might get picked up. He'd said that since installing it, he'd reversed the pumps for three minutes every Monday, and they hadn't had to send a diver down since.

There was a static crackle from a speaker mounted over the hatch. I knew what it was before it came.

"I'll be back tomorrow," I said, running my hand along the sides of four upright cylindrical filters.

"Captain McDermitt to the bridge," my first mate's voice said over the speaker.

I was already on my way. I'd left word with Matt to call me when everything was ready.

A spiral ladderwell led from the crew deck, just above the engine room, all the way up to the command bridge and tactical communications and operations center. It took me less than a minute to ascend three decks.

"Captain on the bridge," the yeoman announced, then turned to pour me a coffee.

Val McLarin was an ambitious young woman who took her job aboard *Ambrosia* very seriously. As yeoman, she was sort of a personal assistant to the captain. She knew the duties and abilities of every member of the ship's crew and if she didn't have a ready answer for any question, she knew who to ask to get it.

"Thanks, Val," I said, accepting the fat-bottomed mug from her as I went to the helm.

My first mate, Matt Brand, stood behind the helm, slowly

turning as he scanned the mouth of the gulf with a pair of large, powerful binoculars.

I sipped at my Hacienda la Minita coffee and waited. Jack had contacted the little Costa Rican farm after trying it once and placed a standing order of fresh-roasted beans, replacing *Ambrosia*'s usual stores.

"*Myttin da*, Cap'n," Matt said, without taking his eyes from the binos.

I'd had trouble understanding some of his Cornish dialect early on but learned the greeting he used each morning.

"Good morning," I said back. "Anything to report?"

Matt put the binos down and picked up his own mug, lifting it in salute. "Nothin' at ull, Cap'n. It's been real quiet. Almost too quiet, mind." His Cornish accent was heavy on the vowels.

"Are we ready to depart?"

"Oye, Cap'n," he replied. "The fo'ard crew is standin' by and Mr. Silva is sittin' on top'o the engines."

"Thanks, Matt," I said, sipping my coffee as I studied the most recent weather fax.

If you accused him of being an Englishman, Matt would correct you and explain that although Cornwall County was a part of the country, once you'd crossed the River Tamar, you were no longer in England. He claimed to be Cornovii and could trace his ancestry on the Lizard Peninsula to the beginning of the Middle Ages, long before the creation of modern borders and maps, when Celtic and Germanic tribes threw off Roman rule, and the peninsula was too remote for the Romans to deem it necessary to control.

"Start main engine one, helm," I ordered.

The helmsman, a young Mississippi man named Axel Troutman, turned a switch, waited a few seconds, then pushed the button to start the port diesel engine, bringing 5300 horses out of slumber.

"Engine one online, Captain."

Through the deck, I could just feel the vibration of the powerful diesel. The low rumble of the exhaust was far astern and three decks down. It was barely discernible—a low bass sound that was felt more than heard. The sound synched with the vibration I felt through my shoes.

"Start main engine two," I ordered, satisfied that the port engine was running smoothly.

The helmsman went through the same process, bringing the second massive V-18 Paxman engine online. The two engines alone weighed more than my forty-five-foot charter fishing boat, *Gaspar's Revenge*, and produced more than four times the power.

I listened for a moment and watched the gauges, but I heard no unusual sounds, and the dull, pulsing rumble of the big engines felt normal.

"Both engines operating normally, Captain," Axel said, confirming my thought. "I don't see any fluctuation in number one's oil pressure like before."

I pushed the intercom button to the engine room. "Bridge

to engineering. Good job, Heitor."

A moment later, his voice came back over the comm. "I will keep an eye on it. But we should replace the bypass filter's oil pump soon. We have several spares aboard."

"How long will it take?" I asked.

"With a solid mechanic, we could do it while underway," he replied. "With just one of the crew to hand me things, it'd take about twice as long as the repair took. Three wicked long days, for me and anyone you can spare who can follow directions. But we're good to go for as long as needed. I will just have to nurse her along."

Having spent almost half his life in the States, Heitor's Portuguese accent was nearly swallowed up by the slang of Massachusetts schooling and wharf-talk.

"What's our schedule look like for the next—"

"Right here, sir," Val said, handing me an electronic notebook.

"Thanks, Val," I said with a smile.

There were times when I thought the woman could read my mind, an excellent quality for a yeoman. The fact that she and Savannah got along very well was another big plus. When she was off duty, Val often spent time with Alberto, so Savannah and I could have some time to ourselves.

The notebook wasn't a Mac or any other name brand, but a wireless handheld computer that Armstrong Research manufactured just for their own use. It was like an extension of every gauge and system on the ship, as well as being an encrypted organizer, sharing data across the entire Armstrong network. With just a few taps on the screen, I could assess the performance of any system on the ship or see where any Armstrong asset was located anywhere in the world. I could even read a short synopsis of their mission and progress.

I scrolled through *Ambrosia's* datebook. We'd been on assignment just off the northern coast of South America for four weeks. Two days earlier, we'd been forced to come into the Gulf of Venezuela on one engine for repairs. We'd lost two valuable days, and time was of the essence.

Two weeks earlier, Jack Armstrong had relayed a message from one of his operatives in the northern Caribbean. From the tone of the communication, I had a good idea who it was from.

DJ Martin and Jerry Snyder worked together in that area. I was confident the message, telling of the capture of a dozen locals from a small village in Guyana, had come from DJ.

We'd been searching for a ship that was moving drugs out of South America. We knew where the drugs ended up, as did the U.S. Coast Guard, the Navy, and the DEA. But we didn't know how the drugs were getting there. The deliveries were massive and so far, undetectable.

I figured the cartel had bought or built a submarine. They'd built them in the past, mostly low-profile boats invisible to radar, not true submarines. But there had been one or two real subs used by the cartels. Those had been small, one- or two-man subs, carrying a few hundred pounds of cargo. But a couple of years ago, I'd come across a couple of divemasters who'd claimed to have sunk a large, Russian-designed sub capable of carrying several tons.

The DEA had reported two large seizures in two different American ports. More cocaine than could be moved in half a dozen standard shipping containers was found at each location—about what a modern, full-sized nuclear attack sub could carry. Only none of the world's navies had reported the sale, loss, or disappearance of any subs.

Jack told me that the relayed message from DJ wasn't the first. He thought that the cartel responsible for moving those drugs was now branching out into human trafficking. So, DJ's message about multiple abductions in Guyana had heightened each crew member's determination.

The thing about a research vessel, especially one that used research as a cover to carry out more nefarious missions, was that it didn't just sit idly for any great length of time. And its appearance, ostensibly to conduct oceanographic research, wasn't surprising to officials.

I pushed the button on the comm again. "If we don't find what we're looking for soon, Heitor, you may have to nurse her along for a couple of weeks. We're not scheduled for three days of maintenance downtime until the first of September."

"She can make it till then, Captain," Heitor replied, a note of confidence in his voice.

"Schedule it," I said to both him and Val. "Order what you need and while we're back in Bimini, the rest of the crew can go ashore or return home for a few days."

"I'll be turnin' in, Cap'n," Matt said. "Call if you need me, yeah?"

"Thanks, Matt."

He patted Axel on the shoulder. "The cap'n has the conn, mate."

Matt left the bridge, and I took his spot behind the helmsman. Conn was an old naval term I was familiar with from my days as part of the Marine Security Detachment aboard the *USS Enterprise*. Passing the conn was a verbal acknowledgment of the transfer of control of the ship from one deck officer to another, so that others on the bridge weren't confused. Only the officer in control can give bridge orders.

"Weigh anchor, helm," I ordered, looking through the binos at the water directly in front of us.

Axel activated the windlass and pushed the intercom button for the speaker mounted just below the Portuguese bridge. "Windlass active. Hoist anchor."

Ambrosia had been designed as a private yacht to be operated by her owner. Originally, all the controls and instruments were within reach of the opulent helm seat. But when Jack bought her, she'd undergone a complete refit. The bridge deck was broken up into sections, with all the navigation instruments moved to starboard, relieving much of the navigation burden from the helmsman. The setup was similar to the bridge of a small warship.

But she wasn't a warship. At least, not outwardly. She still looked like a yacht, with all the refined lines of a luxurious toy for the wealthy. But beneath the outer veneer, she was a dangerous vessel. Still, she was a documented, corporate-owned, civilian research vessel and as such, was operated a little differently than a warship.

I was familiar with how the bridge worked on Navy ships, having served on a few, and during my internship on *Ambrosia*, Nils taught me the differences. Many things were similar but not quite as rigid as on a warship.

The binos I was looking through were color night-vision optics, which brought the whole gulf into clear, sharp focus. But I was only concerned about the quarter mile directly ahead of the ship.

We were in almost two hundred feet of water, so we had over a thousand feet of chain anchor rode out. The chain began to rattle over the rollers as the powerful windlass hauled it up. Two crewmen on the foredeck used high-pressure water hoses to wash down the chain before it disappeared through the deck. A third man operated the remote windlass control.

When I felt the ship start to move, I ordered the helmsman to engage the starboard engine at dead idle, so the windlass didn't have to strain as much. Pulling up the anchor and two hundred feet of heavy chain was hard enough without pulling the five-hundred-ton vessel through the water.

It took fifteen minutes but finally, Axel announced,

"Anchor aweigh, Captain."

"Starboard engine stop," I replied.

He took the engine out of gear, and the ship drifted as the last two hundred feet of chain and the heavy anchor were lifted from the depths of the gulf.

A green light appeared on the helm console and Axel looked up at me. "Anchor's secure, Captain."

"Make your course zero-one-five degrees, true. Speed fifteen knots."

"Zero-one-five degrees at fifteen knots. Aye."

Another vibration could be felt through the deck as the big impellers were engaged, forcing thousands of gallons of water through directional water jets at the stern. Slowly, the ship gathered speed, as Axel moved the throttle controls forward incrementally to the halfway position; fifteen knots was *Ambrosia's* most economical speed.

"Fifteen knots, Captain," Axel reported.

"Take us out of the gulf, Axel. Manual control."

"Aye, sir!"

Though his back was to me, I knew he was smiling. No helmsman ever wanted to turn control of the ship over to the computer. The mouth of the Gulf of Venezuela was almost fifty nautical miles wide and the only thing that lay ahead was the Los Monjes Islands, a small archipelago fifteen nautical miles west of our course. The Spanish explorer, Alonso de Ojeda, had discovered the archipelago in 1499 and thought the rocks looked like the hoods monks wore.

I turned to another crewman sitting in front of the expansive electronics array. "Passive sonar, Ross. Three-sixty degrees, top to bottom."

Ross Mosely nodded. "Passive sonar. Aye."

Ross was a long way from his roots in central Oklahoma. But he had an ear for the very subtle differences in underwater sounds, particularly those made by ships. He'd studied under John Wilson, the man who'd trained me in operating the submersible. John had finally retired completely.

Active sonar sent out an audible "ping" that bounced back from solid objects. The time it took the echo to return and the direction it came from could pinpoint an object's location in the water. Using passive sonar, Ross was just listening to the sounds in the water.

"Take us to where we broke off our search," I told Axel. "Then resume course toward the southeast, just outside territorial waters."

I turned to Val, standing behind the navigator. "You have the conn, Val. I'm going to get some breakfast." Then I gave her a wink. "Don't run over the monks."

Aft the command bridge, I went through a hatch next to the operations center, noting that most of the techs were drinking coffee and going over information on their Metis tablets, dark computer screens at most of their consoles. Early morning hours were usually quiet in the op center.

The technology aboard *Ambrosia* rivaled that of any

Fortune 500 company and most countries. All the stations in the op center were tied into the ship's main computer system. Chyrel had schooled me on what it all did and how it worked, going on about terabyte speed and zettabytes of storage, but most of what I heard barely slowed down as it went in one ear and out the other.

I did remember the name of the system—METIS—which stood for Multi-Encrypted Technical Interface System. All the hardware and the software it ran were designed and built by Armstrong Research. All the wired and wireless devices and systems on board were connected and linked to the computers in the New York headquarters. I remembered the name because of stories I'd read about mythology.

During the Greek philosophical era, about 2500 years ago, Metis was a Titaness, an Oceanid, the daughter of Oceanis himself, and the first great spouse of Zeus. She was the mother of Athena and known as the matriarch of wisdom and deep thought. Aboard *Ambrosia*, the little tablets all the crew used were simply called Metis.

The inside passageway was as long as the op center. When the Saudi prince had *Ambrosia* built, the aft part of the large bridge deck had a bar, restaurant-style seating, a dance floor, and even a stage. The op center took up what was once the bar area and the aft half of the bridge deck had been converted to quarters for the captain and first mate. Those quarters had been joined before I'd taken command, creating a suite for me, Savannah, and Alberto.

"Good morning," Savannah said with a smile, as I entered our quarters. "We're underway?"

"Yeah," I replied, kissing her, and then going to the small galley for more coffee. "We'll be resuming the search in less than an hour."

"Who's on the bridge?"

"Axel's at the helm with Ross navigating," I replied. "Val has control."

She looked up at me, surprised. "She's awfully young."

"Yeah," I agreed. "But she's bright and the crew looks up to her. Besides, there's nothing out there this morning. Almost no shipping traffic this early, and the weather's going to be clear."

"Breakfast is almost ready," she said, turning back to the small stove. "Go get the bottomless pit up."

When I opened the door to Alberto's room, Finn and Woden, lying on either side of his bed, lifted their heads. Since coming aboard, the two dogs had decided on their own that they'd watch after him at all times. They'd been around boats all their lives and somehow sensed that Alberto was new to life on the water.

"Which bottomless pit did you mean?" I asked back over my shoulder.

CHAPTER THREE

Another group had been brought aboard the previous night. They'd been sequestered with the others in the bilge area of the middle hold, the heavy steel plate that made up part of the deck lowered back into place, and the containers lowered back on top of it.

Mauricio knew how dark it was down there, even with the panel removed. The bilge access was the only way in or out.

Mauricio didn't care about them, who they were, or what would happen to them. Sometimes they were there of their own accord, escaping to a better life in America and paying handsomely for it. Other times, they were taken against their will. Some would likely die during the two-week run. Those were almost always from the first groups that were brought aboard. Two weeks in a hot, cramped environment would do that.

Mauricio considered them cargo, nothing more—just

another commodity he was paid to move.

The danger of being discovered was minimal for Mauricio. He was the captain of a small freighter, which moved back and forth from Caracas, Venezuela to Fortaleza, Brazil, at the easternmost tip of South America.

The ship regularly carried a variety of trade goods— lumber, produce, manufactured goods bound for assembly plants in Mexico, Canada, and America, even livestock on occasion. Sometimes, they even carried paying passengers, traveling legally from one port to another. Though the accommodations for passengers weren't the best, they were better than the bilge, and far cheaper than flying.

Security was lax in the smaller ports, and inspections of small coastal freighters was nearly nonexistent.

MV Canopus stopped in more than a dozen ports during her month- long voyage, offloading one type of cargo, and loading another. The human cargo in the bilge was rounded up by members of the crew, using one of the three open emergency lifeboats that were stowed on the roof of the crews' quarters. By putting all three outboards on one of the lifeboats, it was quite fast. At least three times during the voyage, the ship would stop at night, miles from shore, and put the boat into the water.

They mostly raided the poor fishing villages on rivers too shallow for anything but small boats. Few of these villages had electricity, telephones, or police. While the boat was away, the rest of the crew would remove the containers from the middle hold, stacking them fore and aft with a crane, then let the people out for a few minutes before the lifeboat returned with more. They were given food and water then. If any of them died, the body was thrown overboard.

The cargo below the middle hold was always destined for Caracas, though. Not the busy Puerto Cabello, west of the sprawling city, but to the smaller Puerto Borburata. Mauricio knew that the cargo's final destination would be the larger port, but they would go there in small delivery trucks. Once at Puerto Cabello, they would be put aboard a ship bound first for America, to unload their regular cargo, plus a few tons of cocaine, and then the ship would continue to the Middle East, with goods from America and the human cargo still aboard.

What ship that was, he neither knew nor cared. The people in the hold thought *Canopus* was the ghost ship, but Mauricio knew this part of their voyage was nothing compared to what eventually awaited them.

"*Capitão*," the helmsman said, "we are nearing the outer markers."

Mauricio nodded to the man. "I will make the call."

He went out onto the side deck so his phone could reach the satellite in orbit thousands of miles overhead. His satellite phone had only one number stored in its memory; he tapped the *Call* button.

"You are late," the man on the other end of the call said.

"*Si*, we stopped once more, near the border, for an unscheduled pickup. We are entering the channel now."

"What is your cargo?" the man asked.

Mauricio didn't know his name, nor did he know where the man was—either physically, or in the hierarchy of the cartel. But he thought that the man on the phone and the man who always met the ship at the dock, and only called himself Juan, were the same man.

"Four steers and twenty heifers," Mauricio began, speaking in code just in case someone was listening. "Plus, five strong bulls, and nine fine cows."

"That's good," the man said. "When will you reach the wharf?"

"In less than two hours," Mauricio replied.

There was a click and when he looked down, he saw that the call was ended. The man never stayed on for more than a minute, usually half that. How many and when. That was all he wanted to know.

Mauricio reentered the bridge, tallying the numbers in his head. The men and most of the boys were destined to be slave laborers. Few would last two years. He would be paid one hundred American dollars for each of them. The girls and most of the women were destined for some sheik's harem and each would bring two hundred dollars.

Some of them weren't worth the agreed-upon rate. The younger boys and older women, he had to bargain over with the man at the wharf. The younger boys were useless as laborers, but Mauricio knew there was always an occasional Middle-Easterner who liked boys. He had become a sharp negotiator and knew which boys would be desirable to the customers overseas. If any of the women or girls were exceptional, they'd command a much higher price—some as much as five hundred.

Cash in Mauricio's pocket, just for picking them up and taking them to Caracas.

The unscheduled stop had been worthwhile. He stood to make over $6,000 on this one run, on top of his pay as the ship's captain. The extra money every month added up to nearly his annual salary.

But Mauricio wanted more.

He dreamed of owning his own, much larger ship, one that could cross the ocean. Then he could cut out the middleman and keep the best girls for himself, as Juan often bragged of doing.

Soon, the ship entered the port and Captain Mauricio Gonzales moved her alongside the wharf, where lines were thrown to the dock workers. It was still dark, but the sun would be up soon.

Once the ship was secure, he went down to the deck and ordered the crew to remove the containers from the middle hold first. They usually waited to do this last, but he wanted the human cargo off the ship before the sun came up. Then he went down to meet the man on the dock who would pay him.

"I was told you have thirty-eight," the man said. "The numbers I was given comes to 6,200 Yankee dollars."

Mauricio couldn't tell if he was the same person he had

spoken to on the satellite phone, or another cartel member. The phone distorted the man's voice.

"Let's wait until they are brought up," Mauricio said. "There may be a few you will want to discount."

He always allowed that Juan would want to save money on a few of the smaller boys and older women brought to him. That softened him up to pay more for the women.

After ten minutes, the prisoners were led off the ship, their hands tied together in one long chain of human desperation.

Juan counted them. "There are only thirty-six," he said, as he stood at the end of the line.

Mauricio turned to his first mate, who'd shepherded them from the ship. Miguel was the leader of a gang of cutthroats he'd hired in Cartagena. He had the blackest heart of any man Mauricio had ever met.

Miguel shrugged. "*Murieron dos ancianas.*"

Mauricio turned back to Juan. "It is expected to lose a few of the older ones after two weeks in the hold. It toughens the others for the longer voyage to come."

"We will start the negotiation at six thousand then."

Mauricio nodded.

Juan checked out the last person in the line, a young boy of about thirteen years. He looked him over a moment, then moved on up the line, discounting one small boy and another woman who looked to be over thirty. But ahead of her were three exceptionally beautiful young women.

"Add one hundred for each," Juan said, then turned to inspect the next person.

"Add two-fifty for each," Mauricio countered.

Juan turned and regarded him, then stepped closer to the three girls, none of whom appeared to have reached twenty yet, but all ripe and full. He examined them more closely, groping the taller one. Her eyes flashed in defiance and she pulled away, a stifled scream coming from her gagged mouth.

Juan backhanded her, nearly knocking her down.

"Add two hundred each," he said with a sadistic smile. "This one goes with me. Why should a Damascus sultan get the fiery ones?"

CHAPTER FOUR

W e ate out on the small terrace aft our stateroom, where we could see the sun rising near a group of scattered clouds.

"Know what those clouds mean, Alberto?"

He was lost in the breathtaking dance of light and color but shifted his gaze thoughtfully.

"Land," he declared. "Aruba?"

"Very good!" Savannah said, smiling brightly. "How did you know?"

Alberto shrugged. "I dunno." Then he paused and glanced over at me. "You said we were in the Gulf of Venezuela yesterday and I looked on a map to find it. We started moving before I woke up, so I guessed we were out of the gulf. And Aruba is the only island out there."

"Well, there's also Curaçao and Bonaire," I said.

He nodded. "But they're a lot farther away."

I ruffled his hair. "Alberto, the Navigator."

He smiled and broke a piece of bacon in half, handing a piece to each of the dogs. Neither snatched it from him, as most dogs would, but gently took the pieces from his fingers.

"Can I come to the bridge with you?" he asked.

"For a little while," I replied. "And only if you can be quiet. We're conducting a passive sonar search."

"Is Mr. Ross up there?"

"And so is Val," Savannah said, then turned to me. "Why passive sonar?"

"Jack still thinks it's a surface ship," I replied. "Ross's computer has the sound signature of just about every large ship in the world. We're tracking and identifying each sound he finds and sending it to the analysts in Bimini."

"And you still think it's a submarine?"

I shrugged as I chewed a bite from my omelet. "An educated guess," I said. "Every surface ship operating between South America and ports in the United States is searched fairly regularly, at embarkation, occasionally while at sea, and on arrival. It's standard protocol since 9/11. The odds aren't in the cartel's favor to use regular cargo ships. And the recent drug seizures would indicate large shipments—more than what they can bring in using boats and stolen yachts like they've usually done."

"Like that submarine you told me about that was destroyed by a couple of divers?"

I grinned and nodded, remembering the young couple,

Boone and Emily. He'd been a lanky, easy-going young American and she was a feisty Brit with a penchant for wearing green. Both struck me as highly intelligent.

"If that cartel could do it once," I said, "they can do it again."

"How much would it cost to build one?" she asked.

"A sub like the one Boone and Emily described? Millions, if not tens of millions."

She stared off toward the rising sun, its light bringing out the golden hues in her hair and giving her face a radiance that rivaled any of a woman half her age.

"They have that kind of money?" she asked softly.

"And then some," I said. "Those two big seizures? Each was over ten tons—a street value of about a billion dollars."

She turned her gaze back to me. "They lost two billion in two DEA raids, and they can still afford to build a submarine?"

"First," I said, "the street value isn't the same as what they sell it to an American distributor for. And those twenty tons cost the cartel a small fraction of that to produce and ship."

"And second?"

"What they lost was a drop in the bucket," I said. "The Coast Guard seizes over two hundred tons every year, just at sea. The DEA and other law enforcement, several hundred tons more. It's estimated they don't even catch a fourth of it and up to eight hundred *billion* dollars' worth of it hits Main Street, U.S.A. every year."

"I knew it was big," she said. "But I had no idea of the money involved."

"By comparison, a cartel building a sub like Boone and Emily's would be like you or me building a toy boat with a paper sail."

"But it's still a lot of money," she said. "When they can just steal boats and use them once."

"They lose a lot of product that way," I said. "Some get busted because they're stupid, some toss a few kilos overboard out of paranoia, and some of it is just outright stolen by others. Larger shipments give the cartels more control."

"So, you're convinced it's a sub?"

"Not completely," I replied. "Jack has more intel than I do. So, we're listening for surface ships, three hundred and sixty degrees, top to bottom."

She smiled. "A surface ship on the bottom?"

"He didn't say to *not* look for subs," I replied. "The cartels can't build a nuclear sub, at least not yet, so there will be some noise from an electric or diesel-powered one. And it'll be a noise Ross's computer can't identify."

"Y'all go ahead," Savannah said, rising and picking up the empty plates. "I'll come get Alberto in a little while for his lessons."

"Aw, do I have to?" the youngster whined.

"You know very well you do. Today's Monday. Just because there's something more interesting going on up on the bridge doesn't get you out of your responsibilities."

"Yes, ma'am," he moaned, rising from the table.

He and the dogs followed me back through our quarters

and forward to the command bridge. I glanced into the op center as we passed and saw several of the tech people with headsets on and computer screens lighting their faces.

"Good morning, Alberto," Val said.

"Hi, Miss Val."

The dogs split up and positioned themselves next to the two side deck hatches. They did a lot of things like that without having to be told. Woden had undergone months of intensive protection training, and part of that had been training him to be situationally aware—to always look for and block methods of entry. Finn had just picked up on what Woden did. Over the years I'd seen this same teaching and learning behavior in other animals, like dolphins.

"Contact reports, Captain," Val said, handing me the bridge Metis tablet.

As I scanned the last hour of contacts and maneuvers, Alberto went over to where Ross was hunched over the sonar screen.

Without a word, Ross picked up a second set of headphones and handed them to Alberto, who put them on and took a seat beside him.

"Contact fourteen, bearing zero-four-seven degrees," Ross said. "About two hundred nautical miles. Computer identified as a coastal freighter, the *MV Canopus*. It's a Venezuelan-flagged merchant ship of four hundred feet, now leaving the Port of Borburata."

"It's noisy," Alberto added.

I grinned and looked at the readout on the Metis. The *Canopus* had been built in the early 1960s and carried all kinds of goods back and forth along the coast from Brazil to Venezuela. A sixty-year-old diesel-powered ship would certainly be noisy.

"Is that the fourteenth you've identified in the last hour?" I asked Ross.

"Yes, sir. Monday mornings get pretty busy down here after sunrise."

Ross had been a part of *Ambrosia's* crew for over ten years. He'd started as a deckhand, as most do, but John Wilson had seen something in the young man and had spent time teaching him the finer points of identifying underwater sound. Ross had taken over for another sonarman about the time I first encountered *Ambrosia*. Some ships, like the massive Maersk cargo ships, he didn't even need the computer to identify. They ran regularly scheduled trips and he'd encountered them many times.

"Helm, come right to course one-seven-zero true," I ordered. "If it's busy, let's get in behind the ABC Islands."

"One-seven-zero true, aye," Axel replied and turned the wheel to starboard.

After a moment, Axel straightened the wheel and said, "Course is one-seven-zero, Captain.

"Following a hunch?" I heard Savannah say from behind me.

I turned and smiled at her. "Just being prudent. Ross says

shipping traffic gets busy in these parts on Mondays. We don't want to miss something behind an island."

Sound travels great distances underwater. If the sound is noisy enough, like the big diesel engines in large cargo ships, a land mass is the only thing that can block it, whether that be the relatively tiny island of Curaçao to the east of our position, or the continent of Africa far beyond the eastern horizon.

A submarine operating on electric power underwater wasn't a noisy freighter, but even a rudimentary electric sub's sound would get lost in the background noise of the ocean. We'd have to be within a few miles for Ross to pick its sound out of the clutter. So, if my idea *was* right, it was like looking for a needle in a field full of haystacks.

"Contact fifteen," Ross reported. "Vessel identified as E Pioneer, a Cyprus-flagged tanker, bound for Port La Cruz."

"*Puerto* La Cruz," I corrected him. "You wouldn't call the U.S. island in the northern Caribbean Port Rico, would you?"

"Sorry, Captain," Ross said. "There ain't a lot of Spanish spoken back home in Oklahoma."

Savannah touched Alberto's arm, startling him. "It's time for your lessons," Savannah said, after he'd removed his headset. "But you need to walk the dogs first."

He looked up at me and I only nodded.

"I'm off duty in two hours," Val said to Savannah. "How about I drop in and help Alberto with his math?"

Savannah was an intelligent woman, but math had always been her weakness. She'd struggled to teach Flo, until the advent of online learning.

"Thank you," Savannah replied. "I'll make some tea."

Alberto smiled up at Savannah. "I'll take 'em out now and be back in a few minutes."

He left the bridge by the port hatch, both dogs following dutifully behind him. Having dogs on a boat created a lot of small problems, not the least of which was waste management.

Woden couldn't be bothered about it. He'd grown up on Savannah's big Grand Banks trawler and since he was a pup, his only option had been the swim platform, where Savannah would just wash it down with a hose.

But Finn preferred something more natural. On the aft end of the side deck was a patch of real grass, often the only grass for hundreds of miles.

Growing grass on a boat wasn't easy, but Jack also had a dog, a golden retriever, and assigned one of the crew to maintain the turf patch to the same standards as most golf courses. The large tub it was built in drained overboard through a hull fitting below the waterline or into the ship's holding tank.

We continued south-southeast for another three hours, and the monotony began to set in. Val left the bridge. The sea flowed past. The never-ending blanket of blue reflected the sunlight, sparkling at times. I had Axel turn east-southeast, to follow the coast a little closer.

I'd had men under my command in the past. Before

retiring from the Marine Corps, I'd been a scout/sniper instructor. After that I'd worked with Homeland Security on occasion, and for several years now, Armstrong Research. But the crew of *Ambrosia* was exceptional. Jack Armstrong had hand-picked nearly every man and woman on board. They were mostly college-educated, intelligent, and well-paid.

They seemed to revel in the technical abilities of *Ambrosia* and worked tirelessly through long, monotonous periods. Many of the crew were scientists, perfectly suited to conducting slow, methodical searches.

This wasn't the kind of action I enjoyed, though. It was tedious work. Fifteen knots covered less than four hundred miles of ocean a day and we'd been on assignment for a long time already—searching and listening. I was more of a kick-in-the-door-and-bust-some-heads kinda guy. I had a methodical mind, but monotony got under my skin. Long periods of repetitive work made me edgy—unless it was mindless work with my hands.

"Contact thirty-one," Ross's voice droned, describing the ship I instantly saw on my Metis, another container ship hundreds of miles away to the east.

All the information Ross was compiling was compared to AIS locations, shipping manifests, and schedules. This was performed by technicians in the op center, as well as analysts on Bimini and in New York. The Automatic Identification System reported commercial ships' locations, courses, speed, and a few details about the ships. More and more boats of all sizes also used AIS.

Finding the right set of connections between increased drug activity at home with the timing of a ship leaving the two countries whose coasts we searched would eventually indicate what ships were likely suspects to be carrying the drugs. Even if the drugs weren't discovered and confiscated, the increased presence on the streets of American cities was a good indication of when big shipments arrived and where the drugs were distributed.

Additional data and information such as this were analyzed by both computers and humans, searching for any anomaly or consistency that would tie one particular ship, out of the tens of thousands arriving in hundreds of American ports, to the big cocaine deliveries.

Where the coke came from was easy. Colombia and Venezuela produced most of the world's cocaine, and users in the U.S. consumed more of it than anywhere else. Just in the United States, over 130 billion dollars' worth of cocaine is consumed each year— about the same as new car sales.

Sniff...another SUV up the nose.

But the Coast Guard and DEA were over-taxed, undermanned, and underfunded. Richard Nixon had first coined the phrase "war on drugs," and since the 1960s, billions had been spent trying to stem the tide. But when hundreds of billions in profit were at stake, the cartels spent more.

At noon, Matt returned to relieve me for lunch. After I'd

eaten, I went back to the bridge and he turned in for the day. Later, once I went off duty and before going to bed, I'd come back up to allow him to get lunch. Sometimes Val or one of the other senior crew would fill in, controlling the ship while either Matt or I took a break from the boredom and just walked around *Ambrosia's* decks.

We alternated our schedule every week, moving forward six hours, so no crewman stood the same monotonous duty each night. The switch was always during my watch, so I was the only one pulling a double on the bridge. The rest of the crew worked four hours on and eight off.

In the early afternoon, I turned the conn over to the helm and took a stroll around the boat's vast decks. At 199 feet in length and having a thirty-two-foot beam, one lap around was nearly a tenth of a mile.

Alone on the foredeck, I looked out over the water around us. The sea state seemed agitated, but it was nothing to *Ambrosia.* Aside from the wind and the sound of the bow wave, movement was barely noticeable. She was a big boat, with an aluminum hull and superstructure to keep weight down, but she still displaced over 450 tons.

The sky was clear, save for a few scattered clouds off to the south, where I could just make out the foothills of the Venezuelan Andes rising above Puerto Cumarebo. Off to port lay the Dutch island of Curaçao, with a few puffy white clouds floating above it.

As I started to turn aft, something ahead caught my eye. I

stopped and watched but saw nothing for a moment. Then it appeared again; something on the water, just to the right of our course and a good mile away. Each second brought it closer.

Still a half mile away, I recognized what it was.

I turned and raced back along the side deck, taking the steps to the main deck two at a time. Entering the hatch, I went up another set of inside steps to the bridge.

"Reverse engines!" I ordered, grabbing up the binoculars.

"Reverse engines, aye!" the helmsman repeated.

The boat began to slow as I scanned the water ahead of us.

"Ahead slow, helm. Right ten degrees."

He again repeated my commands and *Ambrosia* crept forward, turning slightly. Through the binos, I found the object, dead ahead, just four hundred yards.

"Steady as she goes, helm."

Axel centered the wheel. "Steady ahead. What is it, Captain?"

"Small craft dead ahead," I said. "At least five people aboard. It's not moving."

Savannah was suddenly beside me. "What are they doing way out here?"

"All stop," I ordered, then turned to my wife. "I don't know, but we're stopping to check it out."

I took one last look to see which way we and the small boat were drifting, then pushed the intercom button. "Security to the port side aft."

I went down the spiral ladderwell to the main deck and hurried aft, Savannah following close behind me. When I came out onto the fantail, two armed men, both dressed in black, stood waiting.

"Sorry if I woke you, Travis," I said to the taller of the two.

Travis Stockwell was older than me, but not by a lot. The skin of his face looked like old leather—tanned, with deep lines. He still wore a regulation crew cut, but it was nearly completely white now. The colonel's years meant nothing where his physique was concerned. He worked out daily and hard. I knew, because we often worked out together.

"Not a problem," he growled. "Whatta you got?"

"A small boat with at least five people aboard." I moved over to the docking controls at the port rail, just ahead of the steps down to the big work deck mounted to the stern.

I plucked the mic from its holder and pushed the button, speaking into it. "Captain has the conn."

The controls here were simple and didn't involve the main engines, just the bow and stern thrusters, and a comparatively small, auxiliary electric motor for maneuvering. We were still drifting toward the boat, now just a few hundred feet ahead of the bow.

The boat was small, less than fifteen feet and crudely built. The rough chop was threatening to swamp it, given the number of people aboard. It had a small outboard, but it wasn't running.

I moved the joystick forward and a little to the right,

bringing *Ambrosia* broadside to the little boat. I continued to maneuver her so the big steel platform was close to the boat.

I pushed the button for the bridge again. "You have the conn, Axel. All stop."

"Aye, captain," Axel replied.

"Let's go see who they are," I said to Stockwell.

We went down the steps to the platform, where a crewman stood ready with a line in his hand. I gave him a nod and the line uncoiled perfectly as it sailed through the air to the outstretched arms of a man kneeling in the bow of the little boat.

A few minutes later, we had the boat, really no more than a homemade raft, tied up to the platform.

"Who are you?" I asked the man who'd caught the line.

His blank expression caused Savannah to repeat my question in Spanish.

"*Mi nombre es Marcos Santiago,*" he said. "*Me llevo a mi familia a Curaçao, lejos de Venezuela.*"

"Venezuelan refugees," Savannah said. "They want to go to Curaçao."

CHAPTER FIVE

The political climate in Venezuela had been getting bad for some time. There was corruption from the top of the nation's leadership down to the lowest police officer. Outlaws and drug cartels ran the country. The cartel leaders lived in opulent luxury, as did the politicos who accepted their bribes. Those who hadn't, wound up dead or in the same situation as most of the country's inhabitants—impoverished.

Venezuela had once been where refugees from other Latin American countries escaped *to*. But now it was estimated that nearly half a million Venezuelans lived abroad, having fled their homeland with little more than the shirts on their backs.

We got the people aboard and moved them up to the cockpit. There were seven of them. Marcos Santiago did speak a little English; he'd only been surprised when I'd spoken it earlier—he'd thought we were a Venezuelan ship.

With him were his wife, Mayra, and their three daughters,

a son-in-law, and a grandson, who was about Alberto's age.

Mayra explained that she and Marcos had worked in hospitality, managing a five-star resort in Maracaibo. Their daughters had also worked with them at the resort. The daughters were all in their early twenties, I guessed, beautiful and intelligent.

"Please," Mayra said, once we were all seated at the table in the covered cockpit, "do not return us to Venezuela. We will be killed if we return."

"Why were you going to Curaçao?" I asked her.

"To be free from the *carteles*," she said. "They came for our children."

"Don't you know what has been happening to your people who go to Curaçao?" Savannah asked. "They are jailed or forced into hiding."

She looked at her husband and spoke in rapid-fire Spanish.

Marcos turned toward me, his eyes blinking. "I not know."

"*Estás a salvo aquí con nosotros*," I said, realizing that the majority of the Spanish I *could* speak were words of comfort.

"Where will you take us?" Mayra asked. "To America?"

"For now," I offered, "you are guests aboard *Ambrosia*. You can eat and rest. We are not bound for anywhere at the moment, though. So, we will have plenty of time to decide where you want to go."

"We want to go to America," she said. "Marcos thought he could get us there from Curaçao. *Por favor, señor*. We have money."

For someone in their situation, admitting they had money was a great sign of trust.

"Hold onto your money," I told her. "You are our guests, *mi invitada*."

"Hello," Alberto said from behind me.

I turned and motioned him over. He came and stood between me and Savannah, our dogs sitting behind him.

"This is our son, Alberto," I explained.

More rapid-fire Spanish was exchanged, mostly between Alberto and the Santiagos' grandson.

"I know boats," the boy's father told me. "I have worked on marine engines." He looked at his wife and in-laws. "We will all work. We seek refuge, but we are not *mendigos*—beggars."

He'd been quiet for the most part and when he spoke, he had little accent. Offering to work seemed to be a natural thing for him. I remembered Pap telling me that any time I saw a man struggling to do something, I should pitch in and help. We weren't struggling, but he was offering. I liked the young man.

"Crew accommodations aren't much aboard *Ambrosia*," I said. "The crew doubles up, two beds in each cabin." Then I turned to Savannah. "Do we have three adjoining cabins?"

"Three, yes," she replied. "But only two are adjoining."

The two boys had moved around to the side of the table, where they were talking quietly in Spanish, Alberto introducing his new friend to Finn and Woden.

"We can sleep anywhere," one of the two unmarried daughters said.

The three sisters looked nothing alike but seemed to be almost the same age. The one who'd spoken had black hair, light brown eyes, and was slim, almost waifish, whereas the third sister had a more voluptuous figure and auburn hair.

She spoke with barely a trace of an accent, as well. "Yes, Crystal and I shared an apartment before things turned bad last year."

The married sister also spoke with only a slight accent. She had long, wavy black hair and eyes as dark as obsidian.

"Please, *Capitan*, if we are returned to our country, we will be killed," Marcos said in halting English. Then he looked sadly at his three daughters. "Or worse."

"We won't take you back," I said. "If that's what you want. Our home port is Bimini, in the Bahamas. In two weeks, we'll return there for routine maintenance. You're welcome to stay with us until we get there."

"*Graçias, Capitan*," Marcos said, relief evident in his eyes. "What Ricardo said is true. We can work. Before becoming manager at Mayacoba, I was the *cocinero*... how you say? The main cook."

I looked up to where Val stood behind the couple.

"Grady would relish having help in the galley," she said.

Grady Lawson was the ship's cook. He'd only been a part of the crew for a little over a year and his assistant in the kitchen had left shortly after he'd come aboard.

"Will you show them to their quarters, Val?" I asked, then turned to Mayra. "And would you and Marcos join us for dinner in our quarters? And please bring Fernando. Alberto has nobody close to his age to talk with."

She smiled feebly and nodded.

"Good," I said and stood up. "Yeoman McLarin will show you to where you will be staying. She can also show you where the laundry is. Get settled in and feel free to look around the ship. But the bridge deck is for crew members only."

Val led the family through the big doors into the salon, and I turned to Stockwell. "What do you think, Colonel?"

His steely, blue-gray eyes cut to the retreating family. "I don't know, Jesse. We've never had guests aboard. They seem genuinely afraid to go back."

My relationship with Travis Stockwell stretched back to long before either of us had ever heard of *Ambrosia*. We chewed some of the same sand in the Middle East, me as a Marine scout/sniper, and he as an Army infantry officer. Later, he took over as assistant deputy director of Homeland Security, overseeing Deuce Livingston's hand-picked team.

The fact that I was in command of *Ambrosia* made no difference to the colonel. He was the head of security for all of Armstrong's assets. *Ambrosia* was just where he controlled things. I didn't second-guess his deployment of security teams, and he didn't question my orders on the bridge.

We were co-workers and also friends.

"And his comment, 'or worse'?" I asked.

He looked at me, and his eyes turned cold. "I agree with Jack. There have been abductions all over South America. Hundreds have disappeared, mostly young women. It's assumed the men are used as forced labor somewhere and the women as..." He glanced at Savannah, then back at me. "Well, you know."

"Sex slaves," Savannah said. "No need to couch the truth, Travis. Flo and I have come close to being a part of it on more than one occasion."

His face maintained its usual impassiveness as he looked into my wife's eyes. "But you survived," he finally said.

"And those who wanted to take us didn't always fare so well."

One of Stockwell's eyebrows moved slightly, almost imperceptibly, as he appraised Savannah again.

"Yes, ma'am," was his only reply, before turning to the other security man and nodding his head toward the salon.

The two men disappeared, headed back to their quarters. Stockwell and his security team weren't needed often on *Ambrosia*. But there were five of them and one was on duty at all times, with the other three within seconds of being ready to turn out in the event of an emergency.

Stockwell's office and his team's quarters were in the forward-most part of the boat, as was the armory and gym. That part of the boat was accessible only through a locked hatch at the end of the forward passageway, where most of the crew stayed. The security team could also deploy through a deck hatch in the middle of the foredeck.

"Alberto and I will go and check on our guests," Savannah said.

I turned and started to go back up to the bridge.

"Excuse me, Captain," one of the deckhands said. "What should we do with their boat?"

"Did they get all their belongings off it?"

"Yes, sir."

"We should just sink it," I said, then reconsidered. "But pull the outboard and gas tank and take them to Heitor. Then see if you can stow the boat in the garage."

That evening, when Matt relieved me on the bridge, I told him about our passengers.

"I don't see what else ye could've done," he said. "From the description of their boat, it's not likely they'd have made it, yeah?"

"Taking them to Curaçao was out of the question," I said. "As is returning them to their homeland."

"Aye, Cap'n. If the cartel pillocks wanted the girls, their fate would be far worse than death."

"Pillocks?"

"Oye," he replied. "A pillock is what you might call someone who's not all that bright."

"You expand my vocabulary every day, Matt. I'll be in my quarters if you need me. See you at twenty-three-hundred."

As I headed for the interior passageway, the sonarman announced the eighty-third contact of the day.

"You're grilling," Savannah announced as I entered our cabin.

"I am?"

"Yes. Those people looked famished. I have six big rib eyes marinating, and the potatoes have been in the oven for half an hour."

"Then I'd better get a move on," I said, tossing my cover on the coffee table.

Alberto was on the terrace with Finn and Woden. His back was to me with his nose in a book. The two dogs were looking up at him, as if expecting him to give them a treat or something.

I opened the hatch quietly, but the dogs heard me and looked my way. Alberto was reading aloud and after a moment, I recognized the prose.

"*The Old Man and the Sea*?" I asked, stepping out onto the terrace.

Alberto jumped slightly. "They like me to read to them."

"I wasn't aware Finn and Woden were such fans of the classics."

"It's a good story," Alberto said. "You have read it?"

"Quite a few times." I opened the small gear locker at the side of the terrace and removed a stained Rusty Anchor grilling apron, slipping it over my head. "The first time, I was about your age."

Alberto looked down at the book. "It's that old?"

I couldn't help but laugh. "Hemingway wrote that ten

years before I was born."

"Wow," he said, softly, then looked up as I tied the apron in place around my waist. "Are you grilling tonight?"

"Yes. The admiral wants beef."

He grinned. "She's not really an admiral. You just call her that."

"We're having guests for dinner," I said. "Marcos and Mayra will be joining us. How about you go get them? I don't think they know where we live."

He dropped the book on the table and started to go inside.

"That's not where that goes," I reminded him.

Alberto picked up the book and carried it inside, speaking to Savannah as he closed the hatch.

With little more than the turn of a knob and the pressing of a button, the stainless steel propane grill ignited. I preferred charcoal or hardwood, but on a boat, that was dangerous. The movement of the boat would cause the hot coals to roll around. After closing the lid to let it heat up, I went back inside.

"Did you give him the Hemingway book?" I asked Savannah.

She dumped vegetables from a cutting board into a steamer pot and looked up. "No, he found it in the little library in the crews' lounge." Then she smiled. "He said he thought it was about you."

"I'm nowhere near as old as Hemingway's Santiago."

"And Alberto is no less devoted than Manolin."

I smiled and took her in my arms. "You really think that?"

"I do," she replied. "Maybe he isn't as outward with it as 'the boy' in the book, but I've watched the two of you together. He adores you, Jesse. You're his hero."

I started to kiss her, but there was a sound at the door.

"Shoo," she said. "Get those steaks on."

The door opened and the dogs came in first, followed by Alberto and Marcos and Mayra Santiago, along with their grandson, Fernando.

"*Bienvenidos, Marcos*," I said, reaching a hand out. "*Por favor entra.*"

"*Graçias,*" he said, shaking my hand. "You are a kind man, *Capitan.*"

I opened the refrigerator and took out the bowl with the steaks. "Care to help me at the grill?"

He nodded and I led him toward the terrace.

"Alberto, go show Fernando your room," Savannah said. "We'll call you when dinner's ready."

Woden followed the two boys into Alberto's room and Finn curled up on the floor by the hatch to the companionway.

I slid the glass door open and stepped out onto the terrace.

"Your ship is beautiful," Marcos said, measuring his words.

"It's not mine," I said. "I'm just the captain."

"Still, it is a beautiful boat to care for."

"I'm afraid your English is better than my Spanish," I said, closing the sliding door to the stateroom. I set my phone on the table and swiped the screen. "But we have an app for that."

A slightly mechanical woman's voice spoke from my

phone. "*Pero tenemos una aplicación para eso.*"

Marcos smiled knowingly. "*Es una época maravillosa en la que vivimos.*"

"It is a wonderful age in which we live," the phone translated.

Marcos reached down and closed the app. "Is a crutch, no?"

"*Si, es una muleta,*" I replied.

We both laughed.

Marcos wasn't a young man. I guessed him to be in his late forties, maybe early fifties. Like me, he'd grown up in a time without computers and instant information. I agreed with him that using a translator to exchange thoughts and ideas diminished a person's ability to learn new things in some ways.

"I want to learn to speak English like my wife and our girls."

"Where did they learn?" I asked, making sure to speak slowly and clearly. "They barely even have an accent."

"Mayra attended university in Miami. It was before we met in Maracaibo. Our daughters went there, as well."

I opened the grill and started to put the steaks on.

"*Eso es demasiado, señor,*" Marcos said.

I looked at him questioningly. "Six people, six steaks."

"Too much," he insisted. "Mayra and Crystal will take only half, as will Giselle and Fernando."

I ignored his protest and put the sixth rib eye on the grill. Alberto could eat a whole one, easily. "I've decided to take you up on your offer, Marcos. You will all eat enough to give you the strength to give a full day's work."

I knew he was just being polite. They'd had no food on the boat and few belongings. They'd likely left in a big hurry.

He smiled. "*Graçias, Capitan.* Crystal worked in the… *ropa sucia* at Mayacoba."

"The laundry?

"*Si, Capitan,*" he replied. "She was much impressed with the one on this boat."

I waved a hand toward the stateroom. "Here, I am just Jesse."

He nodded. "*Si*, Jesse. Kassandra, my middle daughter, worked with me in the kitchen, making sure we had all we needed and she made the menus for our guests."

"Sounds like a ship's purser to me," I said. "But we have everything aboard that is needed for a month at sea. Mostly frozen, so knowing when to get it out and how much is one less task for Grady. For the last six months, he's done that, as well as prepare four meals a day for our around-the-clock crew."

He looked at me, dismayed. "That is too much for one man."

"What about Fernando's mother? And your wife?"

"Giselle was… How you say? *Empleada de escritorio.*"

"She worked the front desk?"

"*Si.* Much organized, my Giselle. And Mayra, she is teacher."

"How's her math?"

"*Que?*"

"*Matemáticas?*" I said, as I opened the grill and started turning the steaks. "Is she good with numbers?"

"Very good," he replied. "Mayra studied hard and is very smart."

CHAPTER SIX

We ate on the terrace and I told Savannah about what Mayra and Marcos and their daughters did in Venezuela.

"We are very short-staffed in the galley," Savannah said. "Any help would be appreciated."

"I would like to meet your *cocinero*," Marcos said.

"After dinner," I said, "I can take you to the galley and introduce you to Grady. I'm sure he'll be happy to meet you."

"If it is good with him, I will start *mañana*."

After dinner, Alberto and Fernando took the dogs down to the aft deck to do their business and Savannah opened a bottle of wine, inviting our guests back out to the terrace to watch the sun go down.

I went to the small but well-stocked bar and opened the cabinet. "What's your preference, Marcos?"

His eyes went straight to one of my favorites, as if it were the only bottle on the shelf.

I grinned and reached for the squat, gray bottle of *Diplomático Reserva Exclusiva* rum.

"Mine, too," I said, taking down two highball glasses.

Later, as the sun was beginning to reach the horizon, Marcos leaned toward me. "Is the owner not aboard?"

"No," I replied. "He rarely is."

"You are going to Bimini to pick him up? Is only a few days in a boat such as this."

"Not exactly," I said.

These people were refugees from a tyrannical government that bent to the will of the drug cartels. Their future was uncertain, but I was sure of one thing—they would never see Venezuela again. At least not while the country was under the control of those who made the lives of its people so intolerable, they'd risk everything to escape.

Savannah was talking with Mayra at the other end of the table, telling her how we'd come to adopt Alberto.

I leaned toward Marcos slightly. "This vessel is owned by a man who would like nothing more than to see the cartels destroyed."

Marcos's eyebrows rose, creating lines across his forehead. "Is that why you have armed men aboard?"

I looked him in the eye for a moment, but I already trusted the man.

"We're looking for a ship that carries drugs and people away from Venezuela."

"*El barco fantasma*," he breathed softly.

"A ghost ship?"

"It is rumored that the people who disappear are taken to a ship," he said. "They are herded into the bottom like cattle."

"The hold of a cargo ship?"

"*Si*," Marcos said. "They are never seen again. The cartels have tried three times to take my daughters. Giselle once, and Crystal two times."

"What stopped them?"

"It was two days ago," Marcos replied. "Ricardo stopped the men from taking Giselle." He made a diagonal slicing motion across his chest. "He was cut with the *machete*."

Either the wound was superficial, or Ricardo had a remarkably high tolerance for pain. He hadn't acted as if he were injured in any way.

"And Crystal?"

"Do not underestimate *mi hija mas pequeña, señor*," he replied with a proud grin. "She is small but a fierce fighter." Then he shrugged. "They were but two men. She beat them both."

"This also happened two days ago?" I asked, wondering how a girl so small could ward off two cartel thugs.

"*Si*, and again later that night. That was when we took the boat and fled."

"It wasn't your boat?"

"Ricardo built it," he replied. "He'd planned to take Giselle and Fernando away. We were only a few miles off the coast when the engine failed."

"You were a good twenty miles from shore when we found you."

He shrugged. "I was smart to have brought a paddle."

We watched, each lost in our own thoughts, as the sun slipped below the horizon in a magnificent display of color. Marcos closed his eyes, his mouth moving silently.

The boat they'd been on was okay for two people and a boy but adding four more adults had severely overloaded it. The small outboard might have been overtaxed, pushing that much weight that far out into the sea.

In just a few minutes, it was dark, and low-level deck lights started coming on all over the ship, including the terrace.

"Come, Marcos," I said, rising from my chair. "You and Mayra must be tired from your ordeal. I will introduce you to Grady, then you should turn in for the night."

Savannah and Alberto said goodnight to our guests, and then I led them to the galley. Grady Lawson was busy when we arrived. When he wasn't busy, he was sleeping. Serving breakfast, lunch, and dinner every four hours for a constantly rotating crew of thirty-four had put him under a lot of strain. Other crew members helped in the galley whenever they could, but everyone on board knew it was only a matter of time before Grady would disappear while at some port.

"Grady, I want you to meet someone," I said, as I led Marcos and Mayra into his galley.

"I already heard, Captain," he replied, not looking up from

a cutting board where he was furiously chopping carrots. "More mouths to feed."

"This is Marcos Santiago and his wife, Mayra," I said, ignoring his attitude. If anyone on board was entitled to have one, it was Grady. "Marcos is a *cocinero*, the former head chef at a resort in Maracaibo."

Grady stopped and looked up from his task. "A cook?"

"And his daughter was his sous-chef and purser."

A slow smile spread across the young black man's face. "Really?"

Grady had grown up in Atlanta's inner city. At an early age, he'd found that he liked being in the kitchen more than playing games with other neighborhood kids. At twenty-two, he'd landed a job in an uptown, five-star restaurant, where his talents were soon brought to light and his skills honed.

"Yeah," I replied. "They need to get some rest, they've been through a tough day, but Marcos will help with the cooking starting at zero-six-hundred."

Marcos turned to his wife and spoke to her in their own language. I caught a few words—*trabajo* for work and *dormir* for sleep—but not much else.

She nodded and he turned back to face me. "With your permission, *Capitan*, I will start now."

"You're sure?"

"*Si*," he replied with a curt nod. Then he looked at Grady. "I think he is more tired than I."

Grady picked up a towel and wiped his hands, then

extended one to Marcos. "You're standing, so I won't argue that point, my man."

Marcos shook his hand then turned to his wife. "Mayra, *por favor trae mi gorro blanco.*"

She started to turn, but Grady hustled to the corner of the kitchen where his desk was. "Wait! I got a coupla spare toques right here." He yanked open one drawer after another. "Where are they? Ah, here they go."

He turned and presented a folded chef's hat to Marcos.

"*Graçias,*" Marcos said, taking and unfolding it.

"*De nada, amigo,*" Grady said. "We can work in English or Spanish; I can speak both, just a little bit ghetto."

Marcos looked at me and smiled, putting the hat on, and pulling it slightly to one side. It suited him well.

"I enjoyed working in the kitchen more than running the resort," he said. "I will work now and rest later."

I nodded and held the hatch for Mayra. "I will see that your wife finds her way back."

I escorted Mayra and Fernando to their quarters. When the boy opened the door to his parents' cabin, Ricardo was lying on one of the bunks, his shirt off. Giselle was removing a bandage that was wrapped tightly around his chest.

"Do you need help?" I asked. "We don't have a doctor on board, but one of the crew used to be a medic in the Army."

"I found him," Giselle said, without looking up. "He gave me the things I need."

She carefully peeled off the bandages, revealing a long but

shallow gash starting at Ricardo's left shoulder, then crossing diagonally over the left side of his chest.

He'd been cut by a right-handed man, in a downward slashing motion meant to go deep into the shoulder and sever the spine, but the wound didn't look deep. I guessed that Ricardo, who I could now see was built like a bull, had managed to step back enough so only the tip of the blade had made contact. The skin was held together with a number of butterfly bandages.

"It looks worse than it is," Ricardo said, as his wife flushed the wound with an alcohol solution.

"*Maldita sea!*" he said, wincing. "That hurts more than the blade."

"You're a lucky man, Ricardo," I offered with a grin.

He put a hand on his wife's knee. "*Si, Capitan.* I am lucky to have such a woman to take care of me. When can I start work?"

I'd noticed this generational ethos among many people. A hard- working man and woman raised hard-working children, who in turn looked for the same qualities in their spouses. They then passed their work ethic on to the next generation. Unfortunately, the same held true for lazy people.

"Tomorrow," I said. "I'm up at zero-five-hundred, and if you feel up to it, I can take you to meet the ship's engineer then."

"*Gracias, Capitan,*" he said, as Giselle placed fresh, sterile bandages over the cut. "I will be ready and able."

I closed the door and turned to Mayra. "Get some rest,

Señora. Grady will only keep him a few hours."

"Thank you, Captain," she said. "You have done so much. The smile on my husband's face when he put the hat on his head was his first in many weeks. You have given him back his dignity. Ricardo, as well."

"You have a hard-working family," I offered, then we said goodnight and I returned to my quarters.

Later that night, after Alberto had gone to bed, I went to the bridge to relieve Matt so he could go down to the mess deck for lunch.

"Nothin' to report, Cap'n," Matt said as I entered. "Sonar has identified 148 vessels. No contacts have gone unidentified, mind."

"That seems a lot."

"Oye," he replied. "About normal for these waters, yeah?" He handed me the binos. "I'll be back dreckly."

When he left, I looked at the water all around us, then used the night- vision binoculars to scan the sea ahead.

The first quarter moon was astern, nearing the western horizon, but the stars provided enough light for the optics to show the surface in great detail. The wind had died down after sunset and the sea looked like a pond, barely a ripple on its vast surface.

I picked up the bridge Metis and scrolled though the dozens of contacts. Most were far off, but nearly twenty were near shore, arriving or leaving the seaports along the Venezuelan coastline.

Looking closer at the water all around, I saw the lights of a ship moving in the same direction, about halfway between us and the mainland.

I tapped the sonarman on the shoulder to get his attention. "What ship is that due south of us?"

He moved to his left and looked at the chart plotter. Radar and AIS imagery was laid over the chart. He touched a boat-shaped icon on the screen and it displayed the ship's name—*MV Canopus*, a coastal freighter.

I remembered the name from earlier in the day, as the ship was coming out of the small seaport just west of Caracas. It made regular runs from there to the eastern tip of Brazil, with many stops along the way.

Looking up, I searched the stars to the south and easily found Carina, the keel constellation. Canopus was the brightest star in that group and the second brightest star in the sky, after Sirius, in the constellation Canis Major.

The star Canopus was directly above the ship *Canopus*.

Glancing down at the chart plotter, I saw that *Canopus* was making fifteen knots, matching our own speed. Unless she stopped at a port on the way, they'd be with us for a while.

Looking at her through the binos, I couldn't see much in the way of detail. In fact, most of the hull seemed to be under water.

Standing on the bridge, my head was about thirty feet above the water, so the horizon would be a little under seven miles away. The plotter showed *Canopus* to be about ten miles south of us, which would explain why she appeared to be sinking. She was beyond the horizon.

The distance to the horizon is a fairly simple calculation. On the water, where everything can be measured in height above sea level, the distance to the horizon in miles was the square root of one and a half times the observation height in feet.

It was dark on the bridge at night. All the gauges and screens were in subdued tones of red, as were the two overhead lights above both side hatches. Glancing back into the op center, it was the same. Indirect red light doesn't interfere with our eyes' natural night vision, when the pupils are fully dilated to allow as much light to reach the optic nerve as possible.

"I'm hearing a whale, Captain," the sonar man said. "Dead ahead, one thousand meters, near the surface."

"Idle engines, helm," I ordered, scanning the water ahead. "Transmissions to neutral."

"Neutral idle, aye," the helmsman replied.

"What kind of whale, Bernie?" I asked.

He looked at me and put his right hand to his headphone, listening for a moment. "A blue whale, sir. Mother and young calf."

"Heading?"

"Stationary, Captain. Probably nursing. It's very early in the year."

"Active sonar," I ordered. "Give her one ping to let her

know we're here."

"One ping active," Bernie said. There was an audible sound from his console. "Ping sent."

Although we could hear other ships through the sophisticated passive sonar, *Ambrosia* herself was much quieter. Instead of noisy, cavitating propellors, she used water jets. And the engine room was extremely well insulated from the rest of the ship, to cut down on interior noise while underway. She'd also had a good bit of sound-deadening insulation added to the inside of the hull, as well. There was a chance the whale hadn't yet heard us and I didn't want to frighten her.

Ahead, I saw a disturbance in the calm water, and then she appeared, surfacing for a breath with her calf as the two swam away toward the north. I recognized the blow as that of a blue whale, and from the swirl of her tail to her head, she was probably eighty or ninety feet long.

"Good ear, Bernie," I said. "A blue about eighty feet with what looks like a newborn calf. Let me know when they're clear of our course. Ahead slow, helm."

"Ahead slow," Kris repeated.

Kris and Bernie had joined *Ambrosia's* crew just a few months before I did in January. They'd both come from one of Armstrong Research's true oil exploration ships.

Though oil exploration was the stated goal of the company, it was known by a few people in law enforcement and government intelligence agencies to be much more than that. Finding oil helped fund Armstrong's other projects.

"Clear and moving away," Bernie reported.

"Resume course and speed," I said.

"Resuming course and speed, Captain," Kris replied.

For the next half hour, nothing at all happened. *Ambrosia* rode quietly and steadily eastward. Only the stars and the water occupied my view. It was no wonder that early man saw pictures in the stars at night. When they were the only thing to see, they seemed to come alive.

Matt returned to the bridge and headed to the coffeemaker to pour himself a mug.

"Nothing to report," I told him. "Except a whale in our way."

"Ah, that explains our slowing down, yeah? Emmets are always gettin' in the bleddy way."

I'd heard him use the term before and had asked him about it. An emmet was Cornish slang for a tourist or newcomer.

I doubted if many on board had even noticed that we'd slowed. But like me, Matt was very attuned to the ship's movement, even if there were no sound.

"I met Mr. Santiago," Matt said. "Seems a proper bloke and the food was hell-of-a-good. Too bad he won't be stayin' on."

"I'll get a chance to try his cooking in the morning," I said. "I'm going to turn in now. It's been a long day."

"I'll see ye at sunup, yeah?"

It's been said that the dialect of Cornwall was what led to the fabled pirate language, and indeed, at times, Matt sounded like how I imagined Blackbeard would have.

When I got to our quarters, Savannah was lying in bed, reading.

"Why'd we slow down a few minutes ago?" she asked, putting a bookmark in the novel, and placing it on her lap.

"A whale," I replied, "nursing her calf. What are you reading?"

She rolled over to place the book on her nightstand and the sheet slid down, exposing a bare breast. She turned back to me and gave me a wicked smile.

"It's the latest by Chelle Bliss," she replied. "Called *Singe*."

"*Singe*?" I asked, as I got undressed. "What's it about?"

"Difficult to say," she replied, lifting the sheet so I could slide in beside her. "It'd be easier if I just showed you."

CHAPTER SEVEN

The drive from Puerto Borburata to Puerto Cabello was only twelve kilometers, but it took twenty minutes on the winding mountain road. The two vans that were transporting the live cargo had the logo of a local fish company on the sides, and each had a large refrigeration unit mounted on the roof. These two mingled in with several other vans on the way to the busy seaport.

When they arrived, they lined up with other similar trucks, all bringing iced-down snapper, grouper, dorado, ribbon fish, mackerel, corvina, octopus, kingfish, wahoo, and other local seafood to the port to be shipped to markets in America, Europe, and Southwest Asia.

Security was lax at the port entry. Occasionally, a guard would ask to see the cargo, and when the back doors were opened, all he'd see were stacks of bins, filled with fish and ice, stacked floor to roof. Each van carried forty-eight of the large plastic tubs, completely filling the inside of each van. In the two Nissan vans, the ones carrying the live cargo, there were only eight containers, packed tightly just inside the rear cargo doors.

The line of delivery vans crept forward as each one backed up to a refrigerated cargo container. The driver and assistant unloaded the catch, moving their tubs of fish deep into the cavernous and cold interior until it was full. Then the container would be lifted and moved onto the ship, as another empty container was lowered into place.

The process continued most of the night, six nights a week. Each evening, the catch was brought to local markets all along the coast, where buyers waited to sort through it, purchasing what their customers wanted and then loading it onto waiting vans and trucks.

On Sundays, nobody worked. The country was over seventy percent Roman Catholic, and even among the drug cartels, the day of rest was strictly adhered to.

The first of the two Nissans pulled up and the assistant jumped out to guide the driver back as close to the container as they could get and still open the doors. Once parked in the right spot, the driver got out and they quickly unloaded the eight bins in the back of the van.

From his vantage point, next in line, only Juan Espinoza and his driver could see movement beneath the other van. He watched the two men's feet disappear as they climbed inside. A moment later, a door in the vehicle's bottom opened and one of the men reached down to lift a manhole cover beneath the van and set it aside.

One by one, the live cargo was forced to climb down into the darkness. When they were all out, the cover was replaced and the door in the bottom of the van secured. Then the two men exited the back of the vehicle, closing the doors.

When the first Nissan van drove away, Juan's driver pulled up and Juan jumped out to guide him back. It was important to park in the right position over the manhole cover. Plus, being in the right spot insured that the back doors could be opened to just inside the container, shielding their work from view.

When the driver joined him at the back of the van, they swiftly moved the bins of fish into the container, then climbed into the back of the van to open the inner door.

Juan moved quickly through the knot of people crammed into the cargo van, pushing anyone down who got in his way. At the front, he lowered the false floor and, lying on his belly, he removed the manhole cover and set it aside as Enrique readied the cargo to be moved.

Juan stood and pulled a suppressed semi-automatic handgun from behind his back. Several of the people near him gasped.

"Your restraints will be removed so you can climb down the ladder," he said in Spanish. "Do not try anything foolish. I will shoot anyone who does and dump your body head first down to the bottom. It is ten meters down. If my gun doesn't kill you, the fall will. Do as you are told!"

Enrique began cutting the bonds of those nearest the front of the van, forcing each down into the floor opening. A weak light shone from far below. They worked quickly until they reached the ones in the back of the van.

"Not this one," Juan said, pointing to the girl he'd hit back on the dock. "She will stay with us for a while."

"No!" she cried. "Please, I want to stay with my fam—"

Juan backhanded her again, silencing her protests.

"You do not have a say," he growled. "Sit there and shut up."

Once everyone was out of the van, the two men exited the rear, and closed both the inner and outer doors.

The young woman stayed inside.

"That one has fire," Enrique said. "How long do you think she will last?"

"A week, perhaps," Juan replied as they pulled away and the next van backed in. Many of the dozens of vans in line were similarly equipped but carried tightly packed bricks of cocaine.

The cartel had gone to great expense to create the new shipyard. The plans incorporated the tunnel, and Juan knew that the whole project was basically built around it and what it led to.

Far more money had been spent for the parasite ship.

It had been Juan's idea. Submarines and low profile boats had been tried and most had failed. He'd been up in the mountains overlooking Puerto Cabello and marveled at the number of ships coming and going when the idea just hit him.

The water at the dock was twenty meters in depth—deep enough for even the largest container ships to dock. After selling the idea to his higher-ups, the first expense had been to find and purchase the right container ship, then refit it to suit their needs.

The ship the Maracaibo cartel bought and used wasn't one of the big Suezmax ships, nor even as big as the Panamax line. But *Canadian Gold* was massive, nonetheless. Measuring over three hundred meters in length with a beam of thirty meters, she could carry 2,250 standard twenty-foot containers.

Canadian Gold was moved to a dry dock and work had begun two years ago, while at the same time, a new shipping facility was being constructed at Puerto Cabello.

The ship went into service a year ahead of the shipyard, carrying legal cargo to and from America and also to contacts in the eastern part of the Mediterranean. This continued for a year, despite the low profits, as the parasite ship and the other two facilities were being built.

For six months now, the cartel had used *Canadian Gold* to transport drugs to America and human cargo to the Middle East, safely tucked into the parasite ship attached to her belly, completely under the noses of the authorities.

Canadian Gold had a draft of only fifteen meters when fully loaded, leaving plenty of room beneath its massive hull and the bottom. During the time in dry dock, while the ship was being repowered and having all new wiring and rigging installed, the ship had several strategically placed eyes welded into the bottom of its hull; fifteen in all. Juan had seen them up close as the ship was being refitted for its new purpose.

Deep below the surface, divers would attach thick cables to the eyes, and once the cargo was loaded into the parasite ship, the watertight hatch would be sealed and the remote operator would disengage it from its docking port, then use onboard winches to lift it off the bottom until it was pulled up snugly to the hull of *Canadian Gold*.

There it would stay until the ship reached its destination.

The parasite ship was small when compared to the container ship it attached to. It was seven meters wide—not even an eighth of the cargo ship's beam—and was just over ten meters in length, which was nothing compared to the 350-meter length of the ship that carried it, stuck tightly to its bottom.

A man of average height could stand up inside the parasite ship but would likely have to keep his knees bent or head bowed. Still, it added well over a hundred cubic meters of cargo space that would never be searched. Enough room to transport eighty tons of cocaine, or up to fifty slave laborers. Twice that if they were forced to lie shoulder to shoulder. Usually, the parasite ship carried a combination of the two. The slaves' beds were burlap-wrapped bundles of cocaine.

The winches and cables attaching the parasite ship to the larger vessel were the only mechanical things on board. There was no need of heating or cooling. The surrounding water kept the interior cool when it was just filled with cocaine. But with more than fifty people, it quickly became sweltering.

An umbilical, disguised as a thru-hull fitting for a bilge pump, provided air from the cargo ship, which helped to keep the temperature low enough that only a handful would die in transit.

Losses were expected.

In fact, if discovered, the captain of the ship could disengage the parasite and let it fall to the bottom. The parasite's strength was in its design to withstand the forces of moving at up to forty knots, while attached to the mother ship. If disengaged while at sea, the great pressures of the ocean's depth would crush it like an aluminum can. So far, that had never happened, or even come close. The cartel was now building another parasite ship and looking for another container ship to dock it to.

The trip from Puerto Cabello to the newly constructed shipyard in Miami would take only three days, running at a steady twenty-five knots. The parasite ship had enough water and food on board, mostly in the form of bread, dried fish, and fruit, to last fifty people for several days if they conserved it. The twenty tons of cocaine had been loaded before the people, stacked in lines that allowed room for them to sit or lie down. The slaves would be told how to ration their supplies just before they closed the hatch. After that, they were on their own until the ship reached another similarly designed port in Syria.

Juan, formerly a nautical engineer, had personally

supervised the shipyard construction in Miami, where much of the work had to be hidden from American authorities.

Slave labor had built the one in Syria. The tons of concrete poured into the forms became the final resting place for most of them when the project was completed.

Juan's van returned to Puerto Borburata with the Guyanese girl in the back. Enrique pulled up next to Juan's car, a black Mercedes with dark- tinted windows.

"Give me a moment to open the trunk," Juan said, climbing out of the van.

He moved quickly, checking the area for prying eyes. He saw nothing. When he opened the trunk lid, Enrique climbed into the back of the van.

"Get up," Juan heard Enrique order from inside.

A moment later, he appeared at the back doors, practically dragging the girl by the hair.

Juan took her by the arm and snatched her out, where she tumbled to the ground. As Enrique had done, he grabbed her hair and pulled her to her feet, moving her toward his car. There, he forced her, headfirst, into the trunk.

As he looked down at her, the bright light of the trunk's interior shining on her face, he saw how beautiful she really was. She cowered in fear as a slow, menacing smile crept across Juan's face.

"Perhaps you will last more than a week," he said, then slammed the trunk lid closed.

CHAPTER EIGHT

I woke early, nearly as tired as I'd been when I'd gone to bed. But it was a good sort of weariness. I stretched and flexed, then quietly dressed for the day.

My choice of work clothes was a little different than Nils's starched white pants and shirts. I opted for dark blue. I tended to get up close and personal with *Ambrosia* at times, and white would show stains too easily.

My denim work shirt did have the four gold captain's stripes on the epaulettes, so there was no mistaking who was in charge when we encountered someone at a port. I also wore a white yacht captain's cover with gold braid on my head.

It had taken some time to get used to wearing a uniform again, such that it was, after more than twenty years as a civilian. I was more comfortable in bare feet and shorts. But after trying several styles, I found the dark blue cargo pants and denim work shirt suited me best.

As I'd done the day before, I headed to the engine room to further familiarize myself with the water maker system. But I had to make a stop on the way.

Instead of using the inside companionway to the bridge, I exited our quarters, then stepped out onto the side deck through an exterior hatch. I went down the aft ladderwell to the cockpit on the main deck and entered a hatch beside the big, glass sliding door to the salon. At the bottom of another companionway, I went forward toward the crews' quarters.

Ricardo was waiting outside his cabin. "Good morning, Captain."

"How are you feeling, Ricardo?" I asked. "I wouldn't hold anything against you if you decided to take more time to heal."

"I'll be fine," he replied. "I'm grateful to you for allowing me and Marcos the opportunity to work off our passage."

"Follow me, then," I said, and turned back the way I'd come.

Halfway down the long passageway, lined with nearly twenty hatches to the crews' quarters, we came to a side passageway to port. Going down it, I opened a hatch on the left and motioned Ricardo through.

Inside, we descended a few steps to a grated landing overlooking the engine room.

"*Madre Dios*," Ricardo breathed softly. "I have never seen such equipment."

"Good morning, Captain," Heitor called from below, his voice rising above the drone of the engines. "I heard we had guests aboard. Who is that with you?"

I started down the last few steps to the engine room deck. "Ricardo, I'd like you to meet Heitor Silva. Heitor, this is Ricardo…" I paused and looked up at him, still staring at the two big turbine engines forward of the main diesel engines. "I don't even know your last name, Ricardo."

He snapped out of it and came down beside me. "Lopez," he said, extending a hand to Heitor. "I am Ricardo Lopez."

"Good to meet ya," Heitor said, shaking his hand.

"Ricardo is a mechanic," I told the engineer. "He and his family will be staying with us until we reach Bimini and he's offered to help you down here."

"Help me what?" Heitor asked. "I mostly just keep an eye on things."

"Didn't you say you could replace the bypass filter pump while underway if you had another mechanic?"

Heitor eyed the young man next to me. "Do you know anything at all about bypass oil filtration?"

"*Si*," Ricardo replied. "To take oil from the sump and slowly move it through a very fine filter and return it to the sump."

"Ever change the pump while the engines were running?"

It was Ricardo's turn to study Heitor. "No," he finally said. "It would be dangerous to both the person doing it and to the engine itself."

Heitor grinned. "A little dangerous, maybe. But if done correctly, by two competent engineers, not so much."

"I'll leave you guys to talk," I said. "I have a date with a water maker."

I went around the port diesel engine, glancing at the tachometer, oil pressure, and temperature gauges. The engine was chugging along at an easy 950 rpm, with the oil and temperature gauges both right in the middle of the green. There were also panels for each engine that provided information digitally, but simple green and red analog gauges required only a glance, without needing to know what the optimal range was. If the gauge was in the green, it was good to go.

Opening a hatch, I entered the mechanical room, with all its intricate wiring, cables, and hoses. I closed the hatch behind me and sat down in the spot I'd chosen the previous morning, laying my cover beside me.

"Now, where were we?" I asked *Ambrosia*.

I wasn't exactly sure if Nils had been right, in that every vessel had a soul. But I'd been on a lot of boats and have owned quite a few. Even boats of the same manufacturer and model had subtle differences in the way they handled and reacted to different waters. I doubted that any two boats were the same and I often talked to my boats.

Not, long, drawn-out conversations, where I hear their voice responding in my head. I think that'd be borderline nuts. The conversations I had were one way, and usually one sentence, like, "Start dammit!" or "Come on, baby, you can do it, just another few miles."

While I studied the hoses, filters, and valves again, I heard Ricardo ask Heitor what I was doing,

"Don't bother him," Heitor replied. "He's new and chooses to learn the equipment in his own way. Come, I will show you where the pump and filters are; then I will ascertain if you have the ability to help with this project."

Their footsteps receded as they proceeded forward and over to the starboard side.

I stood and moved closer to the reverse osmosis system to peer behind the large cannisters. Each had individual inlet lines attached to a large manifold mounted behind them. The inlet lines from the manifold were also large. The cannisters themselves were six inches in diameter and nearly as tall as I was. Each housed its own pump and membranes.

A reverse osmosis unit, or water maker, worked like a filter, except the openings in the mesh of the filtering membranes were much smaller—so small that a single molecule of dissolved salt couldn't pass through.

Water is made of a single oxygen atom bonded to two hydrogen atoms. Size-wise, hydrogen and oxygen are two of the smallest atoms on the planet, perhaps even in the whole universe. Even when joined together to make water, those molecules are smaller than nearly anything else. A single molecule of something like salt or iron would be much larger. That's why water is considered the greatest solvent. Given time, it can dissolve anything.

How they made these microscopic filtering membranes and what they're made of, I didn't know. But they were expensive. I had water makers aboard three of my boats—

Gaspar's Revenge, Salty Dog, and *Floridablanca.*

Due to the size of the membranes in *Ambrosia's* water maker, water moved very slowly through them, as the membranes trapped the salt molecules and any other dissolved elements, producing fresh, pure water. To eliminate having to constantly clean and replace the membranes, the raw seawater entering the system passed through a twenty-micron filter, then a finer one of five microns—which was far less expensive to replace—to filter out any solid matter, like plankton or small bits of seaweed.

It was a simple enough system, not much unlike the ones on my own boats, only far larger. The system on the *Revenge* produced enough water that I could fill the cistern above my house in less than two days. Yet, I could remove it and work on it while it rested on my knees. The filter membranes were miniscule by comparison to *Ambrosia's.* Her water maker could completely fill both of my largest boats in a single day. Not just their water tanks—the entire boats' interiors.

The center cannister had a pressure gauge on top, where the outlet lines joined another manifold to carry fresh water to the ship's tanks. The gauge had a green section, spanning about ten degrees of arc, at the twelve o'clock position of the analog dial, while the rest of the face of the dial was red. The needle was dead center in the green, indicating the system was operating at the perfect pressure. Too high meant the membranes were full, too low could mean a failing pump.

The gauge, like all other analog gauges aboard *Ambrosia,*

was redundant. Beside the canisters was a console where performance was monitored digitally, telling the user the current membrane saturation, and expected time until they'd need to be cleaned.

The back flush pump Heitor had installed greatly lengthened the time between cleaning and replacement, as it moved fresh water backward through the membranes and carried much of the dissolved salt back out into the sea.

Satisfied, I rose and rested a hand on the manifold next to the pressure gauge. "Thanks for the lesson, ma'am."

I patted the manifold, then let myself out of the mechanical room, and headed toward the stairs.

I raised a hand to Heitor and Ricardo. "Off to work now. Have a good day, gentlemen."

Heitor raised a hand in return. "Did she tell you all you wanted to know?"

"And then some," I replied over my shoulder as I ascended the stairs.

CHAPTER NINE

I opened the hatch and entered the bridge just as the sun began to peek over the horizon, almost directly ahead of us.

"Captain on the bridge," Val said.

Then, as she always did, whether I had the day watch or the night, she poured strong, black coffee into a fat-bottomed mug. Being wider at the base, it was much less likely to tip over on a moving boat.

"Thanks, Val," I said, accepting the steaming brew.

She handed me the Metis, while Matt continued his slow study of the waters around us.

"We identified 189 vessels yesterday," Val said. "So far, only a small number of private watercraft have not been identified by either sound signature or AIS. None of those fit the criteria of what we're looking for."

Matt lowered the binos and turned to face me. "All clear

for ten nautical miles around the ship, Cap'n. Ross has only picked up ten new contacts since midnight."

"Mondays are really busy," I said.

"Oye, Cap'n," he confirmed. "Devout Catholics make up most of the people of South America. They celebrate the Sabbath on Sunday, and that's forced on the bleddy heathens."

I grinned at Matt, knowing he was as agnostic as they came, but being Cornish, he'd probably had a strong Catholic upbringing.

"Is the *Canopus* still shadowing us?" I asked, scrolling through the list of contacts from since I'd checked it last.

"Just thirty minutes ago, she slowed and turned toward Golfo Cariaco," he replied. "According to her logs, it's one of her regular stops, mind."

"Good," I said. "It irritates me to be within eyesight of another ship."

"Same 'ere, Cap'n. All night long, whenever I'd look over, I'd get a bit teazy seeing her bleddy lights out there." He handed me the binos. "I'm goin' down to the dining room, yeah? I hear tell the new chef is puttin' together a proper job for the night watch. Call if ye be needin' me. Otherwise, I'll spell ye for lunch."

Matt left, and I took the binoculars to do my own scan of the waters around us.

Ambrosia had the newest and most sophisticated radar and navigation systems available, with backups to even the redundant systems. But I still wanted to have a look around with my own eyes.

I could see nothing but water. Even the high peaks of the northern Venezuelan Andes had fallen far behind us during the night.

I pressed the private intercom button to my quarters and waited for Savannah to answer. When she did, I asked if she'd like to have breakfast with the crew in the mess hall one deck below.

"I spoke to Mayra just a moment ago," she said. "She and their daughters are going there in thirty minutes. Can you wait till then?"

"Perfect," I said. "See you down there."

"If I may, Captain," Val began.

"Yes?"

"I met the Santiagos' daughters last night, while I was out on the foredeck stargazing. I spoke at great length with the oldest one, the one who has the little boy."

"Giselle? What about?"

"Many things," Val replied. "She's a highly intelligent, organized person, Captain. I think she would make a good assistant on the bridge during the night watch."

Exactly what Marcos had said about her, I thought.

"You mean as assistant yeoman, right?" I asked.

"Yes. I can show her what I do during the day, and she can do the same for you and Mr. Brand when I'm off duty."

"I don't know, Val," I said, then jerked a thumb aft. "There's a lot of sensitive communication going on back there in the op center."

"Very little at night," she countered.

"True," I said, rubbing my chin in thought. "And the partition can always be closed."

Between the bridge and operations center, there was a folding partition that was seldom used, since only certain people were allowed on the bridge.

I turned to face her. "But they're only going to be with us for a couple of weeks, Val. Do you really think she can pick up enough to make it worth the effort?"

She nodded. "I think so, Captain. Even if she only takes a little of the burden off your and his shoulders for one or two nights, it will help."

Finally, I nodded my assent. "If she's game, make it happen. Work out your own schedules."

I looked back at the Metis and checked its chart plotter interface. We were twenty miles from the island of La Orchila, a little over an hour, and our course would take us eight miles south of it. The island was owned by Venezuela and they had an air base there. In recent years, they'd leased part of it to the Russian Air Force.

"Come right three degrees, helm," I ordered.

"Right three degrees, aye," Axel Troutman replied, adjusting the wheel for a moment.

"Steady up on course zero-nine-eight."

He turned the wheel back the other way. "Steady on course zero-nine-eight, Captain."

Looking down at the Metis again, I could see that our projected course would take us almost fifteen miles south of La Orchila's five-mile restricted area. I didn't want to have any sort of run-in with the fighter jets I knew might be there.

While I could just as easily have adjusted our course using the Metis tablet, some things were better left to humans. Axel had a feel for the way the ship handled that no computer could understand. Besides, it was better for everyone on the bridge to know.

A few minutes later, I turned over the conn to Val and told her I'd be back after breakfast. As I went down to the mess deck, I knew she'd been right. Val worked four hours on and six off, and her schedule and my and Matt's twelve-hour schedules meant that she was unavailable to either of us at times. Her primary function on the bridge was as a second pair of eyes to monitor everything and everyone, even me and Matt. She was solid and analytical in her job—a great benefit when others might be stressed.

When I got to the mess deck, Savannah and Alberto were already seated. Finn and Woden had positioned themselves on either side of the main entry hatch and, to all outward appearances, seemed to be napping. Their heads were on their paws, but their eyes were open, and their ears twitched with every sound. Both dogs rose and greeted me by leaning against my legs and offering their throats. I gave them both quick scratches, then made a beeline for my son and my wife, kissed her on the cheek and sat beside her. Finn and Woden resumed their faux naps.

One of the ship's stewards, a young woman from Bimini, greeted us with a handful of menu sheets in her hand.

"Pleased to have you, Captain. Everyone is raving 'bout what Grady and Mistuh Santiago are doing down dere in dat galley. Will you be havin' breakfast?"

"Yes, Emma," I replied. "Tell Marcos we'll have omelets. Whatever he feels like making will be fine."

I knew that Savannah wasn't a picky eater and Alberto would eat anything that wasn't moving.

When he'd come to us almost four months ago, he'd been near death—emaciated from a lifetime of poor nutrition, starved and dehydrated for days in a small boat. Since then, he'd put on weight and maybe even grown a little in height.

"I will let him know," Emma said, then hurried off to the galley to give our orders.

"Anything going on today?" Savannah asked.

"We'll be passing La Orchila soon," I replied. "I changed course to steer clear."

"Why?"

"The island's a former Venezuelan Navy base with an airport. In the past, it was mostly a place for high-ranking officers to vacation. Even the president had a compound there. But two years ago, they invited the Russians to post some of their supersonic strategic bombers on the island. They haven't done it so far, but there are Russian fighters there."

"Can I go listen with Mr. Ross after breakfast?" Alberto

asked.

"After your chores and studies," Savannah replied, then turned back to me. "Russian fighters?"

"Don't worry," I said. "They have a five-mile restricted area around the island, and we'll pass it nearly twenty miles to the south."

Mayra and her daughters entered the mess and came toward our table, with little Fernando stopping to pet the dogs. I rose and asked them to join us. In seconds, Emma had moved a table adjacent to ours, the six of us sat down, and Emma took the women's orders.

"Do I have to do math today?" Alberto asked, a bit of a whine in his voice. He was bored and wanted to go play with his new friend.

I looked at him and grinned. "Math is something you'll use every day of your life, son. I know it sucks, but sometimes you just have to embrace the suck."

"Captain McDermitt is right," Mayra said. "Without math skills, you would not know if someone were cheating you at the market."

"We don't have a market on *Ambrosia*," Alberto countered.

He'd be ten in a couple of months, and kids at that age would argue that black was white and up was down.

"How do you think Mr. Ross knows how far away a sound is?" I asked him.

"The computer tells him."

"Yes, but he could do it in his own head if he needed to.

Sound travels through seawater a little less than a mile per second. When he uses active sonar and it takes one second for a ping to be sent and then bounce back and be picked up by his hydrophone, that tells him the object is half a mile away."

"Perhaps I can help," Mayra said. "I have always loved solving math riddles. It was one of my minors in college. In Maracaibo I was a teacher."

"We'd love to hire you as a tutor," Savannah said, as Marcos approached our table. "I'm not very good with numbers."

Mayra shook her head. "I would not accept payment. But I would love to help. I teach Fernando."

Marcos was smiling as he reached the table. Behind him came Emma and another steward, both carrying large trays.

He stopped short and bowed his head slightly. "It pleases me that you are here, *Capitan*. I am very much enjoying working with *Señor* Grady."

The dishes were distributed, and Marcos sat down next to his wife, removing his chef's hat.

The omelet was delicious, and I told him so. It was filled with diced peppers and onions, thin slices of pork, and seasonings. I was half-finished when Val's voice came over the intercom.

"Captain to the bridge."

I rose from the table. "Please excuse me," I said. "Something's come up." I turned to the oldest daughter. "Giselle, when you have finished, would you mind coming up to the bridge? Savannah can show you the way."

"Not at all, Captain," she said, starting to rise. "I can come now, if you like."

"No, please. Finish your meal. It's nothing pressing."

I kissed Savannah's cheek once more, and ruffled Alberto's mop, then turned and went to the winding staircase.

"What is it?" I asked, stepping into the command bridge.

"I'm sorry for interrupting your breakfast," Val said. "But you seemed interested in the ship *Canopus*. She's already coming back out of Golfo Cariaco."

She handed me the Metis, already running the chart plotter interface app. On it, I could see the AIS icon for *MV Canopus*, now fifteen nautical miles behind us.

"Wonder why she put back to sea so quickly," I said, thinking aloud.

Val looked at her watch. "She started to slow fifty minutes ago. They wouldn't have had time to even get into the port, much less load or unload anything."

"Maybe their appointment was canceled," I said.

"I don't think so, Captain," Ross said. "There's a slight difference in her sound signature."

"What do you mean?" I asked, going over to the navigation desk. "I thought a ship's sound signature was constant."

"Yes, sir. It is. But there are very minor fluctuations, like when a ship is fully loaded and riding low in the water, or empty and the props are closer to the surface."

"They picked up something without going all the way into the port?"

Ross looked up at me, then pointed to a panel to his left. "This is the *Canopus's* signature from an hour ago, just before she slowed down." He typed some commands on his keyboard and a second sound graph appeared. "And this is her audible signature now."

I leaned in and studied the two graphs. They weren't much different from the sound pattern of music on some stereo systems, using green bars rising and falling slightly, to show the highs and lows of the music. *Canopus's* signature had a slightly irregular pattern. It was this irregularity that gave each ship its own sound signature. I remembered John Wilson explaining that even with a brand-new ship, there would be differences, caused by slight variations in each blade of the propellers.

"This one's digging harder," I said, pointing to the second graph.

Ross tapped the *Canopus* icon on the chart plotter. The readout showed she was making the same fifteen knots as she'd been doing before.

"Engine revs are up about two percent," Ross said. "But she's going the same speed."

"An increase in weight?"

"I estimate she's about two tons heavier now," Ross said. "I'd gotten so used to hearing her from before that the difference was noticeable."

"So, they went into the gulf opening, stopped and loaded something from another boat?"

"I think so," Ross affirmed. "There was an unidentified pleasure craft in the area when she started heading toward the gulf."

"How do you know it was a pleasure craft?"

He shrugged. "Coulda been commercial, I guess," he admitted. "But it had triple outboards."

CHAPTER TEN

I continued to look at the two sound charts. In these waters it probably wasn't unusual to load and unload from a smaller boat. Fishermen did it all the time.

A whole class of boats was built in the Chesapeake Bay area for just that purpose. They were called "buy boats" and would rendezvous with large fishing ships at sea to buy seafood and bring it back to local markets.

Most likely, that was the case with *Canopus*. She'd met with a boat outside the gulf and loaded cargo.

One of the analysts from the op center stepped out. "Communication for you, Captain."

He handed me a sheet of paper.

"Thanks, Chip," I said, looking down at the paper. As he started to turn, I stopped him. "Oh, close the partition, Chip. And tell everyone back there to keep their voices low. We'll have a guest on the bridge shortly."

"Yes, sir," Chip replied, his voice breaking a little.

Chip McAllister had been with *Ambrosia* for a couple of years, though he didn't look old enough to drive a car.

The communication was an email from Savannah's and my daughter, Flo. In it, she said that she and her boyfriend David would like to visit *Ambrosia* before classes started. She'd made arrangements with Charity, who was due to fly out to meet us tomorrow. She also asked if it would be okay if Tank and Chyrel came, along with an old friend of Tank's.

"I need to make a call," I told Val. "Savannah's bringing Giselle up in a few minutes. You can ask her then."

I stepped out to the side deck, where I'd have an unobstructed signal, and went forward to the Portuguese bridge, fished my sat phone out of my pocket, and called Flo.

"Hey, Dad! That was fast."

"Why didn't you just call my sat phone?" I asked.

"You're sometimes sleeping in the daytime," she said. "It wasn't urgent. Chyrel told me Charity was going to be flying out to meet y'all and I called her to see if she had room before asking you."

"How's Tank doing?"

My friend, Owen "Tank" Tankersley, had moved to the Keys nearly a year ago, after his oncologist had given him only a year or two to live.

"David and I went to see them on Friday. He's not doing well, Dad."

Very soon, I knew I'd be called away from *Ambrosia*. I'd already told Jack, and he'd said that when that day came, he'd send a helicopter immediately, and would be on it to look after things while I went to my friend's funeral.

"How bad is he?" I asked.

"He can't get around like usual," Flo said. "He gets tired very easily and has coughing fits."

"Did his doctor okay him to travel?"

She laughed. "Would it matter?"

"No, probably not. Who's the friend he wants to bring?"

"His name's Bud Ferguson," she replied. "A friend of Tank's from Vietnam."

I didn't have to ponder her request. We were on a routine "patrol and listen" assignment until it was time to head to Bimini.

"Sure," I said. "It might be a long, cramped flight in her Huey, though."

"She's not bringing the Huey," Flo said. "She relayed our request to Mr. Armstrong and he's flying us to Grenada, where one of his helicopters is located."

I grinned. "So, why'd you even bother asking me?"

"Thanks, Dad. We'll be there tomorrow. Charity said to look for us about eight o'clock."

"That'll be about noon UTC," I acknowledged. "See you then."

Jack Armstrong had a fleet of helos and corporate jets stationed all around the world and often moved them around so he could visit his many financial investments. With his wealth, it was comparable to me driving the Beast from Rusty's place to Skeeter's, on Big Pine Key, to get a fuel filter for an outboard.

We ended the call, and I went back inside the bridge. Savannah was there with Giselle.

"Flo's coming for a visit," I told Savannah. "Charity's bringing her and David, along with Chyrel, Tank, and an old friend of his."

"Oh, it'll be good to see them again. When will they get here and how?"

"Charity was scheduled for more computer training later this week. They're arriving tomorrow morning."

"Oh, dear," she said, then turned to Val. "How many empty cabins do we have available?"

"Two doubles," she replied without having to check the Metis tablet.

"That's a problem," Savannah said. "They're two couples and two single people—a man and a woman."

"Easily remedied," Giselle interjected. "That is, if you wouldn't mind Fernando staying with your son while your guests are aboard."

"Alberto would love that," I said, curious. "Go on."

"Kassandra and Crystal can share Fernando's bed in our cabin. They used to sleep over in our apartment all the time. Would the single man and woman be okay sharing a cabin?"

"Tank's friend could stay with him and Chyrel," Savannah said. "And Charity could bunk with Flo and David."

"There are several crew members who are alone in double cabins," Val offered. "Mr. Brand and I, for instance. Charity has stayed with me before."

"More than enough room," I said. "Thank you for the offer, Giselle. You too, Val."

"It will be like old times," Giselle said with a smile.

"Val was just explaining to Giselle her idea of using her as a backup yeoman," Savannah said. "Until we reach Bimini."

Giselle turned to face me. "May I speak to you privately, Captain?"

I waved a hand toward the side hatch, and we went forward to the Portuguese bridge.

Giselle stood looking out over the foredeck for a moment. I gave her time to gather her thoughts.

"You have no idea the impact you have made on my family," she finally said, without looking at me. "The resort had been closed for over a month. We were living hand-to-mouth when we decided to flee Venezuela."

"It's that bad there?"

"Si," she said with a nod. "Even worse. Many men have been taken and forced to work in the coca fields. Women dare not go out alone. We had run out of options."

"We just happened to be in the right place at the right time," I said.

She turned to face me. "No, Captain. It is much more than that. You didn't have to take us aboard. Nobody forced you to extend such generous hospitality. My husband and father are so incredibly happy that you have allowed them to work to pay for our passage. We all want to."

"Is this your way of saying you'll accept the temporary job?"

She looked down at her feet, the wind coming over the bow blowing her long, black hair over her face. Finally, she looked up and pushed her hair back over her shoulder. Her eyes were luminous with tears.

"Would it be asking too much if these positions could become permanent?"

"Permanent?"

"We have no place to go, Captain. My mother lied a little when she said we have money. What we have wouldn't pay for even one of us to get to America."

I didn't have to consider the question long. We were short-staffed in a few areas, not the least of which was the galley and engine room. If Ricardo proved to be as capable a mechanic as he claimed, Heitor would appreciate the help. And I already knew Marcos would be a benefit.

"Have you talked this over with your parents?" I asked.

"With my mother, yes," she replied, almost sheepishly. "My husband and my father are proud men. They would never—"

"What if I asked them?" I interrupted.

I looked into her dark brown eyes as a single tear rolled down her cheek. She quickly turned away and wiped at it. I took her shoulders and turned her to face me.

"I understand a man's desire to work and provide for his family," I said. "And I also understand a man's pride. I think I'll talk to your dad first. If he is willing to stay on and work in the galley, do you think he can convince your mother and your husband?"

Giselle fell into my arms and sobbed for a moment. All I could do was hold her and pat her shoulder. It was uncomfortable, to say the least.

A Portuguese bridge is an open area immediately in front of the windows on the bridge. It has a low bulkhead at the front about waist high, where you can look down on the foredeck.

Finally, Giselle stepped back and wiped her eyes. "Thank you, Captain. We will all work hard, and this ship will become our home."

We returned to the bridge, and I walked Savannah back to our quarters.

"What was that all about?" she asked once we'd reached the interior companionway.

"Mayra lied when she said they had money. They have practically nothing and nowhere to go."

"Then they should stay here," she said. "Or maybe Jack can arrange jobs for them on Bimini."

"That was what Giselle wanted to ask me," I replied, opening the door to our quarters. "If Ricardo's and her temporary jobs could lead to permanent ones.

Alberto and Fernando were at the small dinette, a chess board between them. Finn and Woden were lying next to the table.

"I'm teaching Fernando how to play chess," Alberto said.

I smiled at our son. "Don't show off. Teach him well, so you'll have a worthy opponent."

"He is a good teacher," Fernando said in halting English.

I turned to Savannah. "I'm going to ask Marcos if he'd like to stay on permanently. It'll be up to them after that, but I sense a strong family bond between them."

"Good," she agreed. "But don't make it seem like a handout. Hispanic men are enormously proud."

"That's what Giselle said."

I left her there and returned to the bridge, heading straight to the coffee maker. There was a covered dish beside it. I lifted the cover and saw my unfinished omelet.

"Giselle was worried that you hadn't finished," Val said.

"Where is she?" I asked, picking up the fork and taking a bite.

"She went below to compose herself," Val replied.

"Contact fourteen," Ross interrupted. "An unidentifiable small boat, less than a mile off the southern coast of La Orchila."

I looked at the chart plotter. There wasn't a corresponding AIS icon where Ross had indicated. Nor was there any radar return. We were nearly due south of the island.

"It's a single outboard engine, Captain," Ross said. "Turning slow revs, probably making about ten knots. It's too small for the radar to pick up at this range."

The radar antenna was a good fifteen feet above our heads. That meant the distance to the horizon for it was over eight miles. The boat was at least fifteen miles away. If it were as big as *Ambrosia*, the radar would barely reflect off the upper deck.

"Probably a small fishing boat," I said. "Ignore it and continue your search."

"Aye, Captain."

"Helm, come left three degrees and steady up on your original course."

Axel turned the wheel. "Left three degrees to nine-five degrees true, aye."

Giselle returned, smiling sheepishly at me, then she and Val went to the port side of the bridge, talking in low voices next to the spiral staircase.

As the morning wore on, I thought about how best to approach Marcos. He'd worked late with Grady the previous night and likely started early this morning. Odds were, he was napping in his and Mayra's cabin. I'd wait until lunch time, then go down to the galley.

There were far fewer contacts than the previous morning and the routine on the bridge settled in. We made minor course corrections to avoid ships in the area, mostly out of an abundance of caution. I really felt uneasy being within eyesight of other vessels.

Val explained to Giselle in great detail what each person's job was on the bridge and how control of the ship was handled by more than just the helmsman. She made a point of telling her that while all were good at what they did, each did just the one thing.

"A good yeoman is like a backseat driver," I overheard Val explain. "One who observes and only makes suggestions when necessary. The main thing is to always assist the captain, to anticipate his needs before he does, so he can concentrate on controlling the ship."

I also thought about Flo's upcoming visit. She was about to start her sophomore year at University of Florida and David would be a junior. He worked remotely for Armstrong Research on occasion and had been extremely helpful to the analysts in the op center when they needed computer help. Chyrel did basically the same thing and was impressed with David's abilities.

"Cap'n," Matt said, entering the bridge. "If you don't get things sorted with Marcos before we get to Bimini, we'll lose out on a bleddy good cook, yeah?"

He froze when he saw Giselle.

"Matt," I said, "say hello to *Ambrosia's* newest crew member, Assistant Yeoman Giselle Lopez, Marcos's oldest daughter."

"You mean you already—"

"Not yet," I said, cutting him off. "I planned to do so when I went down for lunch."

He grinned. "Don't let me hold ye up, Cap'n. Go get some denner, yeah?"

I made a perfunctory scan of the waters around us, then handed Matt the binos. "You have the conn."

When I got to the galley, I could hear laughter through the hatch. The laughter was punctuated with rapid-fire Spanish. When I opened the hatch, I saw Grady and Marcos, both dancing around the prep table as they talked and joked. Salsa music played from a small radio.

"Captain!" Grady said, grinning and reaching to turn the music off. "I wasn't expecting you."

"How are things here?" I asked.

"Man, it's so much easier with two of us in here. I mean, well..."

"I understand what you mean, Grady."

"It's just that me and Marcos get along really good, Captain. He's a lot better cook than me."

"*Señor* Grady is too kind," Marcos said. "I have never worked where time seemed to move so quickly."

"Do you have a minute?" I asked Marcos. "I need to speak with you privately."

"*Si*," he replied, picking up a towel and wiping his hands. "Is there a problem?"

"No, nothing like that," I replied, holding the hatch open.

We walked out into the companionway, and I led him forward to the crew's lounge. One of the deckhands was just exiting with a book in his hand, leaving the room empty.

"Have a seat," I told Marcos, then sat at a small table.

Marcos sat opposite me, his face bathed in concern. "What is it, *Capitan?*"

"You've probably noticed we're short-staffed in the galley," I began. "But that's not the only place."

"*Señor* Grady is a fine *cocinero*. But yes, he seems overworked."

"He could probably use *two* more people full time," I said, rubbing the back of my neck. "And we only have one engineer and one yeoman. That's what you call the assistant to the captain and first mate—a yeoman. I don't know how well you know boats, but even a small one requires a lot of work; my engineer is overwhelmed. Don't even get me started on the laundry—it's always backed up."

"But I thought Ricardo was helping with the mechanical work."

"He is," I said. "And I appreciate the two of you pitching in very much. But what happens when we get to Bimini and you and your family fly off to America? I'll be short-handed again."

He cast his eyes down for a moment. "I do not know what will happen to us when we get to Bimini."

"Have you ever been there?" I asked. "It's a small island, but there are lots of things to do. And plenty of work for someone who wants it."

"No, *Capitan*, I have not."

"After Bimini, we're supposed to go to the Mediterranean," I said. "Some of the crew are from Bimini and will likely stay at home once we arrive. We'll probably hire others, but good help is hard to find on a small island. Have you ever seen the Med? Morocco, France, Italy, the Greek islands?"

"No, *señor*," he said. "I have only read about such places."

"The crew earns a good living on *Ambrosia*," I said. "Meals and housing are included, but only a few have been aboard for more than a year. I really need to find more loyal, hard-working crew members."

"You go to these places often?" he asked.

"All over the globe," I said. "Primarily here in the Caribbean, but *Ambrosia* has been to the Pacific and Indian Oceans as well."

Marcos sat up straight in his seat. "*Capitan*, I would like to... How you say? *Solicitar*?"

"Apply?"

"*Si, Capitan* Jesse. I would like to apply for a job."

"What about your wife and family?"

"Mayra will do what I do," he said. "We don't need much."

"And your children?"

He thought for a moment, rubbing his chin. "We will go to America sometimes as well?'

"It's where my home is," I said. "Savannah and I live in the Florida Keys."

"I am a hard worker," he said. "And very loyal. So too are my children and Ricardo. I would like to feed your crew good meals and I will stay as long as you will have me."

"I'll accept your offer on one condition," I said, leaning forward.

"What is that?"

"You discuss it with your wife and family first. Your daughters and Ricardo might not like the idea, and how will you handle it if they go on to America?"

"I will," he replied. "I think I can convince them."

CHAPTER ELEVEN

T he rest of the day went by slowly. With fewer and fewer sonar contacts, it became monotonous. Ocean crossings were long and boring for the most part. But usually, there was an objective, a place you were going to. We had no destination. Our mission was to listen and identify.

At noon, Val handed me the Metis. "Message for you."

It was an email from Charity. *All arrived safely and checked into the resort on Grenada for the night. See you in the morning.*

The next day, once Flo and the others were aboard, we'd continue east until we reached Trinidad and Tobago, the southernmost group of islands in the Lesser Antilles. Then we'd turn southeast, following the coasts of Guyana, Suriname, French Guiana, then on to the eastern tip of Brazil, where we'd turn around. The run from Trini to the turnaround, with family and friends aboard, would take us a little over four days, and we'd find even fewer contacts along that more desolate stretch of coast. Then another four to five days back to the Antilles, where Flo and the others would return to Grenada.

Just before the tip of Brazil was a place called Lençóis Maranhenses National Park, or *Parque Nacional dos Lençóis Maranhenses*, in Portuguese. *Lençóis* meant linen in English, and Maranhenses meant it was in Brazil's state of Maranhão.

The park was a vast area of sand dunes, stretching over forty miles along the coast and up to thirty miles inland. The sand was carried to the coast from the continent's interior by two rivers, the Parnaíba and Preguiças. There, the sand was pushed up onto shore by long, almost perpendicular wave action into a high dune. Wind then carried it inland, creating more dunes and valleys. Some of the dunes rose as high as 130 feet.

From what I'd read, it looked like a desert, but got more rainfall, sometimes creating freshwater pools up to ten feet deep in the hundreds of little valleys between the dunes.

I'd planned to give the crew a couple of days rest there, allowing them to go ashore, explore, sleep, and just unwind. It wasn't exactly permissible without first clearing into the country, but the place was so remote, we'd be long gone before anyone raised a fuss.

Finally, Matt relieved me at 1800, and I went to my cabin, where Savannah was already making dinner.

"Long day?" she asked, as I tossed my cover on the table.

"Boring day," I replied, putting my arms around her from

behind and kissing her neck. "And tomorrow will be even more so."

"But we'll have Flo and the others aboard."

"I'll still be on the bridge," I reminded her. "At least until we get to the dunes."

"I'm looking forward to seeing them," she said. "Are they as impressive as they sound?"

"I've never actually been there myself," I replied. "I've only read about them. So, a first for both of us. Where's Alberto?"

"He and Fernando took the dogs for a walk," she replied. "Did you talk to Marcos?"

"I did," I replied. "He promised to talk to Mayra and their kids before giving me his final decision."

"I hope you didn't make him feel like you were being charitable."

I grinned. "I can be sneaky and underhanded when I need to. It was actually his idea."

"That's good, because—" A knock on the hatch interrupted her. "I wonder who that is?"

I went to the hatch and opened it.

"*Hola, Capitan,*" Marcos said. "I was about to go to the kitchen to help Grady with the evening meals."

"Please, come in," I said. "What's on your mind?"

"I can only stay a moment," he said, entering our quarters. He nodded at Savannah, twisting his chef's hat in his hands. "*Buenos dias, Señora.*"

"*Que bueno verte, Marcos,*" Savannah said.

He smiled at her, then turned to me. "I spoke with my family, *Capitan*. If you will have us, we would like to work aboard this *barco magnifico* for as long as you find use for our labor."

"That's good news, Marcos," I said, clapping him on the shoulder. "I'll let the owner know we have a full crew once more. He will be very pleased. *Gracias*."

Marcos left us and Savannah took my hands. "You do have your moments, my captain."

"What's for dinner?" I asked, looking over her shoulder.

"Food," she replied. "Now pour us both a sundowner and I'll bring our plates out to the terrace in a minute. The boys should be back soon."

Opening the little mini fridge in the bar, I found a pitcher of some sort of frozen concoction. It was kind of greenish-yellow, and I could instantly smell the mango and coconut. Savannah was quite the mixologist, always trying new drink recipes.

I filled a pair of Collins glasses, adding a straw to hers, and carried them outside just as Alberto and Fernando entered, the dogs right behind them.

"We were up on the bow with Miss Val," Alberto said, removing his compact life vest and hanging it in the wet locker on the terrace. "We saw a whole bunch of dolphins. Thousands of them! They raced in front of the boat for a while, then swam away."

I sat down in one of the deck chairs and waved a hand at

the boys to join me. "What kind were they?"

"I don't know," Alberto said, pulling a chair out. "They were smaller than the ones I've seen before. But real fast. And they jumped completely out of the water."

"What did they look like?" I asked, grabbing my personal Metis tablet. "Can you describe them?"

"Well, they were small, like I said. And they had kind of yellowish or tan sides that went back under their tails. I know because sometimes they'd do flips, and I could see their bellies."

"Did they have a longer nose than the bottlenose dolphins you're used to seeing?"

"I think so," he replied. "What are they called?"

"Sounds like the long-beaked common dolphin," I replied, scrolling through a list of dolphins I'd pulled up on my Metis. I found the right picture and turned it around to show the boys. "Like this?"

"*Si*," Fernando said, enthusiastically. "That is it."

"They're usually found in shallower water nearer shore," I said.

Alberto turned to Fernando. "*Mi papá dice que por lo general se encuentran en aguas menos profundas cerca de la costa*," he told him, translating what I'd said.

I only caught a few of his words, but the word *papá* resonated in my mind. Alberto had called me his dad.

"It's not shallow here," Alberto said. "Mr. Ross said it's over a thousand feet deep."

I pointed off to starboard. "We're just a few miles off the continental shelf. There, it's only a couple hundred feet deep. Maybe they heard us and came out to play."

Savannah slid the door open with her bare foot, carrying a plate in each hand.

The dogs looked up expectantly.

"I'll get the others," I said, starting to rise.

She pushed me back down, both hands on my shoulders. "You just sit tight. I'm already a step ahead of you." She placed one in front of each of the boys, then turned to go back in. "I'll have ours in just a sec."

When she returned, we ate our fish sandwiches as the sun slowly slid toward the horizon. As it disappeared, I noticed that Fernando closed his eyes for a moment, his mouth moving silently, just as his grandfather had done.

"What is that you do, Fernando?" I asked. "Just as the sun set."

"*Qué?*"

"Closing your eyes," I said.

He looked at each of us in turn. "It is custom with my people," he replied. "In case of the...*destello de verde*. We wish for good luck."

The green flash was a rare phenomenon at sunset. When atmospheric conditions were exactly right and the sea state was calm, if a person looked closely, they might see a faint flash of green light just as the sun disappeared over the horizon. I'd only seen it a few times in my life, though I made it a habit to watch the sunset as often as I could.

"We have the same custom," I told Fernando. "We make a wish at sunset and if we see the green flash, it's supposed to come true."

"I have never seen it," Fernando said. "*Mi abuelo tiene.*"

"Keep looking for it," I said with a smile. "One day you can tell your grandfather that you have seen the *destello de verde* as well."

After the dishes were done, the boys went to play in Alberto's cabin, and Savannah and I went out to the foredeck. At night, the lights on the foredeck were extinguished and those from the bridge created nothing more than a dim, red glow. So, the foredeck was in complete darkness. Even the moon was invisible, obscured by the ship itself as it followed the sun toward the western horizon behind us. Stars provided the only light on the foredeck, but it was more than enough to see by. And the water all around us was illuminated by the moon.

There were a few others on the foredeck. Marcos's oldest two daughters, Giselle and Kassandra, sat with Val and Axel, staring up at the night sky.

"Please join us," Val said, when she noticed us.

The four of them were sitting on a wide deck cushion, their backs against the raised superstructure of the forward part of the main deck.

"Thank you," Savannah said, taking a seat next to the youngest, dark-haired Venezuelan beauty.

I sat next to her, and we held hands as we gazed up at the dazzling display. Words weren't needed. Everyone there sat just as I did, their heads tilted heavenward and eyes wide open. Some were even slack- jawed in amazement. It was nightly entertainment for most of the crew.

Even on my island, which was miles from the lights of Big Pine Key and Marathon, the glow could be seen from the two towns and even from Miami, far to the east. The light pollution diminished the number of stars you could see from there.

But out on the ocean, a hundred miles from any man-made light source, the stars shone in full brilliance, all the way down to the horizon.

"I never get tired of looking at the stars from a boat at sea," Savannah said softly.

"I have never seen so many," Kassandra acknowledged, her voice low, almost reverent.

"It's one of the main reasons I stay on," Axel said. "I look forward to coming out here to watch the stars when I'm not on duty. And they're a bit of a distraction when I'm on the bridge at night."

"It's beautiful," Val added. "Sitting here for hours watching them move across the sky makes me feel very small."

A few minutes passed, then Heitor and Ricardo joined us. Ricardo kissed his wife and squeezed in between her and Kassandra.

"Nobody's in the engine room?" I asked. "I thought you said

you were going to have to sit on that bypass pump until we reached Bimini."

"Oh, I think it's going to be just fine now," Heitor replied, taking a seat beside Savannah.

"Why's that?" she asked.

"It's on my workbench in pieces," Heitor replied. "Ricardo and I replaced the pump an hour ago."

CHAPTER TWELVE

The next morning started the same way as before—me rising early to have a little alone time with my ship. On this particular morning, I decided to spend it in the forward part of the crew deck.

"So, you hired them without knowing anything about them?" Travis asked.

He sat comfortably in an overstuffed chair. Each member of the security team had their own small room in this section of the crew deck, with Stockwell having a double stateroom and office. We were in the office.

"You know how you can get a good read on someone right off the bat?" I replied. "They're good, solid people."

"Sounds to me like providence put them right in our path," he said, his hard, steely eyes giving away nothing. "What do you think the odds are of finding just the people needed, floating in the middle of the Caribbean?"

"Are you thinking one of the cartels sent them and they're here to slit our throats while we sleep?"

One corner of his mouth turned up slightly. "You said it, not me."

"Why would they send a cook, a teacher, a mechanic, and a laundress?" I asked. "It's more likely they'd send hardcore mercs."

"We've known each other a long time, Jesse. I'll be blunt. You're in command of a large vessel with a crew of thirty-four, many of whom are highly-trained operatives."

"And you think taking the Santiagos aboard is a threat?"

"Not a threat," he said, looking around the office. "Within easy reach, I have two handguns and an Uzi. My men are armed in their sleep. We train constantly for anything that might happen, including infiltration. In a pinch, you and a few others in the bridge crew, each with similar backgrounds to yours, can be armed and manning the rail."

"So, what then?" I asked. "Do you think it was irresponsible to bring them aboard?"

"No," he replied, rising, and moving over to a coffee maker. He held the pot out, offering me a refill. I extended my mug and he filled it, then poured his own. "Jack saw leadership potential in you," he continued. "I happened to agree with him. He wouldn't have spent all the time, energy, and money molding you into a ship's captain if he didn't trust your judgment.

"It would have been irresponsible of you to not take them aboard," he added. "The first rule of the sea is to never leave a mariner adrift. I'm just an old dog soldier, but I've learned a lot being on this tub."

"Tub?" I asked, taking a sip of my coffee.

"You know what I mean, Jesse. You, and you alone, are responsible for the well-being of the thirty-four souls aboard. Now you've made that forty-one. You've increased your responsibility by twenty percent."

"Soon to be forty-seven souls," I said. "We have visitors arriving in a couple of hours."

"I've heard," Travis said. "I'm looking forward to meeting your friend Tank. Is it true what they say? That he somehow knew where all those mines were?"

I grinned as Travis sat back down in his chair. "I'll let him tell you that story."

"The thing is," he began, "Jack put you in charge for a reason. It's your job to hire crew—at least those outside the more technical positions, and of course, my security team. Jack hired you, Brand, Val, and most of the guys in the op center and on the bridge. I hired my security team. You should vet the crew you hire. That's all I'm saying."

"I have," I replied, looking over my mug at the retired spec-ops Army officer. "Let me ask you something. Did any of your guys come to you looking for a job, and hand you a resume?"

"Point taken," he replied. "I searched them out."

"I found solid people to fill at least four vacant positions," I said. "The fact that none of them were looking for a job when I found them doesn't make them any less qualified."

"I agree," Travis said. "From what I heard, Mr. Silva was very much impressed with your new mechanic. And I've seen firsthand what Mr. Santiago can do."

"Then what's the problem?"

"The girls," he replied, his eyes boring holes into mine. "They'll be a distraction."

"They're not the only women aboard, Colonel."

He sat forward and put his mug on the table between us. "Has being married affected your eyesight, Gunny? I'm old enough to be those girls' grandpa, but even *I* can see they're more than just beautiful. A lot more. My men are professionals, but they have eyes. Meachum and Duster are young and far from home."

I took a slow sip from my mug, then put it down. "They're all young, Trav. When did we get so old?"

The lines in his face seemed like they might crack as a rare smile came slowly to his lips. Then it went away, as if it were never there. "For me, it was in the Sinai Peninsula, nearly forty years ago. For you, I expect it was in Beirut a year later."

He rose and looked down at me. "You didn't come down here to chat about crew hires. What is it you want?"

I stood and faced him, our eyes at the same level. We were two old warriors, cut from the same cloth.

"I want to inspect the armory."

"No need," he said. "I check it daily."

"Have you done that today?"

"Not yet," he replied.

"Then we can do it together. I have thirty minutes to kill, and the armory is the last thing on this tub I haven't gotten up close and personal with."

"Tub?" He paused and grinned. "Okay, let's go have a look at *Ambrosia's* weaponry."

The armory was next to his office. Stockwell punched the code into a pad next to the hatch and pushed it open. Walt Meachum was at a table, reassembling an M-249 Squad Automatic Weapon, or SAW, a crew- served machine gun requiring two men to operate.

"Colonel," Meachum said, "I wasn't expecting you for nearly an hour."

"Captain McDermitt wanted to inspect the armory, Walt."

Meachum faced me. "Any time, Skipper. I have a couple of sweet long guns I know you'd be interested in."

"With only five security people aboard," I said, "including the Colonel, why would we need a SAW?"

He grinned. "It's not for us. If the shit hits the fan, Axel Troutman and Bernie Knight would man the SAW up on the roof of the flybridge."

"How long would it take to deploy it?"

He pointed up to a hatch in the overhead, a ladder leading up to it. "It can be deployed in less than three minutes. They do time tests once a month, and they don't stop until they get it under that."

The M-249 is a smaller caliber machine gun than the M-60, used by Marines during my time in the Corps. It had variable rates of fire—the highest nearly double that of the familiar chug-chug-chug of the 60, and it had a slightly higher muzzle velocity. Personally, I preferred the M-60. Nothing instilled fear in the enemy more than the sound of the larger and louder 7.62 mm rounds it fired. That is, unless you could deploy a Ma Deuce. The M-249 was kind of an M-16 rifle on steroids.

"What would your team deploy ahead of the shit hitting the fan?" I asked.

"Each man on the security team is armed with an M-9 at all times," Walt replied, unholstering his own Beretta. He dropped the magazine out and racked the slide, catching the cartridge as it was extracted from the chamber. Then he placed the weapon on the table.

The Marine Corps was just changing over from the M-1911 .45 caliber sidearm when I'd retired. So, I was familiar with the 9mm Beretta. The venerable old Colt .45 had been in service for nearly a hundred years.

I picked up the weapon and had it disassembled in seconds. I looked into the chamber and through the barrel. It was as clean as a whistle. I quickly reassembled it, racked the slide, and test-fired it, hearing a satisfying click, then laid it back on the table.

"What else?"

"The M-16 would be the weapon of choice on the battlefield," Walt replied, reloading and holstering his sidearm. "But in the confines of a ship, we opted for the Wilson SBR, chambered for the five-fifty-six NATO cartridge, same as the SAW. The short-barreled rifle isn't as accurate at long range, but on a moving deck, accuracy beyond three hundred yards is nearly impossible."

"Anything heavier than the SAW?" I asked.

"We can deploy two M-2 .50 caliber machine guns," Walt said. "There are stanchions for each Ma Deuce fore and aft. We also carry a pair of FGM-148 Javelins, with heat-seeking missiles."

"Impressive," I said, picking up the SAW's receiver assembly and inspecting it. As with Walt's sidearm, there wasn't a speck of dust or grime. "And the long guns?"

He grinned and jerked a thumb toward a cabinet next to the workbench. "Have a look."

I opened the cabinet. It wasn't locked.

"In the event of a pending attack by hostile forces," Walt began, "the Colonel will order me and you to the armory from wherever we are. It will be our job to deter and discourage the attackers long before they get into range of the SBRs."

The locker contained a pair of Barrett .50 caliber semi-automatic rifles, six ten-round magazines, and several large ammo boxes.

"What are they zeroed at?" I asked, taking one out.

"Zeroed to the maximum effective range," he replied. "Almost two thousand yards."

"One thousand, nine hundred, and sixty-nine," I said, lifting the heavy rifle to my shoulder and peering through the scope at the bulkhead.

"That looks damned sweet welded to your cheekbone, Gunny," Walt said.

"You used the Barrett in Afghanistan," I said, lowering the rifle and putting it back into the cabinet. "Two confirmed kills from over a mile."

Walt looked at Travis and then back at me. "I'm flattered you know that."

"Don't be," I said coldly. "There's nothing flattering or sweet about taking a human life, son."

"No, sir," he replied.

"We have guests coming aboard shortly," I said. "Maybe after they leave, later in the week, you and I can go out on the aft work platform and put some tow targets out."

Walt smiled broadly. "I'd be honored."

"Will there be anything else?" Travis asked.

I looked at my old dive watch. It read 0555. "No, I have to relieve Matt on the bridge."

Once we left the armory, I stopped at Travis's office and turned to face him. "One of those Barretts is brand new," I said.

"Nils couldn't hit the broad side of a barn," he offered. "Jack sent the new one before you came aboard."

"I haven't fired a rifle in several months."

"I've seen you hit a target with a cold, unfamiliar barrel at five hundred yards, Jesse. With no more information than someone else's word on what the weapon's dope was."

"Your armory is very impressive, Trav. Hopefully, it'll never be needed."

"From your mouth to God's ears," Colonel Stockwell replied.

CHAPTER THIRTEEN

An hour and a half after sunrise, Ross reported an incoming radar contact approaching from the north at 145 knots.

"Roger that, Mr. Mosely," I said. "Dead slow, helm. Turn us into the wind for helo recovery."

"Dead slow, aye," Axel repeated, pulling back the throttles to idle speed and turning the massive yacht into the wind. "Heading to windward, Captain."

I checked the radar screen, then pushed the button for the intercom to my quarters. "Flo will be here in five minutes, Savvy."

A moment later, her voice came back over the comm. "Can Alberto and I join you on the helipad?"

"Yes," I replied. "Is Fernando with him?"

"No, he went to breakfast and is going to spend the day with Mayra, studying."

"I'm headed that way now," I said, then released the button and turned to Val. "You have the conn, Val. Have two crewmen meet us up there."

"Aye, Captain," she said. "I have the conn."

Going aft, I opened the hatch and started down the long, inside passageway. Savannah and Alberto were just coming out of our quarters, so I waited by the exterior hatch. Together, we made our way up to the expansive flybridge.

The flybridge covered the entire command bridge, op center, and my quarters. The helipad took up the aft part of it, a big round circle with an H painted in the middle of it. The flybridge itself was relatively small, just two forward-facing seats at the helm and a small table and L-shaped seating behind them.

"Where are they?" Alberto asked. "I don't hear it."

I scanned the sky off to the north and behind the ship, until I spotted the sleek, executive helicopter. Then I knelt beside my son and pointed. "There she is. See that black dot turning behind the boat?"

"I see it!"

"Stay here with Savannah until the pilot shuts down the engine," I warned him.

Then I stepped aft, removing the cable that separated the flight deck from the flybridge. Opening a small locker, I removed two yellow-and-red-striped paddles, then moved aft to the forward edge of the slightly elevated helipad.

I stood facing aft, the paddles alongside my knees, as the

Bell 222 approached. It flared and began to slow down over our wake. I could see the pilot and copilot in the front seats, both wearing reflective aviator shades and ball caps.

At about a hundred yards out, I raised both arms until they were horizontal to the deck, paddles facing the incoming bird. It flared again, until its speed matched *Ambrosia's*. Then I bent my elbows and moved the paddles up and down, signaling the pilot forward.

The nose dipped slightly, and the chopper moved toward me. It started to drift a little to port, but before I could signal that to the pilot, he corrected and continued to approach.

The landing gear came down just fifty feet beyond the helipad. When it moved over the edge, I stopped my forward signal and again signaled it to hover.

The bird held position ten feet above the deck, matching the boat's movement perfectly. I slowly lowered the paddles, and the pilot brought the chopper down closer to the deck. As soon as the wheels made contact, I brought the paddles together in front of my legs.

The pitch of the rotors changed, and the full weight of the helo compressed the shocks in the landing gear as it settled fully onto the deck.

Two crewmen came from behind me and ran in a crouch to the helicopter, attaching straps to four points in the bottom of its fuselage and to recessed rings in the deck. In seconds, they pulled the straps tight.

With the bird secure, I raised the paddle in my right hand

and did a sawing motion in front of my neck, signaling the pilot to cut the engines. The high-pitched whine of the turbines ceased, and the rotors began to slow, the transmission now disengaged.

After stowing the paddles in the gear locker, I approached the chopper's right side to congratulate the pilot on a perfect landing.

When I opened the door, Charity pulled her cap and sunglasses off, shaking out her blond hair and smiling at me. "You're still a pretty good marshaller."

"I didn't know you'd be flying," I said. "I was expecting you to be a passenger and the chopper to return to Grenada."

"Dad!" Flo yelled, as she stepped out of the bird's rear door.

I turned as 120 pounds of excited girl jumped and flung her arms around my neck, while David stepped down beside us.

"It's good to see you again," I said, hugging my daughter tightly.

She released her stranglehold and I shook David's hand as Chyrel stepped down and helped Tank out. He wore one of those tube things that provide oxygen to the wearer's nose. The end of it went to a small box strapped at his waist. Tank looked old and frail, a far cry from the man I'd last seen just four months earlier.

"How are you feeling, Tank?" I asked hesitantly.

He removed the tubes looped around his ears and stuck the nasal cannula in his pocket. "Not dead yet," he said, as the man who'd been in the copilot's seat came around the nose. "I want you to meet a friend, Gunny. This is Bud Ferguson. Bud flew choppers in Nam."

"Any friend of Tank's is a friend of mine," I said, shaking the man's hand.

Bud seemed a few years older than Tank, which made sense if he'd been a chopper pilot when Tank was a PFC. But Tank now looked to be a decade older than his seventy years. Bud was tall and stood erect, with silver hair pulled back in a ponytail.

"Tank's told me a lot about you," he said.

Just then, Alberto came running up. He stopped short beside me, looking up at Tank and the others.

"Hey there, Alberto," Tank said, dropping down to one knee. "How've you been?"

The boy smiled. "Right as rain, Master Guns."

Tank laughed and scooped him into a big bear hug, belying the fact that he should have been on oxygen.

"What's that tube for?" Alberto asked, when Tank released him.

"This?" he asked, pulling the cannula out. "Charity let Bud fly. That old Airedale can scare the pants off a nun."

"Airedale?"

"That's what you call a Devil Dog who flies," Tank replied.

Alberto turned toward Flo. "Are you my sister?"

Flo's eyes brimmed with tears as she knelt in front of him. "Yes, I am. My name's Florence but you can call me Flo, okay?"

"Mom told me how your whole family is named after

cities."

"That's right," she said. "Mine's a city in South Carolina and Mom's is a city in Georgia."

He glanced back at Savannah, who'd now joined us. Then he looked up at Flo again. "And her sister was named after a city in North Carolina—Charlotte. And her mom and dad were Madison and Jackson."

"Come on," I said. "Let's all go down to the mess deck. You can get something to eat or drink, then Savannah and Alberto can show you to your quarters. I'll have to go back to the bridge."

I led the way to the steps down from the flybridge but paused at the helm and pushed the intercom button. "Captain to bridge."

"Bridge," came Val's voice over the speaker.

"Helo recovered. Resume course and speed."

"Aye, Captain," she replied. "Resuming course and speed."

"Follow me," I said to the others, then started down the ladder. "The crewmen will get everyone's luggage and take it to your quarters."

A few minutes later, we were all seated at one large table, which I had no doubt Emma was responsible for arranging.

"Was that your first mate on the comm?" Bud asked. "A woman?"

"That was Val McLarin," I replied. "She's my yeoman and acting first mate at times. My mate's a Cornishman named Matt Brand. He's off duty right now, so I left Val in control of the ship for a while. You'll be bunking with Matt during your stay. I hope that's okay; we're tight on accommodations. Matt works nights, so you'll have the cabin all to yourself."

"I'll be staying in Val's stateroom?" Charity asked.

"Yes," I replied. "We're back to a nearly full crew, so there aren't any private accommodations available."

"That's perfectly fine," she said. "Where did you hire crew from?"

"It's a long story," I said. "Savannah and Alberto can fill you in. But I need to get back to the bridge."

"Would it be okay if we tagged along?" Tank asked. "Me and Bud?"

"Sure," I replied, rising from my chair.

I kissed Savannah on the cheek and guided the two men forward to the spiral staircase leading up to the bridge.

"How big is your ship?" Bud asked, as we stepped out onto the bridge deck.

"*Ambrosia* is a foot shy of two hundred feet in length," I replied. "She has a thirty-two-foot beam and displaces almost five hundred tons when fully loaded."

The two men looked around at the modern equipment in front of the helmsman and sonar man. I'd told the bridge crew that I might be bringing guests up, so Axel and Ross had removed all the sensitive information from their displays.

"When we first spotted you on radar," Bud said, "you were making fifteen knots. Is that her top speed?"

"That's her cruising speed on the main diesel engines," I

replied. "She can reach twenty on those."

"And on the auxiliaries?"

"Classified," I replied. "But suffice it to say that the Saudi sheik who had her built was a speed junky. So, you were a chopper pilot in Vietnam?"

"Hueys," he replied. "Tank was my crew chief for a while."

"Bud was flying the day we picked up those Marines in the mine field who'd gotten pinned down," Tank explained.

"Is that right?" I said, turning to face Bud. "Thank you for what you did that day."

Bud jerked a thumb toward Tank. "He's lucky I didn't bust his ass. I ordered him not to leave the aircraft."

"I'm a little tired," Tank said. "I think I'll go find my cabin and lie down for a bit."

"Sure, Tank," I said. "Matt usually relieves me at eleven hundred for lunch. I'll catch up with you then, okay?"

"Mind if I hang out?" Bud asked, as Tank went back down the spiral staircase.

"Suit yourself," I replied. "Most of the ship is open to you."

Giselle entered the bridge, wearing the standard blue shorts and white button-down blouse of the crew, her dark black hair a sharp contrast to the crisp linen.

"Do you want to take control, Captain?" Val asked from behind us. "I was going to show Giselle more of the ship and introduce her to some of the crew and what they do."

I turned and nodded. "I have the conn."

The two women disappeared into the op center, closing

the folding panel behind them.

"What's back there?" Bud asked.

I studied the man for a moment. I'd always been good at reading men. Not women so much—on that front, I was usually way off base. But I could size a man up rather quickly and Bud struck me as trustworthy.

"This isn't a yacht," I said. "*Ambrosia* is a research vessel."

"I figured that out when I saw the submersible on that big, ugly work deck. How deep is it rated?"

"Eight thousand feet," I replied, then moved aft, to get out of earshot of the bridge crew. "Back there are a half dozen technicians," I whispered. Then I nodded toward Ross, bent over his sonar screen with his headphones on. "We're currently conducting a sonar search of the entire northern coast of South America."

"Looking for oil deposits?"

The way he said it made it obvious he didn't think that was what we were doing.

"How long did you serve, Bud?"

"Thirty years in the Corps," he replied. "I retired as a lieutenant colonel."

That struck me a bit odd. Usually, a Marine officer would be a full-bird colonel by thirty years, maybe even a brigadier general.

"The first ten were active," he said, as if reading my thoughts. "I spent the last twenty in the reserves, where I worked out of Langley, Virginia, at the behest of the president."

"CIA?" I whispered.

"Although my address was Langley," he said, then looked southward out the starboard hatch, "I spent most of those twenty years right down there."

"*Ambrosia* isn't just a research vessel," I said quietly. "And Armstrong Research does more than look for oil deposits."

He looked around the bridge. Axel and Ross had their backs to us. The two men were like bookends, both over six feet tall, broad- shouldered, and very fit. Not your typical helmsman and sonar man.

"I know who Jack Armstrong is," he said. "You're looking for drug smugglers or pirates."

It wasn't a question.

"We're looking for anything out of the ordinary," I replied.

He gave me a knowing look. "Like the ghost ship?"

CHAPTER FOURTEEN

An hour earlier than usual, Matt relieved me for lunch. "I met me cabin-mate a bit earlier," he said. "A proper bloke, 'e is."

"I'm sorry about that," I offered. "We're suddenly a little short on accommodations."

"Hunky-dory, mate," he said with a grin. "I ain't there at night, an' he promised 'e'd not disturb me kip during the day. A bit of a spooky geezer, mind."

I couldn't help but grin. "He is that," I replied. "He's a retired CIA spook."

Matt looked at me puzzled. "A spook, ye say? You mean like a ghostie?"

"A spook is an undercover agent," I explained.

"A birdwatcher? That's what we call 'em, yeah." Then his face became serious. "I 'ear CIA agents *never* retire."

"They have to at some point," I said. "Ferguson's gotta be at least in his mid-seventies."

"A proper double-oh-seven, yeah? Take a few hours, Cap'n. Spend some time with yer emmets."

"Thanks, Matt," I said. "I will. You have the conn."

"I have the conn, oye," he replied, picking up the binos and scanning the sea ahead. "What's the count up to, Ross?"

"Twelve contacts so far, Mr. Brand," Ross replied, as I headed for the corridor.

When I reached our quarters, Flo and David were both there, getting to know Alberto.

"An early lunch?" Savannah asked.

"Matt has the conn for a few hours," I replied, tossing my cover on the little coffee table. "He said I should spend time with my emmets."

"What's an emmet?" Alberto asked, looking up at me with a puzzled expression.

"It's a Cornish term," I replied. "An emmet is a tourist."

"Tank's friend seemed nice," Flo said. "Did you know he was seventy-five?"

"No, but I figured he was a bit older than Tank, who was only seventeen when he enlisted. Chopper pilots are college-educated officers, so he'd have to be at least four years older to serve with Tank right after he enlisted. Have you seen either of them around?"

"They went down for lunch," David said. "Chyrel and Charity are in the op center. Would it be okay if I joined them?"

"Sure," I replied. "I figured you'd be there sooner or later."

He left us and I joined Flo and Alberto on the sofa. "It's Wednesday," I said. "Aren't you supposed to be studying?"

He grinned at me. "The admiral said *I* could take a long lunch, too."

I put an arm around him and pulled him close. "She did, did she?"

Woden's head came up, his ears perked.

"I'm just playing with him," I said to the dog.

"Woden takes his job very seriously," Flo said to Alberto. "He was my protector when I was younger than you. He and Finn won't let anyone hurt you. Not even dad."

"He'd never hurt me," Alberto said. "Him and Mom saved my life."

Savannah let out a little gasp, trying to hide it with her hand. It was the first time he'd directly referred to her as his mom. Until today, he'd never referred to us directly by anything and when talking about either of us to the other, he'd used our names.

"Mine too," Flo said.

"Really?"

She looked over at me for a moment, then back at her adopted brother. "Yes, really."

"How's the swim training going?" I asked Flo, changing the subject.

She grinned. "Swimmingly!"

Savannah laughed.

"Sorry, I couldn't help it. It's going really well. Last week, I swam a two-hundred-meter freestyle that tied the school record

147

and was just a little over a second off the U.S. record."

"Whoa! That's excellent," I said. "I'm sorry you didn't make the team for the Tokyo games."

"Coach didn't think I was ready to try out," she said with a shrug. "He thinks I'll grow another inch this year."

Using my best Bogart impression, I said, "We'll always have Paris."

She laughed. "Well, it gives me another three years to prepare for the Paris Olympics."

"I'd much rather visit Paris anyway," Savannah said.

"You're gonna be in the Olympics?" Alberto asked, in awe. "We watched some of it a few weeks ago."

"She will," Savannah said. "She had one of the best trainers when she was little."

"Who?"

"Charity," Flo replied. "She swam in the Sydney games twenty-one years ago."

"The lady who flew the helicopter?"

"Yep," I replied. "She won a medal, too."

Wow," he breathed softly.

"Why don't you men leave us girls to talk?" Savannah said. "Tank told me he and Bud were going to try to catch a fish or two after lunch."

"Can we go too?" Alberto asked, excitedly. "I saw them headed down there a little while ago."

The kid enjoyed fishing as much as I did.

"For a little while," I agreed. "You have to get back to your schoolwork and I have to go back up to the bridge."

He turned and looked at Flo. "I'm glad I finally got to meet you. I think I like having a big sister."

She smiled and rose with us. "You have three," she said. "And two brothers-in-law, and a nephew."

"I haven't met them, yet," he said. "We've been on *Ambrosia* for a while now."

She smiled. "Soon, you might have another brother-in-law."

"Huh?" Alberto and I said at the same time.

She took Savannah's and my hands. "It was David's idea to come and see y'all." She turned and faced me. "If he asks for a few minutes of your time, Dad, please don't put him off. He might be too scared to ask a second time."

"He proposed?" Savannah asked, hugging her tightly.

"Not officially," she replied, pushing her mother away and looking up at me. "But we have talked about it. He said his dad told him he'd have to ask you first."

I looked over at Savannah, who was smiling brightly, then back to our daughter. "He damned sure better."

"There's one more thing," she said, looking down at the deck.

"What is it, sweetie?" Savannah asked.

She looked at her mom. "I changed my name last week."

My chest swelled with pride.

"As I get married," she continued, "I want my name to be McDermitt. Is that goofy?"

Savannah looked over at me and we both smiled.

"Not at all," Savannah said. "It's what your name should

always have been."

I hugged both of them and then guided Alberto toward the door. When we reached the large, aluminum work platform attached to the stern of the boat, Tank and Bud had set up the two chairs and had lines trolling out behind *Ambrosia*.

"Any action yet?" I asked, as Finn and Woden lay down beside the two outboard stairwells.

"Bud put a wahoo in the cooler," Tank said, nodding toward a six-foot Igloo mounted at the side of the work deck.

Many of the crew members enjoyed fishing and it supplemented our provisions. Between the two sets of stairs was a large door that could be raised to access the "garage," where the submersible was usually kept, along with an assortment of other things, including fishing and dive gear, an air compressor for filling scuba tanks, two twenty-four-foot tenders, and a mini-sub. One of the crew must have shown them where the gear was located.

I flipped open the lid on the Igloo. The fish was nearly as long as the cooler and probably close to a hundred pounds.

"Hell of a catch, Bud," I offered.

"Would you like to take a turn?" he asked Alberto, as he unclipped himself from the fighting chair and rose.

"Thanks," the boy replied. "But if I catch one that big, I don't think I could get it on the boat."

"Have a seat," Tank said. "Me and you can fish together like we did back in the Keys, and if you get a big one, we'll all help you get it aboard."

Alberto settled into the chair and adjusted the straps to fit his smaller frame.

"A couple of fine animals there," Bud said, nodding toward where the dogs lay watching everything that went on.

"Thanks," I replied. "They've sort of taken it on themselves to stay close to Alberto. They're both boat dogs and until recently, Alberto's never been on one."

"But Tank said you used to be a charter captain."

"Savannah and I adopted Alberto a few months ago," I replied, lowering my voice. "His father died when he was six and his mom was recently murdered."

"No other family?"

"None fit to take care of him," I replied. A silence hung between us for a moment or two before I said, "You mentioned a ghost ship earlier. What was that about?"

He looked up at the cockpit, inscrutable eyes scanning for anyone listening, then lowered his voice. "It's no secret in certain circles that the drug cartels down here have expanded into the slavery business."

"What do you know about it?"

"More than most," he replied. "Maybe more than you."

"We picked up a family of rafters two days ago. One of them mentioned a ghost ship where kidnap victims were taken to."

"It's a coastal freighter," Bud said. "But that's not how the drugs and people are transported away from here."

I faced the older man and searched his dark eyes. Though he was American, I could see how he could easily pass himself off as

Hispanic. The fact that he'd worked for the CIA in South America reinforced that.

"Did you just *happen* to drop in to visit Tank?"

"Actually, no," he replied. "We'd been talking about getting together again for some time and when he told me he'd settled in the Keys and had cancer, I made it a point to arrange a visit. Why do you ask?"

"I don't buy into coincidences," I said.

He shrugged. "Well, I can assure you that's all that's going on here. Two old Nam vets getting together one last time. So, am I to take it that you're looking for this ghost ship?"

"Take it any way you like," I replied, as Tank's rod bent and his reel started to zing.

"Wahooooo!" Tank yelled, his exclamation explaining how the fish got its name.

The wahoo was one of the fastest-swimming fish in the sea. Not just in spurts, either. They could sustain high speeds for great lengths of time, and pound for pound they were one of the most powerful game fish, highly prized for their flaky white flesh.

I moved quickly behind Tank's chair, ready to help him if needed.

"Pull your line in," I needlessly told Alberto. When I looked over, he was already reeling furiously.

Ambrosia wasn't a sportfishing boat. Aboard the *Revenge*, I could slow or turn to keep a fish astern. We were making fifteen knots, a good speed to catch wahoo over steep, underwater ledges, like the one just to our south. But the ship wasn't going to slow or turn to help Tank get the fish aboard.

It tired quickly from straining against the continuous pull, and when Tank got it close to the stern of the platform, I was able to gaff it and bring it aboard, flopping wildly. I quickly got the fish into the cooler and removed the hook. It wasn't as large as the one Bud had caught, but we'd soon be adding enough meat to the freezer to feed the entire crew for a couple of meals.

"I thought I heard a shout," Marcos said from behind me.

I turned and saw him coming across the platform, eyes on the two fish in the cooler.

"*Magnifico*," he said, admiring the cooler's contents. "I have a special recipe for the *peto*."

He looked up and smiled at me. Then he saw Bud and his eyes went wide. It was obvious he recognized the man. But he quickly recovered and introduced himself.

"I am Marcos Santiago," he said to Tank. "I am one of the *cocineros* aboard the ship."

"*Cocinero?*" Tank asked.

"That means chef," Alberto said.

He shook hands with the two men, but I could tell that he'd met Bud before. Not so much from Bud's reaction, but from Marcos's.

"I'll have a couple of the crew bring these fish to you," I said. "Along with anything else we catch."

Marcos looked back at the churning wake of the ship. "At this speed, *Capitan*, you will only catch the *peto* or the *picúa*. Few can swim so fast."

"He means wahoo and barracuda," Alberto translated.

"Let's get another one," Tank said, putting a hand on Alberto's shoulder and guiding him back to the fighting chairs.

Marcos disappeared quickly up the steps and I nodded for Bud to follow me out of earshot of the boy.

"You know my cook," I said.

He looked me right in the eye and lied. "I have no idea what you're talking about. I just met the man."

I knew a little about CIA spooks. They lived a life of total anonymity and secrecy. Often, failing that resulted in their death. Lying came as easily as breathing for them. Those I'd met would disavow knowledge of their own mothers if they hadn't just introduced her to you. It was that engrained in their training and discipline.

One CIA operative I knew had gone rogue and murdered a friend of mine, a young Marine corporal he'd shafted in Afghanistan. Charity and I had tracked him all across the Caribbean until we finally caught up to him and she'd disarmed and killed him, barehanded.

CHAPTER FIFTEEN

Crammed into the confined space, the people had little room to move around without bumping into one another, so they didn't. The heat was unbearable, and the stench of sweat permeated the thin air. Cries and moans from the frightened and those who were ill echoed off the steel walls, creating a miserable, mournful sound.

The crowd of people were mostly women, the majority of them young, but there were a few men and even some children—all crammed into a space dimly lit by a single light near the door, and barely the size of a small house.

After a while, they began to talk, some finding friends or loved ones, or just a comforting person to be close to. They came from different backgrounds and from all areas of the coast of South America, mostly from small fishing villages on the many rivers that flowed down from the mountains of Brazil and Colombia through to the sea. Some spoke English, while others spoke Spanish or Portuguese.

After an indeterminable amount of time, the talk ceased.

They'd been forced to simply lie on the rough burlap bags stacked in rows, each bag no bigger than a pillow. They had no way of knowing the contents of the bags. They also couldn't tell how long it had been since the door had been closed and their fates sealed. Beyond the confines of the room, it could be day or night. The dim light over the door never turned off.

There was food and water, but they'd been told to use it sparingly, because it would have to last for several days. Their captors had said the best use of their time would be in simply doing nothing, conserving energy so they might live to complete their voyage.

Nobody knew where the voyage would take them.

Once the door had been closed, it was silent for a long time, except for the occasional whisper. Then a mechanical clang came from the door and a whirring sound emanated from several places along the sides of the room. This had frightened many of them, and several screamed for help. There'd been a sensation of motion, but in the near total darkness it was difficult to tell if the movement was real. That had been followed by metallic clangs and then the moving had ceased.

After some time, there came a vibration and a noise had filled the close air—the sound of an engine. Again, a slight movement was felt, but it quickly dissolved into nothing.

The engine sound droned on for what seemed like hours. Then it increased slightly, and the room began to move up and down, rolling slightly from side to side. The constant movement had made a few ill and the stench of vomit mixed with the reek of urine, feces, and body odor.

To most of the captives, the closing of the door had seemed like days earlier. Time didn't exist. Whether it'd been days or hours, they had no way of knowing.

It was decided that the constant rolling motion meant that they were on a ship of some kind, though only a few fishermen in the room had ever been on one.

The people had slept fitfully, some clinging to one another. In the near total darkness, eyes reflected desperation, sadness, and a loss of hope.

At some point, a Spanish-speaking man took charge, positioning himself near the stores of food and water. When he was thirsty, he passed the water around, telling everyone to take no more than a sip. When he was hungry, he passed food to the others, dry bread, fruit, and smoked fish.

Nobody argued with him.

The overall mood was one of utter despair. They could only guess at where they were being taken, how long it would take to get there, or what their fate would be when they arrived. It was maddening.

Most had heard stories about or even witnessed the taking of other people. Those who were taken by the raiders were never seen or heard from again, and no bodies were ever found. One moment they were there and the next, they were gone. The realization of what those people had gone through was slowly unfolding to the captives.

After what seemed many days, the water supply began to get low, and the food was nearly gone. Finally, the rocking motion began to subside, and the engine sound diminished.

Just by the amount of time between eating, the Latino man, who called himself Jorge, said they must have been locked in the confined space at least three days, maybe longer.

It didn't matter.

Soon there were other sounds and sudden bumping movements. Finally, the sound of the engine stopped, and it became deathly quiet. Huddled on a makeshift bed with a young woman and a little boy, an older woman coughed. The three had cried for most of the trip, having had another girl taken from them before they'd been forced down the ladder.

The whirring sound they'd heard before started once more; the sensation of movement was felt by many. After a few minutes, there was a jarring bump, creating a clang that ricocheted off the walls, as if they were inside a giant bell. There were more jolts and jangles, then everything went still.

Finally, a mechanical sound came from the door and everyone stepped away from it. The door swung outward and the people cringed at the bright light that flooded the room.

"Everyone out!" a voice shouted in English.

It was followed by poorly-spoken Spanish words repeating the order as a man with a gun stepped into the room. He grabbed the first person within reach by the hair and forced her brutally through the door.

"*Fuera!*" he shouted. "*Rapido!* Everyone out! Now!"

The knot of people was herded through the door into a much larger area, lit by overhead fluorescent lights. There were stacks of metal boxes along one wall and many strong-looking men, some with guns.

The captives were pushed and shoved into a smaller space with concrete walls, floor, and ceiling. There was a large drain opening in the middle, covered with a steel grate.

Suddenly, two large water hoses were turned on them by two laughing men. Others, wearing masks over their mouths and noses, began to move the burlap bags out of their prison, stacking them on the floor beside a ladder.

The spray from the hoses nearly knocked people over and they all scrambled to get away from it, packing themselves into the two far corners. As they pushed and shoved, others were moved into the blast from the hoses, gasping and trying to stay on their feet.

The ordeal lasted only a few minutes, then the hoses were shut off and they were forced to sit on the cold, wet floor. Nearly everyone was sobbing at that point, even some of the men. The powerful force of the water hoses had torn shirts open and ripped seams apart.

Outside the shower room, the men quickly removed everything from inside, passing the burlap bags out in a chain until they were all stacked along the far wall.

The man with the gun approached, looking over the huddled mass of terrified people, hair hanging over their faces, some partially naked from the violent shower. Nobody made eye contact.

"Who speaks English?" he demanded.

Jorge looked up. "I speak English, Spanish, and Portuguese."

"Stand up before you talk to me!" the man roared, pointing the gun at Jorge.

Slowly, he got to his feet and faced the gunman. Behind him, the people whimpered and sobbed.

With the unloading finished, the dock workers began to move other boxes into the room. They were square and looked to be made of steel, painted black—each the size of three of the burlap bags they'd removed. The boxes had carrying handles and at the bottom of each was a small opening, covered with a wire mesh. They were all numbered, and the workers carried them in order.

"Those are battery-powered refrigerated containers," the gunman said to Jorge. "Do you know what that means?"

He nodded. "*Si.*"

"Inside each container is enough food and water to last five people for just one day. *Comprendo?*"

Jorge nodded again.

"They have timers. Each day, eight of them will open. That will be all the food and drink you will have for that day. Do you understand?"

Jorge looked over the gunman's shoulder, seeing one of the workers carrying a box with the number "100" stenciled on the side. The men continued loading more.

Again, Jorge nodded.

"Explain back to me what I just told you," the gunman ordered.

Jorge blinked and looked back at the man.

"There is food in each box for five people," he said, his voice cracking slightly as he watched the last box being loaded. It was marked with the number 120 on the side. He stared at the gunman for a long moment before speaking again, realizing that they were loading supplies to last forty people for fourteen days. "Each box is for one day and eight of them will open each day."

There was a commotion behind the man, as a woman stepped down from the ladder. She had blond hair and fair skin and was wearing a short yellow dress with thin straps. Three more women came down behind her and the workers surged around them, pawing and grabbing at their bodies.

The gunman turned. "Enough! Get them aboard."

"Tell us where you are taking us," the blond-haired women pleaded.

The gunman covered the distance between them in three quick strides, then backhanded the blonde, knocking her into the men, who took advantage of the situation and groped her even more.

"You were told not to speak!" the gunman roared at her.

Then he took one of the others by her dark, auburn hair, pulling her head back so she stared up at him. She wore tight jeans and a brightly colored tank top. He dragged her by the hair to the open door and threw her inside, then turned on the other three.

"The rest of you!" he shouted. "Get in there."

They moved without force and entered the room. Then the gunman returned to stand in front of Jorge.

"There's enough food and water in there to last forty people for two weeks. That's how long it will be before you see daylight again. Now get the rest of these slaves back inside!"

CHAPTER SIXTEEN

A lberto and I fished with Tank and Bud for about an hour. Alberto caught a forty-pound wahoo and he managed to get it close enough to the stern for me to gaff.

Not long after that, Tank boated a large barracuda, but I could see the fight had sapped his strength.

"I think I need a rest," Tank said, looking up at me, his features gaunt. "Will you tell Chyrel I went to our cabin?"

"Sure thing, Master Guns," I replied, concerned for my old friend and mentor. "You go get some rest and I'll see you at dinner."

Alberto escorted him up the steps to the cockpit, both dogs following behind them.

"He doesn't have much longer, does he?" Bud asked.

"No," I replied. "He's already past the time his doctors gave him."

"He refused treatment?"

We sat in the two fighting chairs and swiveled them to face one another, the fishing done for the day.

"By the time the cancer was discovered," I began, "it had already spread to many of his internal organs, his abdominal wall, and into his bones. He told me his doctor had said that the best they'd be able to do was give him a couple of years filled with chemo treatments and radiation—it was terminal."

Bud visibly shuddered. "Not the way I'd want to go either."

"Tank chose to live his last days to the fullest," I said. "He found a place he liked, a woman to comfort him, and friends to go fishing with."

"Not a bad choice, if you ask me."

I stared down at the roiling water just behind the platform for a moment. Then I turned and faced Bud. "The cancer's eating him up. He's in constant pain, though he won't say it. He's lost a lot of weight since he arrived in the Keys just last Christmas."

"I knew him as a young man," Bud said. "He thought he was ten feet tall and bulletproof back then. He was just another FNG when he replaced my crew chief, first time in-country. First time anywhere except Bozeman, then San Diego for boot camp."

I'd heard the old-timers in the Corps talk about the life expectancy of a Marine newly arrived in Vietnam. They said it wasn't much longer than the flight that brought them there. The saltier warriors didn't bother getting to know the "fucking new guy" or even ask his name, because he'd likely be in a body bag the next day. They simply referred to them as FNGs and they died at a rate of nearly ten per day.

"He was bigger than life when I first met him," I said. "He was already a legend in the Corps, just a few years after the fall of Saigon. He was my first platoon sergeant."

"He told me about you," Bud offered. "In letters we exchanged over the years. Said you stood up next to him to face down a bunch of hostiles in Beirut."

I shrugged. "Couldn't let the old man do it alone. Besides, there were a bunch of us on that rooftop that day."

"He said it was a lot more than that," Bud continued, turning to look at the sea. "He said you were the bravest man he'd ever known and he wanted to face his last days as he thought you might—with fortitude. His words."

I looked at the side of the ex-spook's face. I didn't know what to say.

Bud turned and stared into my eyes. "I think he wanted to come out here because he knows his time is up."

"N—" I started to protest, but then realized it was likely true.

"The man told me, Jesse. He said he wanted you to eulogize him. Nobody else."

It was my turn to stare out over the deep blue water. I felt the sting in my eyes, then a single tear trickled down my right cheek. Of all the people in the world, the man I considered the greatest and bravest, next to Dad and Pap, wanted to be near *me* in his last days.

Rising suddenly from the chair, I turned and crossed the deck in three strides, then took the steps two at a time to the cockpit, and from there up the outside ladderwell to the bridge deck.

"Where's Val?" I asked Matt as I burst onto the bridge.

"On the mess deck," he replied. "With Giselle and her family, yeah?"

I went to the console and pushed the button for the intercom speaker in the mess hall. "Bridge to McLarin."

She responded after a couple of seconds. "What is it, Captain?"

"Report to the bridge immediately. And bring Giselle."

Matt studied my face. "Wasson, Cap'n?"

"I'll tell you all when they get up here," I replied.

Matt didn't have long to wait, as Val and Giselle came quickly up the spiral staircase.

"Gentlemen," I said, loud enough to get Ross's attention over his headphones, "your attention please."

Ross removed his headset and he and Axel swiveled to face us.

"I need your help," I said. "I need you to figure out your schedules, including Giselle here, to properly man the bridge in my absence."

"You goin' somewhere, Cap'n?" Matt asked.

"No," I replied. "But while my family and friends are aboard, I've decided I want to spend some time with them."

Axel grinned. "Val's already thought of that."

"Oye," Matt said, nodding, and looking at Val. "It's sorted, innit?"

"Ross is going off shortly," Val said. "And Axel's pulling a shift and a half. Between the four of us here, plus Kris, we'll have at least two of us here at all times. Mr. Stockwell spends most of the night up here anyway, so probably three on deck at all times."

"He does? When does he sleep?"

"I asked 'im once," Matt said. "Told me 'e gets a short kip in after supper, an' another durin' mid-mornin'."

"As you know, we're not going all the way to Caiçara do Norte as planned," I said. "We'll be anchoring twelve nautical miles off the coast of Lençóis Maranhenses National Park. There's a relatively shallow shoal there, and we can make shore excursions to explore the dunes. It's time the crew took a little break. We'll be there for a few days."

I left them on the bridge to figure the rest of it out on their own. Matt was a licensed 100-ton near-shore captain, and Val held a second-mate rating, as did Axel. I had confidence that I could take some time away from the bridge.

"Tank's dying," I told Savannah as I entered our quarters.

"Yes," she replied. "But not for a while yet."

"No," I said, my eyes beginning to sweat. "He told Bud he came out here to die."

"Oh, Jesse," she said, stepping into my arms. "He doesn't know that. Nobody knows the time they're going to go."

"He knows," I said, my face buried in her hair.

I held her quietly. Tank and I had served together in Beirut and several other places over the years. He'd always been there to give me advice on how to lead my men. The thought that he'd soon be gone was one I didn't want to face.

He'd been almost like a father figure.

I pushed her away and turned, wiping at my eyes. "Chyrel probably knows, too. Where is she?"

"She and David are in the operations center."

"Tank went down to take a nap," I said. "Will you go get her for me? Tell her to come here and leave us for a few minutes?"

"Of course," she said, already moving toward the hatch. "I'll go right now."

She hurried out and I sat on the sofa, tossing my cover on the table. A moment later, there was a soft knock on the door.

Chyrel came in and without a word, sat next to me, pulling my head to her shoulder.

"Let it go, Jesse," she whispered. "Let it all out now. His doctor said it's just a matter of days and we gotta be strong for him."

The tears came then, and my body spasmed with sobs.

CHAPTER SEVENTEEN

O ver the next two days, *Ambrosia* continued steadily toward the southeast. I spent time with my family and made sure to spend as much time as I could with Tank. He and Bud told sea stories of their time in Khe Sanh and the men they'd served with.

When we were alone, Tank told me he'd seen his oncologist the day before they'd left to fly to *Ambrosia*. The doctor had told him then that he only had a few days left. He seemed at peace with that fact.

The evening we arrived and dropped anchor off Lençóis Maranhenses National Park, Marcos prepared a feast for the whole crew. It was a simple dish he called *peto con arroz blanco*. The wahoo was seared to perfection, glazed with a sauce I couldn't identify, and lying on a bed of white rice, the whole thing drizzled with what he called *guasacaca*. It was delicious.

I'd had Emma bring twenty bottles of Aperture Cellars Sauvignon Blanc up from the ship's vast wine cooler. *Ambrosia* wasn't called that for just any reason. The Saudi prince who'd had her built had included the wine cooler in his demands. The tropical flavor of the wine went well with the dish.

After dinner, Emma brought three bottles of Pusser's fifteen-year-old aged rum from my cabin. As she finished serving the rum, I stood and raised my glass, waiting for the conversation at the two long tables to die down.

"By now, you've all gotten to know my family and friends a little," I began. "Some of you have heard the story about how Tank had once saved the lives of a dozen Marines in Vietnam. What you don't know is that by his guidance and mentorship over the following fifty years, he's also saved countless others. Tank is the best and most noble man I've ever had the privilege to know. To Master Gunnery Sergeant Owen Tankersley!"

Cheers went up, glasses were clinked, rum was sloshed and consumed.

Slowly, Tank rose to his feet. For the whole day, he'd worn his oxygen cannula. He'd told me that the device strapped to his waist made pure oxygen from air and delivered it at low pressure. It was battery- powered and lasted eight hours. He had two of them and alternated as the batteries recharged.

He looked tired and worn-out, but he stood erect, with a smile on his face. He lifted his glass and tapped it with his dessert fork to get everyone's attention.

"I've served with a lot of men," he said, his voice raspy. "During my fifty-one years as a Marine..." he continued, but then started coughing. Chyrel rose and put an arm around his shoulders, but he gently pushed her away.

"During my fifty-one years as an active-duty Marine," he began again, speaking slowly, "I've not met a braver man than your skipper." He paused and took a couple of deep breaths. "He stood with me... and he will stand up for you." Another pause to catch his breath. "Jesse is the kind of man... who will always stand up... for those who need help." He looked down the length of the table at me. "To Captain Jesiah Smedley McDermitt!"

I glared at him, though I was smiling, as more cheers rang through the mess hall, accompanied by a few laughs.

Few people knew my full, given name. Not that I was ashamed of it—Smedley Butler was one of the greatest and most decorated heroes of the Marine Corps. It was just such an odd name in modern times that it always required an explanation, so I'd always just gone by Jesse, short for the Hebrew *Jesiah*.

Travis stood. He didn't need to tap his glass or wait until the chatter died down. The room became quiet. He looked at me, then at Tank, his deeply lined face as inscrutable as always.

When he spoke, his voice was low and gravely. "Let's not forget our fallen comrades," he began, "but remember them always. They have earned our respect and admiration with their lives." His eyes went up and down the tables, making eye contact with each person from Matt to the lowest crewman. "We knew them, we remember them, and they will *not* be forgotten. To our fallen comrades!"

Everyone rose and lifted their glasses solemnly. Many of the crew were prior service, but all were true patriots and sailors, working a tough job far from home to help protect what they cherished most and to right the wrongs of the world, with neither fanfare nor recognition.

"To the fallen," many said.

Marcos stood and gave me a quick nod. "I do not have the words as *El Capitan* and *Señor* Tank," he said. "I only want to say *graçias*." He looked around the tables for a moment. "You have all made my family welcome and I am grateful. If *Señor* Grady will help me now, we will serve the..." He looked down at Mayra. "How you say? *Postre*?"

"Dessert," she quietly whispered.

"We will serve the dessert now!"

An hour later, with the two boys asleep in Alberto's room and the dogs having posted themselves as usual—one in the room and one outside the door—Savannah and I went to the foredeck. Most of the ship's lights were extinguished; only the anchor light and a dozen lights below the waterline were on.

Looking over the rail, I could see small fish darting in and out of the glow of lights around the hull. Above, the stars shone as brightly as I'd ever seen.

The foredeck was crowded with stargazers.

"Over here, Jesse," I heard Chyrel call out. "We're watching the Perseids."

She was sitting on the long sun pad with Tank and Bud, two empty spots between them and Charity. We sat down and I stretched my legs out, gazing up at the night sky.

The Milky Way, a dense band of stars making up the galaxy our own sun was a part of, stretched from horizon to horizon.

Every year, the Perseid meteor shower dazzled viewers with up to twenty "shooting stars" per hour during peak activity. It had reached that a week earlier, but there were still the occasional streaks of light across the sky as small rocks burned to dust in Earth's atmosphere.

"Even better than out in the desert," Tank whispered. "It really makes a person feel so tiny and inconsequential."

"The things we do and say don't matter," Charity agreed. "Not in the big picture, anyway."

I took Savannah's hand and squeezed it. A meteor shot across the sky and there was a collective gasp from those on deck.

"Do you know," Tank whispered, his voice soft and reverent, "the light from most of those stars is older than mankind? Some are so far away, the light takes hundreds of thousands of years just to reach our eyes. Looking at the night sky is looking back in time."

My friend Rusty talked about this quite often. He called the stars timeless and predictable and could go on for hours behind the bar about how early mariners were able to use the stars to guide their ships. Today, we used artificial stars, little tin boxes in geostationary orbit, stuffed with electronic gizmos that relayed telephone calls, emails, television, radio, or just their location. GPS receivers picked up these signals from various satellites and computed azimuth and direction to determine their location.

But Rusty had learned to read the stars using a sextant and was amazingly accurate. Of course, he relied on the digital time on his cellphone to determine where a star should be.

"What's the plan for tomorrow, Jesse?" Charity asked, interrupting my thoughts.

"We'll explore the dunes," I replied quietly. "I'll order both tenders launched to take the crew ashore, along with anything else that floats."

"The helo can carry me plus nine passengers," she offered. "I can make two runs before the first launch reaches shore."

"We'll be on the first run," I said. "To make sure the coast is clear."

"What time do you want to start?"

"First light," I replied. "The six of us, the boys, and the dogs."

"I'll be in the left seat," Travis's gravelly voice announced from the side deck.

Bud turned his head and looked up at him. "You're a chopper pilot?"

"No," he replied. "But nobody goes ashore without security."

"Then you'll ride in back," Bud said. "I'll have the copilot's seat."

"Pull up some deck, Travis," I said. "Take some time and contemplate the meaning of life."

He glanced up at the stars a moment, then back at us. "I know the meaning of life," he announced. "Protecting it is my job."

He turned and went back along the side deck. I heard his footfalls on the steps going up to the bridge.

"Officers always got a stick up their ass," Tank said, then turned to the ponytailed CIA spook seated next to his wife. "Present company excepted."

"There was a time I was just like that," Bud said. "The Nam cured me of it. What's his story?"

"Retired colonel," I replied. "Ranger and special forces. Then assistant deputy director at Homeland Security."

"Wait, what? Travis? His last name Stockwell?"

"One and the same," I replied.

Bud looked over his shoulder toward the darkened windows of the bridge. "And now he's working security on a research boat?"

"A little more than that," I said. "Stockwell's the head of security for all of Armstrong Research, overseeing more than fifty operatives in the field and twice that at Armstrong's many operations and command and control centers around the globe."

"So, this is where he disappeared to," Bud said, almost cryptically.

I stared at his profile for a moment, but he said nothing else.

A steady easterly wind held *Ambrosia* pointing to windward and a calm sea gently moved her. It was still early in the evening, a waxing gibbous moon was on the rise, and with every tick of the clock, it was stealing the night sky from the stars. There were a few puffy clouds floating to the south, illuminated by the moon. Aside from them, the sky was clear, and the moon and the stars shone brightly on the sea.

We all chatted for an hour, watching the meteors radiate out from the constellation Perseus. Savannah leaned against my shoulder. I looked down and saw her trying to stifle a yawn.

"We'd better turn in," I said, noticing that others were beginning to retreat to their quarters for the night.

"Been a long day," Tank said in agreement.

Without aid, he rose and extended a hand to Chyrel. She took it and stood next to him, not letting go. "We'll see all y'all in the morning," she said.

"That's Southernese for 'all you nice folk,'" Tank said to Bud, grinning in the moonlight.

I rose and helped Savannah up.

"Is someone on watch tonight?" Charity asked, remaining seated.

As Val passed by, headed to the side deck, she replied, "Yes, Mr. Stockwell has the conn and Axel will relieve him at oh-three-hundred."

"Then I'll stay here for a bit," she said, looking up and back toward the darkened windows of the bridge. "Work on my moontan."

CHAPTER EIGHTEEN

I woke early to the smell emanating from the coffee maker. Savannah had set it up before we'd gone to bed. Pulling back the covers, I rose naked and went to my dresser, picking up our clothes, which were strewn haphazardly across the small room.

I tossed everything in a laundry basket beside the dresser, put on clean skivvies, and made my way to the little galley area of our quarters. There, I poured two mugs of coffee, and returned to find Savannah leaning over the bed, pulling the sheets up.

"Hold that pose," I whispered.

"You just get that notion right out of your head," she said without looking back. "You're too old to survive a second round."

She wasn't far off the mark. Savannah had always been a wild and passionate woman in bed. Our lovemaking the night before had left me completely drained.

I leaned against the dresser. "Doesn't mean I can't enjoy the view. Want some coffee?"

She turned and tossed her golden hair over a tanned shoulder, standing before me in all her glory. Savannah wasn't bashful about her body, as some women might be. Though she'd turned fifty just over a month earlier, she could hold her own with any beach bunny.

"Thank you," she said, taking the cup and setting it on the dresser.

She hugged me tightly, her bare breasts warm against my chest. I could feel a stirring in my shorts, and she felt it too, reaching down to stroke me slowly.

Once she had me fully aroused, she smiled up at me, then picked up her mug. "That should keep you at attention until tonight."

She pushed me aside and opened the top drawer, selecting her clothes for the day. She stepped into a yellow bikini bottom, adjusting it with her back to me, fully aware of what she was doing.

"Get dressed," she said, glancing over her shoulder and catching me looking at her butt. "The boys will be up soon."

"The *boys* are already up," I said, smacking her lightly on a bare butt cheek.

A few minutes later, we emerged from our bedroom and found Alberto and Fernando sitting at the little table, munching loudly on breakfast cereal.

"Are we going to the beach?" Alberto asked, as they both turned to look at us. His voice became concerned as he looked at my face. "You don't look so good. Are you okay?"

Savannah took my empty mug from my hands. "He just hasn't had enough," she said with a lascivious grin, refilling my mug.

Alberto turned to his friend. "*No es humano hasta que bebe su jugo de vida.*"

"*Qué es el jugo de vida?*"

"*Café,*" Alberto replied, and they both giggled.

"*No es verdad,*" I said to Fernando. "I can be very human before having my lifer juice."

"He's right," Savannah said, stretching on bare toes to kiss me on the cheek. "He can often be alert and invigorated before his coffee."

The two boys giggled again and went back to their cereal.

"You're a vixen," I whispered in her ear.

"Want some breakfast?"

Without waiting for a reply, she opened the fridge and took a carton of eggs out, along with a tube of sausage.

I sat down with the boys while she fried the sausage, then scrambled a half dozen eggs in the grease.

As we were finishing, I heard footsteps from above.

"That's probably Charity," I said, looking at my watch. "It's a half hour till sunup; she's probably doing her preflight."

"Go on up," Savannah said. "We'll catch up after the boys help me with the dishes."

When I climbed to the fly bridge, I spotted Charity in the gathering morning light. She had her hair in a ponytail hanging out of the hole in the back of her ball cap. As usual, she was dressed in her tight-fitting black flight suit, a pair of reflector shades hanging from a pocket. She was on a ladder, inspecting the twin turbine engines.

"Everything okay?" I asked, crossing the helipad.

"Yeah," she said. But her voice seemed on edge—kind of cutting.

I looked up at her. "Something's wrong."

She looked down at me, her features masking any emotion. I'd seen that look before. Charity was an extraordinarily complex woman. She'd survived being captured and tortured by the Taliban in the early days of the war. I knew she'd been repeatedly raped during that time, as well. The memory of such an ordeal would be too much for most people. But she managed to bury it deep in her subconscious mind, a place filled with vile and hateful emotions. She could call on it when needed, changing from a happy-go-lucky California girl to an intense warrior like flicking a switch to turn on a lamp. There was no slow burn in Charity Styles, just on and off. She and I had discussed our demons openly with one another many years ago.

That was the look I saw in her eyes at that moment—demonic.

"I have a mission," she finally answered. Then her face changed, and she smiled. "But I don't have to leave for four days, when I get back to Grenada."

Normally, Armstrong's operatives didn't talk about their assignments, not even to one another. Only when they needed help or intel did they contact the guys working in the op center. But Charity and I had a different relationship.

"What's the assignment?" I asked, knowing that was what must have triggered her.

"Observation only," she replied, putting the engine access cover back in place. "Some rich turd fondlers who like little girls."

Inwardly, I grinned at the use of the phrase. It was a favorite of mine, not often used in public.

"And you're only going to be watching them?" I asked.

"One in particular," she said, climbing down. "No danger. The girls these guys are into are almost thirty years younger than me."

Charity had celebrated her fortieth birthday with us in Belize over a year ago. She was talking about a group of child molesters, something I knew she had a more-than-vehement opposition to. I wasn't worried about her safety encountering men like that. I was more worried she'd snap and kill them. Not that they wouldn't deserve it, but it could blow her cover.

"Where?" I asked.

"The Virgin Islands, of all places."

She folded the aluminum ladder and strapped it to the side rail where it was stored.

My responsibility, as *Ambrosia's* captain, was to the ship

and her crew. I wasn't privy to the missions Armstrong's field operators were assigned, though many of them were my friends. But I had to wonder about assigning Charity a mission where the situation might unexpectedly dredge up those suppressed memories.

I pulled open the door on the pilot's side. "Who assigned you?"

She didn't answer until she'd climbed in. "No need to worry, Jesse. I got this."

She flipped on the batteries. The dash and interior lights came on and the few analog gauges on the dash flicked. Removing a laminated sheet, she started going through the preflight instructions. In her own bird, she didn't need a card. Hers was a UH-1 Iroquois, commonly referred to as a Huey. She'd flown a Huey at the age most girls were just getting a learner's permit to drive a car. Her father had used helos in his crop-dusting business, and she'd started flying at an early age, spraying the fields of the San Fernando Valley. After 9/11, she'd accepted a commission in the Army and flew Hueys as a search and rescue pilot.

Finn and Woden appeared at the top of the ladder, with Savannah and the boys right behind them. The boys were talking excitedly in Spanish as Giselle and Ricardo brought up the rear of the small entourage.

"Did you call Chyrel?" I asked Savannah as they joined me beside the bird. "Charity's gonna be ready soon."

"They're on the way," she replied.

Stockwell appeared, wearing shorts, sandals, and a goofy-looking fruit juicy shirt. The contrast between his tropical tourist clothes and face was huge. His tropical attire screamed tourist. But one look at his face would make even the drunkest partygoer on Duval Street step into the road to let him by. The shirt hung loose over his cargo shorts, and I knew he had a holstered handgun under it.

I did too.

"Before you utter a word," he cautioned, "I'm just trying to make the crew feel comfortable. I know a few don't like me and my team being armed all the time."

"I wasn't going to say anything," I said.

"Sure, you weren't," he grumbled, then walked around to the left side of the bird, opened the copilot's door, and climbed in.

So much for Bud riding shotgun, I thought.

Looking east, I saw the sun peeking over the horizon. Savannah joined me.

"It looks like it's going to be a beautiful day," she said, holding my upper arm in her hands. "Please try to enjoy it."

"We're about ready," Charity called out.

I helped the others aboard as I spotted Chyrel and Tank approaching. Bud was a few steps ahead of them.

"Get in back," Travis ordered the CIA man.

He started to protest, but I shook my head, and he kept his mouth shut.

Aside from Charity, everyone was dressed for a day at the

beach, carrying bags with towels and sunscreen.

Ricardo got his son strapped in behind Charity, then leaned in toward her. "He has never flown before."

She smiled at him. "You have nothing to worry about. He'll be as safe in my charge as he is on the boat."

Giselle kissed Fernando on the cheek, admonishing him to do what he was told. "We will be on the first boat," she promised.

"We'll keep a close eye on him," I said to Ricardo. "He'll be fine. Charity's one of the top helo pilots the Army ever had."

The couple retreated to the flybridge and with everyone aboard, including the dogs, I climbed in and closed the door, settling into my seat.

"*Hinlegen*," Savannah ordered Woden.

As one, the two dogs dropped to the floor of the helo right in front of the two boys.

Ricardo turned toward Alberto and asked, "*Que esta hinlegen?*"

"*Es Alemán. Creo que significa acostarse.*"

"That's right," Savannah said. "It's German for 'lie down.'"

Charity donned her headset and opened a vent window. "Clear," she shouted needlessly. There were only four others on the deck, all directly ahead of us. But Charity was a stickler when it came to flight procedures.

Tank opened his armrest, took out a compact pair of headphones, and showed the boys how to plug them into a receptacle in front of the armrest.

The rest of us did the same, donning the headsets so we could talk and be heard over the sound of the rotors and engine noise.

The turbines began to spool up, the whirring pitch getting higher and higher as the rotors turned. When it reached speed, Charity flipped on the fuel pump, then pressed the ignitor, and the turbines roared to life. She nodded at the crewmen standing with Ricardo and Giselle, and the two men raced forward, bent low. They quickly undid the tiedowns and retreated.

Charity twisted the throttle, bringing the turbines up to speed, then raised the collective slightly as she pulled back on the cyclic. The bird rose off the deck, nose high as it moved backward off the helipad.

Moving the stick forward and to the right, she dipped the nose toward the water, and we flew out over the wave tops, heading toward shore.

Fernando stared out the window, waving to his parents. Then he turned to Alberto, and I heard him ask over the intercom, "*Cuánto tiempo antes de que lleguemos?*"

"About five minutes," I told them both, raising a hand showing all five digits.

"Thank you," Fernando said. "This is..." He looked at Alberto again. "*Excitante?*"

I laughed, remembering my first ride in a helicopter more than forty years earlier. I'd jumped out of that one.

"Exciting," I said. "Yes, it is."

The nose remained down, and Charity added more power. Soon, we were skimming across the water at what I guessed to be close to 150 knots.

Before reaching shore, Charity pulled up, gaining altitude to have a look around, but not high enough to appear on any radar system on shore—just a few hundred feet above the water.

Travis scanned the area through a powerful pair of binoculars. "I don't see anything."

"Roger that," Charity said, bringing the nose down again as she reduced power. She flared as we crossed over the beach, turned into the wind, and brought us down gently on a high dune.

CHAPTER NINETEEN

O nce the bird had settled and Charity had given the okay, I put away the headset, unbuckled my seatbelt, and opened the door. The sound of the rotors and turbine were much louder outside.

The dogs leapt to the ground beside me as I helped the boys and Savannah out of the back.

"Head down to the far side of the dune!" I shouted over the noise.

She took the boys by the hands and moved away from the bird, with the dogs trotting ahead. Chyrel and I helped Tank get out. When Bud and Travis joined us, we started down the dune as well.

Charity waited until we were a good distance away before taking off, swooping forward and out over the waves quickly to avoid kicking up too much of the fine, powdery sand.

Together, we all climbed to the top of the dune. The view

was unbelievable. White sand glistened as far as the eye could see, giving way to tiny waves. Beyond the surf, the water looked like gold, colored by the sand beneath the surface. Then it changed to turquoise and a deep, dark blue, no more than fifty yards from shore.

Looking to the south, all I could see was a vast expanse of sand dunes all the way to the horizon. I knew the dunes extended a good ten times farther than what I could see into the interior.

"Can we go exploring?" Alberto asked.

"Don't go far," Savannah replied, her eyes following the contour of the beach. "We'll set up a spot right here on the high ground."

Alberto and Fernando took off like a shot, the dogs spreading out to either side of them, running along the shoreline. Finn and Woden weren't young dogs; they had a combined weight of over two hundred pounds. But the boys weren't fast and the dogs easily kept pace. I realized that they probably needed this as much as the crew. All dogs like to run.

We unfolded two large beach blankets, anchoring them at the corners. The wind off the water was light and refreshing, the sand already warm from the early morning rays of sun. There wasn't a cloud in the sky, and everything seemed right with the world.

Chyrel pulled a folding chair from a long, red, canvas tube and set it up for Tank before sitting cross-legged on the blanket in front of him.

Savannah removed her shorts and T-shirt and lay down next to Chyrel. "It's so nice to be on land again," she said, propping herself on her elbows. "The water looks so beautiful in the shallows."

Bud had brought a chair also and set it up next to Tank's. "You doing okay?" he asked.

Tank watched Chyrel wiggle out of her shorts, tossing them and her tank top aside before stretching out in the sun.

"Right as rain, Captain," Tank replied with a grin. "Savannah hit the nail on the head. This view is gorgeous."

Travis faced the interior of the island, scanning the dunes for any unseen visitors. Finally, he looked at me and nodded his head toward the beach. "Let's walk."

I fell in beside him and we headed down off the dune to the shoreline, in the opposite direction the boys had gone.

"What's on your mind?" I asked, once we were out of earshot.

"Your friend's friend," he replied. "What's a CIA operative doing here?"

"You checked him out?" I asked, getting a nod in return. "He's just a friend of Tank's. They served together in Vietnam. He's retired."

"Spooks don't retire," he grunted.

"He knows you," I offered, getting no reaction. "He recognized your name when you came out onto the foredeck last night."

We walked a while before he continued. "Have you ever

heard of Operation Condor?"

"The guerilla fighting campaign back in the seventies?"

He looked over at me a moment. "It was a lot more than just guerillas. Backed and trained by the CIA, intelligence operatives in Argentina, Chile, Uruguay, Paraguay, Bolivia, and Brazil kidnapped, tortured, and murdered tens of thousands of leftist political dissidents—union and peasant leaders, priests and nuns, students and teachers, intellectuals and yes, a few suspected guerrillas."

I looked back at the group. Bud, with his long, gray ponytail, was staring out over the waves.

"Yeah, he was one of them," Travis said. "What his role was in South America is still classified and even I couldn't access it."

"But you suspect he had a role in it?"

He stopped and turned to look back at our group. "I don't suspect things, Jesse. I simply deal with the facts as they're presented. I do know that this isn't Bud Ferguson's first time in Brazil."

My eyes followed his gaze. "His being here could be happenstance."

"Says the guy who doesn't believe in coincidences," he countered.

I shook my head. "Tank wouldn't cover for him," I said. "He wouldn't lie to me about Bud being his pilot in Vietnam or withhold information on why he went to the Keys to visit. Hell, Tank probably didn't even know where we were when he asked Flo to contact us about a visit."

"That part's true enough," Stockwell said. "He was the chopper pilot your friend served with during the rescue operation that eventually led to his receiving the Medal of Honor. Ferguson left Southeast Asia shortly after that, tapped to work covertly for the CIA while still serving in the Marine Corps as a reservist. He's fluent in French, Spanish, and Portuguese. The CIA sent him to Brazil in 1975, at the start of Operation Condor. I'm just saying, you should watch him."

Woden had returned and sat beside Tank, who draped an arm over the dog's massive flank. The boys and Finn were a hundred yards beyond the group, walking back unhurriedly. There was something odd about the way Woden sat there, looking up at Tank. Since his first visit, Woden had always seemed more affectionate toward Tank than he usually was with strangers. With most people, he was always a bit standoffish.

I could hear the helo returning. Looking out over the water, I saw the two launches in the distance, both heading toward shore. I waved my arms over my head and Charity adjusted her course toward us. I pointed toward the high dune, and she waggled the bird side to side in response.

"I'll keep an eye on him," I said, turning to face Travis. "Maybe Chyrel can find out something."

"Do that," he said, as Charity landed on the dune a hundred yards down the beach. "That's not all."

We started walking back toward the group, the sound of

the rotors diminishing.

"It never is with you, Colonel. What else?"

"Your new cook," he said. "Forty-five years ago, a young Marcos Santiago fled his native Brazil from the region where it borders Venezuela and settled in Maracaibo."

Marcos was Brazilian? I thought.

As we approached, Chyrel got up from her blanket and set up a telescoping umbrella, adjusting it so Tank was shaded from the morning sun. Behind him, she bent and wrapped her arms around her husband, holding him and saying something into his ear. Even from a distance, I could see him smile, tilt his head back, and accept a kiss on the cheek.

"Where did y'all wander off to?" Savannah asked, rolling on her side, and looking up at me.

"Just finding a level spot for Charity to land," I lied.

She eyed me suspiciously, knowing full well that if Charity had a need to, she could land on the side of a building.

"How're you feeling, Tank?" I asked.

Woden turned his big head toward me, the hair bristling along his spine as a low, menacing growl barely rose from his chest.

"Now you stop that," Savannah scolded him.

Tank's eyes were closed, but he was still smiling.

"Tank?" I said, stepping closer.

Chyrel's face was buried in his neck, her arms still holding him in a loose and loving embrace, stroking the side of his face. When she looked up, there were tears in her eyes.

"He's gone, Jesse," she said, a sad smile on her face. "He just told me he couldn't feel the pain anymore and then he stopped breathing."

Savannah and Bud scrambled to their feet as I knelt in front of my old friend. I put a finger to the carotid artery in his thin, frail neck. There was no pulse.

I looked up at Savannah, a tear in my own eye, as the boys came running toward us.

"Look what we fou—" Alberto started to say, holding out a large queen conch shell.

He dropped the shell in the sand and took a step closer, as Charity and the others approached. "Is Tank...?"

"Yes," I said quietly, then looked up at Stockwell. "Will you take Fernando to his parents? They're coming ashore from the launch now." Then I turned to Bud. "Please ask Charity to bring a stretcher from the helo. Tank needs to be exfilled."

He took one more look at his former crew chief, then moved away more quickly than his years dictated. He intercepted the group Charity and Val were leading from the chopper.

Charity had her flight suit unzipped, pulled down around her waist, the sleeves tied. Under it, she wore a lime green bikini. Val was similarly dressed in a blue bikini top and shorts.

The three of us knelt around Tank's still form, Savannah clutching Alberto tightly. I lowered my head and felt three hands lightly touch my shoulders, as I spoke. "At ease, Master Guns."

CHAPTER TWENTY

W e moved away, giving Chyrel some time alone, and joined the crew now milling around the helicopter.

The loss of someone close is never easy, not even when you know it's coming. It'd happened to me more times than I cared to recall. Maybe what Charity had said the previous night was true: that what we say and do didn't amount to anything in the "grand scheme" of things. But Tank mattered to me. He'd mattered to a lot of people. A dozen men owed him their lives. Those dozen men might be the fathers of two dozen or more and grandfathers to more people than now stood on the beach with him. And that didn't even come close to the number of people Tank's life had touched over the fifty years since then. My parents mattered, as did my grandparents. Alex mattered. Russ Livingston mattered.

Matt approached and nodded for me to join him. We

stepped away from the group.

"I know it's a bad time, Cap'n, and I'm truly sorry for your loss. But that freighter almost swamped our boat."

I turned my attention away from where two of Travis's men were bringing the stretcher with Tank's body toward us. Chyrel walked alongside, clutching Tank's hand.

"What freighter?" I asked absently.

"The one was doggin' us all night, several days ago," he replied. "The *Canopus*."

I looked out to sea, though I knew it wasn't likely I'd see anything beyond a few miles.

"It came close," Matt said. "The buggers actually turned toward us. Men on the rails yelled."

"What did they say?"

"Cap'n, they pulled their pants down and shook their willies at us, asking how much we wanted for the women."

I looked back at Matt and could see the fire in his eyes.

"It's the only time since leaving Her Majesty's SBS that I wished I'd had a gun on me, yeah?"

The British Special Boat Service was the equivalent of the U.S. Navy's SEAL teams—the elite fighting element of the British Royal Navy.

"We'll worry about that later," I said, as the two men arrived with Tank's body, now covered in the blanket on which we'd planned to relax and enjoy the day.

Charity opened the back door of the helo and folded two facing seats down, creating a spot where we could secure the stretcher.

The men loaded Tank into the helo and Bud climbed in front. He, Chyrel, and I would escort Tank back to the ship.

I looked back at the sad faces of those gathered beside the helo. Woden sat off to the side, slightly away from the group, as if he knew Tank was gone.

Since their first meeting, the big Rottweiler had bonded with my old friend, surprising everyone, including Savannah. Whenever Tank was around, Woden had stayed close to him. She'd said Woden had never done that with anyone. I think he'd somehow sensed that Tank was sick.

As I helped Chyrel into the back, I wondered if dogs felt loss like we did. When I glanced over, Woden's eyes met mine. He looked sad, but somehow relieved and calm.

"You want to go with him?" I asked.

Woden rose from his haunches, his head high, ears forward.

"Come on," I said.

He sprinted across the sand, as if he'd just seen a prowler, then leapt into the passenger compartment, settling beside Tank's body.

As I climbed in and closed the door, Charity began spooling the turbines up. In just a moment, we were airborne and headed back to *Ambrosia*.

Chyrel sat in her seat, still holding Tank's hand. I'd never pried into what their relationship was like—she was much younger than him. Initially, he'd told me that he wanted to marry her so his pension wouldn't end—a simple business arrangement. He figured that after fifty-one years of service, the government owed him more than just a couple of years of retirement, and by marrying someone younger, he knew that money would continue to fund his charity for a long time.

She'd agreed. But after a while, I knew there was love between them.

Chyrel looked at me and smiled, then put her headset on.

"It was exactly how he'd said he wanted to go," she said. "Sitting on a beach in the sun, surrounded by the people he cared most about."

"I'm so sorry," I said, not really understanding why those words needed to be said.

"Hush, Jesse," she said. "I think he endured the pain beyond what he should have, just to get here. He greatly admired you and wanted to see you one last time. He's still with us, but now he doesn't hurt anymore."

I reached over and took her other hand. "And our pain is just beginning."

Charity settled the bird onto the flight deck. She'd radioed ahead and the same two crewmen were waiting, Grady Lawson and Bernie Knight standing by with them. Once the bird was secure, Charity killed the engine and we got out.

"What happened?" Bernie asked.

He'd agreed to stay behind to listen to the sonar, saying he didn't like beaches and sand.

"Cancer," was all I could say.

"What do we do with him?" Chyrel asked, her voice cracking a little.

"I can clear out one of the coolers," Grady offered.

Her face showed alarm. "He can't be frozen. There has to be an autopsy and a declaration of—"

"I'll take care of it, ma'am," Grady said.

I took Chyrel by the shoulders and looked into her eyes. "Once the crew is back aboard, we'll make for the nearest medical facility."

"There has to be a death certif—"

"I know," I told her. "We'll do everything by the book. Exactly the way Tank would want it done. Leave everything to me."

"Thanks, Jesse."

I turned to Grady. "Go clear the cooler, son. Set it to thirty-six degrees."

"Aye, Captain," he replied, then hurried down the steps.

Then I turned to the two crewmen, Al and Jocko. "Please be careful taking him out."

They both nodded somberly at Chyrel as Bud and Charity joined us.

"Matt just called on the radio," Charity said. "They were able to get everyone into the two launches. It'll take a bit longer for them to return, but they should be here by the time you have the boat ready to get underway."

"Go with him," I said to Bud. "Then make sure Chyrel gets to her cabin."

"I don't want to be alone, Jesse," she said. "If you don't mind, I'd like to join you on the bridge."

"Of course," I said.

"I'll take care of him," Bud said to both of us, then followed Al and Jocko, who were carrying the stretcher toward the steps.

Chyrel and I followed Bernie down the steps and into the empty bridge. I looked back and didn't see anyone in the op center, a first since I'd come aboard. I was suddenly struck with a sense of enormous loneliness.

The man I'd so greatly admired for most of my adult life was gone.

Suddenly, Heitor's voice came over the comm. "Engine room to bridge."

We weren't alone. Bernie, Al, Jocko, Grady, and Heitor had all decided to stay aboard. Our original plan was to stay anchored here for a couple of days and they'd all planned to go ashore tomorrow.

I pushed the intercom button. "Bridge."

"I heard what happened," he said. "My condolences."

"We'll be getting underway as soon as the crew returns," I said. "Maybe twenty minutes. Will you be ready?"

"Whenever you say the word," Heitor replied.

"Bridge out," I said.

Chyrel moved next to me, putting a hand on the back of the helm seat, absently moving it back and forth.

"It all seemed so simple," she said. "When Owen first

explained his great plan to me."

I put an arm around her shoulders and guided her into the chair, then sat down at the sonar station and turned to face her.

"At first, he just wanted someone who would carry on his legacy," she began. "It made sense to me. 'You're only thirty-eight,' he'd said, then explained how his pension could continue to add to his trust fund for a long time if I married him and didn't remarry when he was gone."

She looked up at me. "Was it weird?"

"You know I don't judge," I said. "What two adults do is their business."

"I never wanted a husband," she said. "Still don't. We had different rooms in the beginning. We barely knew one another." She turned and looked out over the bow. "But he made me laugh, Jesse. We watched sunsets, walked along the beach, and he told me stories about his life in the Marines—all the people he'd met and admired." She glanced back over at me, then. "He talked a lot about you."

"Tank was one of the greatest men I ever knew," I said.

"Not really," she replied, with a sad smile. "He said he was just a guy from the Big Sky Country—a simple man with simple needs. He told me that what he did on that one day completely reshaped his life, but he believed it was what anyone else would have done. I didn't know the 'Tank' you knew, Jesse. The man I knew was sweet and gentle and warm and caring. I fell in love with Owen, not the man you stood beside on some rooftop in the desert.

"The first time we were intimate was more than a month after we'd married. It was the day before Valentine's Day. He took me out to that little boat of his. He'd piled the front of it with pillows and blankets, scented candles, and wine. He'd said that he thought I needed romance in my life, even if it was just make-believe. That's why he picked the day before. We were just friends—confidants, I guess you could say. We pretended we were lovers and suddenly, I didn't want to pretend anymore. I know it sounds goofy, but he was actually very sweet and shy, so I had to make the first move. Later that night, I moved into his room."

I reached over and took her hand. "I guess there's a side to all of us that only a few people know. I'm glad he found someone to share his inner feelings and thoughts with."

She smiled again. "And I'm glad you introduced us and I got to know that side of him. I don't think I'll ever know someone who cared so deeply."

The VHF above the helm squawked and Matt's voice came over the speaker. "*Ambrosia, Ambrosia, Ambrosia!* Tender *Calypso*! We are under attack!"

CHAPTER TWENTY-ONE

Springing to my feet, I snatched the mic. "What's going on, Matt?"

"The other boat is under attack!" he shouted. "An odd-looking powerboat with three outboards, Cap'n. I'm turning back to assist!"

I snatched up the binos and scanned the water to the south. I could see our two launches, one turning sluggishly in the swells, both overloaded. The other boat was half a mile behind it. A third boat, looking more like a lifeboat than anything, was bumping the side of *Penelope*, our second launch. There were four or five men aboard.

I was moving before I realized it. Snatching the handheld radio from its cradle, I went down the spiral stairs as fast as I could go, shouting into the radio, "Negative, Matt! Get your boat back to *Ambrosia*!"

When I reached the long passageway on the lower deck, I

sprinted to the end and punched in the code, then opened the hatch and went straight to the locker where the rifles were stored.

A moment later, I was climbing through the deck hatch onto the foredeck, where I dropped into a prone position, inserted a full magazine, and flipped up the lens covers on the scope.

Through the optics, I saw the other boat ram *Penelope* again. Ross was at the helm, trying to maneuver away. But the boat was overloaded and seriously off balance, the crew having moved away from the attacking boat.

All but one man.

I saw a brightly colored shirt rise up from behind the helm seat. Travis Stockwell pointed his weapon at the attackers. Suddenly, he went down.

I racked a .50 caliber round into the chamber and estimated the distance at nearly a mile.

One thousand, nine hundred and sixty-nine yards, I heard my own voice echo in my head.

I aimed slightly below the boat's pilot and squeezed off a round. We called it "Kentucky windage" in the Corps—it was something I tried to teach my Marines when there wasn't time to adjust the weapon's sights.

I barely felt the kick, most of which was absorbed by the recoil spring as the spent cartridge was ejected and a fresh one was loaded into the chamber.

The bullet, as big around as a man's finger, missed its mark but at least hit the boat. I saw a huge chunk of fiberglass fly into the air.

I kept the crosshairs just below the torso of the man at the wheel, trying to predict where the moving boat would be a full second after the round left the muzzle. The wind was light and at ninety degrees. I aimed low and left, then fired three more rounds in quick succession, knowing that there was little chance for a hit at this distance with the way the boat was bobbing and rolling in the swells. But more fiberglass flew up as two of the rounds tore through the boat, splintering everything in their path. At least I was getting the point across.

My crew wasn't unprotected.

With the fifth round, it seemed as if the pilot were suddenly yanked out of his seat, replaced by a fine pink mist as the bullet tore through his body at nearly 700 miles per hour.

The boat careened away from *Penelope*. I continued to fire on the now retreating boat. I had no qualms about taking the enemy out as they fled. They sowed it. They could reap it, too.

One of the outboards erupted in a shower of sparks and flame. Even a mile away, the .50 caliber BMG rounds hit like a bowling ball at nearly supersonic speed.

Just as I was about to fire again, the boat erupted in a fireball, engulfing its occupants.

I took my finger off the trigger, laying it alongside the guard, and brought the scope back to *Penelope*. She was still underway, now running straight. A flash of golden hair appeared, and I saw the side of Savannah's face, looking out to where the other boat had exploded. Then she turned and looked straight at me, her face a mask of concern.

"*Ambrosia, Ambrosia*, this is *Penelope*," Ross's voice shouted over the radio that lay beside me. "We have a man down!"

Leaving the rifle on the deck, I snatched up the radio and tore down the side deck. "Who is it?" I shouted into the handheld.

Ross's steady voice came back. "It's Mr. Stockwell, Jesse."

When I got to the stern platform, I raised the garage door and pulled the dollies out to retrieve the launches. Then I activated the hydraulic lift and lowered the whole platform into the water.

With the deck awash, Matt steered his boat into position as I readied the first dolly, locking it into place.

Matt mashed the throttle and brought the twenty-four-foot tender up onto the platform and into its dolly.

"Everyone out!" I yelled. "Get up to the cockpit!"

The crew scrambled over the sides of the launch as Matt helped me get the second dolly ready.

"Was that you doin' the shootin', Cap'n?"

"Yes," I replied, as Ross lined the second tender up. "How's Travis?"

"Don't know," Matt replied, "It was all I could do to keep the bleddy boat from goin' ass over teakettle."

With a roar from the small inboard, Ross brought *Penelope* up onto the platform, bouncing off one side of the dolly before settling a little off-center.

I splashed around to the side as the crew got out. Savannah knelt on the deck, bent over Travis, applying a gauze pad to his shoulder.

"How is he?" I asked her.

"Damned pissed," Stockwell thundered, trying to push Savannah away. "Let me up, woman."

She put a hand on his other shoulder and forced him back down onto the deck. "*You* are not in charge here, Colonel," she said. "Stay still, till I get this in place or I'll kick your ass."

Travis stared at Savannah in utter disbelief, but he did what he was told.

Alberto climbed out and stood beside me. "Is he going to be okay?"

I looked into Travis's eyes and could see the anger boiling. "Yeah," I replied. "Only his dignity is hurt."

"He's lost a good bit of blood," Savannah said, then looked up at Ross. "Get over here and help me get him out of this boat."

"Yes, ma'am," Ross replied, jumping aboard.

Matt didn't wait for Savannah's order. Together, the two men got Travis out of the boat and up the ladder to the cockpit.

"Are you okay?" I asked Savannah, noting her blood-soaked blouse.

"I'm fine," she said. "It's Travis's blood. Who were those men?'

"I don't know," I said, helping her over the side.

Walt, Travis's armorer, was starting after the others, but I stopped him. "Get the tenders stowed, Mr. Meachum. Then meet me on the bridge."

"I'll take Alberto and Finn up to our quarters," Savannah said.

"Finn knocked Mr. Stockwell down," Alberto said. "He tried to jump in the boat with those men."

"That sounds like Stockwell," I said, as Alberto and Finn started up the ladder.

"No, Jesse," Savannah said. "It was Finn. He was an absolute terror. If one of those men had gotten aboard, I really think he'd have ripped him to shreds after Travis was hurt. If it hadn't been for whoever was shooting at them, I think Finn would have been the only one to protect the rest of us."

I looked up at the big, friendly, yellow dog, his tail wagging as he disappeared into the cockpit with Alberto.

I shook my head. "Unbelievable."

"Where's Woden?"

"On the bridge with Chyrel," I replied.

"Oh, dear," Savannah said. "I must change and go help her."

We went up to the cockpit, where I found Matt. "Where's Travis?"

"His security team took him to his quarters, Cap'n."

"Prepare to get underway," I told him. "Let me know when the garage and platform are secure. I'll be on the bridge."

"Aye," he replied, then turned and started barking orders at the rest of the crew.

When I reached the bridge, Chyrel was still sitting in the helm seat. Val and Charity were with her, and Woden sat with his head on Chyrel's lap as she softly stroked the fur between his wide-set eyes.

Val met me at the hatch. "Will Mr. Stockwell be alright?" she asked quietly.

I nodded. "I think so. How's Chyrel?"

She looked back. "She's okay," she replied. "A bit shaken up by everything, I think."

I went over to her and put a hand on her shoulder. She looked up and smiled. "I've always been behind the scenes," she said. "I'd told Owen what I did to help y'all when we worked for Homeland and later with Deuce and Armstrong. He said you and Deuce were 'men of action,' which I never realized until now."

"You should get some rest," I said, as others began to file onto the bridge, one of them Meachum.

"What are you going to do, Jesse?" she asked, her blue eyes somewhat dull.

"One sec," I said, then strode across the deck to Meachum. "Travis is okay," I told him.

I saw the relief in his eyes.

"He's in his quarters," I assured the armorer. "Your Barrett is on the foredeck. Go get it, then go to Travis's quarters and have him make an announcement that all but bridge, security, and op center personnel are to go to their quarters and stay there."

He gave me a puzzled look.

"I want the crew to hear his voice."

Meachum smiled. "Aye, Captain," he said, then hurried off.

I turned back to Chyrel. I needed her head straight.

She looked up at me. "That boat didn't come from shore."

She was right. We'd have seen it from the chopper if it had come from the mainland.

Canopus, I thought. *The ghost ship.*

I looked over at Ross, standing by his electronics system. "Where's the *Canopus*, Mr. Mosely?"

He checked the chart plotter, but I couldn't see her AIS signature there. "No AIS," he replied, then switched over to radar.

I could see three returns on the screen, all within twenty miles. Ross held one side of his headphones to his right ear and bent over the sonar screen for a moment, adjusting the underwater acoustic sensor.

"She's eighteen miles south-southeast, Captain. Engines at idle."

The *Canopus* could make fifteen knots, slightly less than our cruising speed on the diesels. At full speed, our overtake rate would be barely five knots, meaning it would take almost four hours to catch her. São Luís was less than an hour in the other direction.

Of course, there were the turbines.

Travis needed medical attention.

And then there was Tank.

I leaned on the helm's armrest and pushed the engine room button on the intercom. "Bridge to engineering."

"Engine room," Heitor replied, as though he were sitting there waiting for me to call.

"Start the turbines, Heitor," I ordered.

Chyrel touched my hand. "What are you going to do?" she asked again.

I turned to Axel, who was standing beside her. "Set your course for São Luís, Mister Troutman."

"Jesse?" Chyrel said.

"I need your help, Chyrel," I said.

"What can I do?" she asked, rising to allow Axel to take his position at the helm.

I guided her toward the op center and lowered my voice. "I need to know everything there is to know about the freighter *Canopus*. I want to know who owns it, who the skipper is, the crew, their wives, mistresses, kids, what damned bars they frequent, and favorite stool. Can you do that for me?"

Chyrel looked into the dimly lit room, the nerve center for Armstrong Research. David had taken a seat at a console, the bottoms of his shorts still dripping from the wade out to the tender. Flo stood behind him as both looked at us.

"Yes," she replied, with a knowing grin. "Most of it, anyway. What stool will depend on whether the bar has a security camera."

Chyrel knew what I was up to. She was one of the best computer hackers in the world, and *Ambrosia's* operations center contained some of the fastest, most sophisticated equipment on the planet. I wanted to get her mind off her loss, though we'd all known it was imminent.

She started to turn, but I put a hand on her elbow. "But first, I want you to contact Jack and let him know what's going on, then get his permission to hack the CIA's computer."

Her eyes went wide with excitement. "What?"

I nodded toward where David and Flo stood. "Find out what you can about Bud Ferguson and Marcos Santiago."

CHAPTER TWENTY-TWO

O n another bridge, Captain Mauricio Gonzales smiled, remembering the fancy yacht and the two motor launches he and the crew of *Canopus* had seen earlier in the morning. The small boats had been loaded with people, many of them women.

Mauricio had always believed that when good fortune came along, a man must be ready to snatch it before it passed him by. Second chances were rare.

Mauricio saw the yacht as a big score. From the number of people in the two tenders, he doubted there would be enough crew left aboard the yacht to put up much of a fight.

With a boat like that, he could go into business for himself. The only thing that had ever stopped him from hijacking a big yacht in the past had been the knowledge that it would have a lot of people aboard, and he and his men were few.

When he'd seen the women in the tenders, he'd altered his

plan, instantly morphing it to include the passengers. Once the yacht was his, he could send his men out to take the small boats, one by one.

The captives could be ransomed or sold. Taking captives to Juan would only add a few more American dollars in his pocket. But with the yacht, he could cross the ocean in style, selling the *putas Americanas* directly to those who would pay top dollar.

It was the helicopter that had first drawn Mauricio's attention. Such decadence. As if owning a boat like the one he'd barely seen on the horizon weren't enough. The rich *Americano* used a helicopter to get to shore.

Canopus had then passed quite close to the small boats, caught halfway between the yacht and shore, and he'd gotten a good look with the binoculars. There were probably a dozen women on the two boats, many quite beautiful. He'd seen three dark-haired beauties and two blondes staring up at him and his men, who taunted them with their exposed manhood. An exceptionally beautiful girl with thick auburn hair had shouted obscenities at them in Spanish.

He'd immediately devised a better plan.

Canopus continued on for several miles. Mauricio knew that sooner or later, the two small tenders would return to the yacht. He'd ordered his men to remove the engines from two of the lifeboats and put them on the third. Then he sent them back to wait.

They could easily take the two launches as they returned.

Then, using their own tenders, his men could sneak up on the yacht and take it without giving them time to radio for help.

He'd told Miguel that once he had the yacht secure, he was to kill the men and throw the bodies overboard, with the exception of the captain and two of the bridge crew. They would need the captain to learn how to operate the yacht. If he refused, Mauricio would kill one of his crew.

Miguel and his men hadn't even been gone an hour when his radar showed the helicopter, which they'd seen flying toward the beach earlier, lift off and fly back to the yacht. Minutes later, he'd seen the two small blips on the radar screen moving that way as well, spaced a kilometer apart.

"*Perfecto*," he sneered, thinking how easily his men could overtake and commandeer the overloaded boats.

He contacted Miguel by radio and told him and his men to stop the two boats, then use them to approach the yacht. Once they had control of the yacht, Mauricio would bring *Canopus* alongside, open her seacocks, and order his men into a lifeboat. Then Mauricio would set the autopilot due north and engage the engine before getting into the boat and casting off.

With his men in control of the yacht, *Canopus* was useless to him, and it would steam north for almost an hour before the lower decks flooded and killed the engine. Then she'd sink in water more than two kilometers in depth.

He watched the radar screen, seeing his lifeboat head toward the boat closest to shore. He would have taken the lead boat first, but Mauricio quickly realized Miguel's plan as the lead boat started to turn back.

"He'll lure the other boat back," Mauricio said.

Suddenly, the radio operator sat up in his seat, holding his headphone tightly to one ear.

"What is it?" Mauricio asked, reading the shocked look on the man's face.

"They are returning," Eduardo said, excitedly. "Someone started shooting at them from the yacht. Miguel is dead."

"Shooting? From the rich *Americano's* boat?"

"*Si*," the radioman replied.

"How can that be?" Mauricio asked rhetorically. "They were nearly two kilometers away."

He looked down at the radar screen and saw his men racing away from the two launches.

Suddenly the blip representing his lifeboat disappeared.

Mauricio waited for it to return, assuming it had dropped below a large wave, though the seas were relatively calm. Still, he'd seen big waves on calm seas before. He waited a moment longer, but the radar signature from his lifeboat didn't return.

"Contact the lifeboat," he ordered the radio operator.

He used his field glasses to look in the direction he knew the small boats to be, though he realized they and the yacht were over the horizon.

Through the binos, he saw a black and orange cloud rise up over the horizon.

"They are not responding," the radioman said.

Understanding started to sink in as Mauricio slowly

lowered the field glasses.

"*Esos malditos Americanos.*" He muttered. "I will kill them all!"

"What is it?" the radioman asked.

The rich gringo must have security, he thought. Someone who is good with a rifle. *O muy afortunada.*

A lucky shot from two kilometers? That was more likely, considering the distance the yacht was from the small boats.

Maybe someone on one of the launches was armed. But he dismissed that thought since a handgun wasn't much use against a boat.

He turned to the radioman. "You said they were being fired on from the yacht?"

"*Si,*" he replied. "Miguel was shot and Tomas took over to drive the boat away."

It had been at least ten seconds after the radioman had first said the men were returning that he saw the image on the radar disappear. Not a long time, but a lifeboat with three engines would be out of range of a handgun from the tender. It had to be a rifleman from the yacht.

He stared down at the screen, watching the two small echoes merge with the larger one.

The radioman was monitoring the international hail and distress frequency and the yacht hadn't reached out to report anything. At least not by radio.

Girls from fishing villages had fathers who were poor fishermen. But those from a yacht would have very wealthy families.

Mauricio stared at the blip on the screen, his anger seething. He would follow the *Americano*. Somehow, some way, he was going to take those women from him. He would ransom them to their families in America, and then sell them to Juan after receiving the money.

While the rich yacht owner and his friends searched for their wives and daughters, they'd be locked in a hold, on their way to Syria, playthings for the super-wealthy oil sheiks to use up and throw away.

As he watched the screen, the blip began to move, heading away from *Canopus*.

"Engine ahead," Mauricio said. "Follow that yacht."

"You may run, *mis hermosas putitas*," Mauricio snarled, still staring at the screen. "But you cannot hide."

They had lost five good men, one of their lifeboats, and all three of their lifeboats' engines. The men were his *cazedores*, his hunters, the men who snuck into the villages and grabbed anyone they could, concentrating on younger women.

They would be hard to replace, but every port in South America had its share of wharf rats, men who would do anything for a few *centavos o pesos*.

On the radar screen, the yacht began to accelerate. It went faster and faster, until Mauricio was sure the radar was malfunctioning.

"How fast are they going?" he asked his radar man.

"Forty-five knots," the man replied, anxiously. "And still

accelerating."

Mauricio slammed both fists on the dash.

"How can this be?" he cried out. "Who is this *Americano*?"

The radar man turned on the AIS for just a moment, watching the screen closely. When the identifier appeared, he quickly turned the system back off.

"It is a motor yacht called *Ambrosia, Capitão*," the radar man disclosed. "Its home port is New York, New York."

CHAPTER TWENTY-THREE

I ordered the anchor raised but waited to engage the turbines until Travis's voice emanated from every speaker on the boat. "This is Mr. Stockwell," he said, his voice charged with rage. "We have been attacked, but there are no serious injuries to any of our crew. The captain is going to move the ship expeditiously to São Luís. All on board who are not part of the bridge crew, operations deck, engineering, or security team, please remain in your quarters. The ship will be moving very fast."

"Engage the turbines," I ordered.

Axel moved the uppermost set of throttles forward, and even with the bridge hatches closed, I could hear the roar of water from the giant twin water jets as they were engaged. *Ambrosia* gathered speed quickly.

Moments later, as we accelerated past forty-five knots, Ross looked up from his radar screen. "Captain, *Canopus* just turned on their AIS."

If there wasn't a knot meter on the chart-plotter screen, nobody could guess we were going so fast, except for the occasional jarring motion as the ship plowed through moderate seas.

I moved over next to Ross's station, keeping hold of the grab rails in the overhead. Just as I spotted the identifier on the screen, it disappeared.

"Out of VHF range?" I asked.

"Definitely not," Ross replied. "We should still be able to pick up their AIS transmission to a range of about forty miles."

"They turned it on to identify *Ambrosia*," I said. "But why?"

Val stepped up beside me. "You killed some of their men and sank their boat. *Machismo* revenge?"

"I hope they do," I said, barely whispering, but meaning every word.

"Me too," Charity added.

I hadn't even noticed her step up beside me.

I put a hand on Axel's shoulder. "Hold her steady at fifty knots, Axel."

"Fifty knots, aye," he replied, gently pulling back on the throttles.

Unlike a commercial ship, where a desired engine speed is relayed to the engine room, *Ambrosia* was a yacht, and had two sets of electronic engine controls, one for the diesels and another for the turbines, allowing the helmsman to directly control the boat's speed.

"Fishing vessel eight nautical miles ahead, Captain," Ross informed me. "Three nautical miles south of our course and heading south."

"Gradual turn to starboard, helm," I said. "Give us non-visual separation."

Maneuvering at high speed was something the helmsmen practiced whenever we did our routine maintenance runs on the big turbines. The first time I'd actually taken the helm at high speed, I'd been surprised at how little movement of the wheel was required to turn the big yacht.

All four engines were connected to water jets. The two connected to the turbines were fixed, while the two connected to the diesels were directional and had diverters to reverse the flow of water.

Axel gently turned the wheel a few degrees and *Ambrosia* gracefully heeled into the turn. He brought the rudder back amidship and the line on the chart plotter indicated that we'd pass the fishing boat about six miles north of its present location. If someone were on the roof and had powerful binoculars and sharp eyes, they might see our flybridge roof and radar arch hurtling along the horizon.

"Nicely done," I said.

I looked back into the op center. Chyrel was at a console next to David, both scribbling notes on a pad and reading what the other had written. I had no idea what it was and probably wouldn't have a clue even if I read it.

But she was busy—in her own element—and her mind

was on something else.

Val was reading something on her Metis, then stepped over to the communications system. She plugged a headset into an encrypted radio's jack. The headset was the kind that had only one earphone, like football coaches wore, or anyone else who needed to listen quietly with one ear while maintaining outside hearing.

She handed the headset to me. "It's Mr. Armstrong for you."

I put it on and adjusted the voice-activated microphone in front of my lips. "Jack?"

"Chyrel filled me in on what happened," Jack said. "I'm sorry about Tank. He was a good man and I know what he meant to you."

"Thanks," I said, looking over at Val.

"And Val just reported what happened with the launches. How's Travis?"

"He's okay," I said. "I had him make the announcement that we were going to São Luís, so the crew would know he was okay."

"Good thinking," Jack said. "How long before you get there?"

I looked at the chart plotter. There were numerous radar returns near the busy port city. We'd have to slow down soon.

"Less than twenty minutes," I replied.

"Don't go to the docks," he said. "Drop anchor three miles off the coast of Raposa and wait. A doctor is on the way."

"What about Tank's body?" I asked.

"The doctor who's coming will have the necessary documentation," he replied. "Once he leaves, Charity can fly Chyrel and Tank back to Grenada, where I'll have a jet waiting to take him home."

"And my daughter, David, and Tank's friend, Bud Ferguson?"

"David and Florence are your call," he said. "Ferguson stays aboard until we find out who he is and whether his being there was simply as Tank's guest, or something else."

Even I didn't know all of Jack's operatives and I wasn't privy to all the goings-on in Armstrong's vast network. He directly employed thousands of people, and there were tens of thousands in his network, maybe hundreds of thousands.

I watched Chyrel, busy at the terminal. "I take it you weren't the one who sent him."

"I'll never send someone to *Ambrosia* without clearing it through you first," Jack replied. "Call me when the doctor leaves."

His voice was replaced with static, as he'd switched off the encrypted satellite radio connection.

I handed the headset back to Val and told Axel to start slowing the ship. When we were down to twenty knots, he brought the diesels up to speed, then shut down the turbines.

Twenty minutes later, as we were dropping anchor, a small boat came racing out toward us.

I wasn't taking any chances and ordered security to man the starboard rail and aft platform.

"Take over," I said to Matt. "Let me know if anything comes within three miles of our position."

"Aye, Cap'n," he replied.

I went back to our quarters and told Savannah that Jack had a doctor coming out to meet us.

"It never fails," she said.

"What do you mean?"

"Are there any resources, anywhere, that Jack Armstrong can't provide?"

I grinned at her, understanding that for Jack, it wasn't about the logistics of moving equipment and assets, but more in knowing where assets he didn't control were located. With a single phone call, he could have just about anything available that his operators needed.

"He just knows a lot of people," I said.

"Can I go with you?" she asked. "That last hour was very long for us back here."

"Was it rough?"

"No," she replied. "It's just that knowing we were going twice as fast as *Sea Biscuit* ever could and not seeing what was going on or where we were going was...well, a bit disconcerting, that's all."

"You could have come to the bridge," I told her, hugging her tightly.

"But Travis said—"

I looked into her clear, blue eyes. "Travis's orders don't apply to the captain's wench."

She pinched me hard on the butt. "Wench, huh? I'll show you."

The door connecting our main quarters to Alberto's suite opened and he joined us. "I thought you said she was the admiral."

Savannah and I broke apart. "What've you been doing?" she asked innocently.

He shrugged. "Just watching out the window. Can I go out now?"

"No," I told him. "Not yet. Soon though."

"And me?" Savannah asked. "Whether wench or admiral, I worry about you."

"It's better if you stay here and keep Alberto company," I replied. "I don't trust anyone in these waters right now."

I left them and went down to the cockpit by way of the starboard side deck.

The boat was a small center console with only two men aboard—one at the wheel and the other seated in front of the console. He had a briefcase and a large first aid kit at his feet.

Meachum and another man I'd only heard called "Duster" were at the rail, weapons carried openly, as the boat moved toward the platform. I waited for the two security men, then the three of us went down the steps to the platform.

I was surprised to see Travis waiting there with another of his team, a short, stout black man named Gerald.

The small boat's pilot moved the center console closer, then went forward and tossed a line to me. I made the line fast to a cleat and pulled the boat closer, turning it sideways to the platform.

"You shouldn't be standing, Colonel," the man I assumed was a doctor said. He stood and handed the big first aid kit to me.

"We have first aid supplies," I told him, but took it anyway.

"You guys can stand down," Travis said to Meachum and the others.

The doctor handed the briefcase to me as he stepped over. "I'm sure you have a fine first aid kit," he said. "But Colonel Stockwell is blood type B positive. Not the rarest, but only a small percentage of Earth's population have it."

"I'm fine, sir," Travis said. "No need for—"

"I will be the judge of that, Colonel," the doctor interrupted. "Sit over there on that step."

Surprisingly, Travis did as he was told. I caught a bit of a snicker from Duster.

The doctor, his pale blue eyes charged with electricity, looked back at the man. "That'll be enough of that, Duster. Unless you feel it's time for a proctology exam."

The young man's face went blank and his body rigid. "Yes, sir!"

Who was this guy?

Stockwell sat on the second step and removed his shirt, wincing slightly. There was a bandage over the upper part of his left chest, just below the collar bone. It wasn't the same one Savannah had put on while Stockwell was lying on the deck.

The doctor peeled the bandage down from the top. The bullet wound had been closed with three sutures, which I knew Savannah didn't have time to do.

He nodded approvingly, then grabbed a blood pressure cuff from his kit and fit it onto Travis's upper arm. With the touch of a button, the cuff inflated, then slowly deflated, as sensors measured the BP.

The doctor frowned, then used a stethoscope to listen to Travis's heart.

He frowned again. "Not a through and through," he said. "Who took the bullet out?"

"I did, General," Duster said.

General?

The doctor looked back at the younger man and grinned. "No doubt why the colonel needs blood."

Turning back to his patient, he said, "You're lucky, Travis. A couple of inches lower and we wouldn't be talking."

"The guy was aiming at my face," Travis said, then nodded toward me. "His dog knocked me aside."

The doctor turned to me. "I don't believe we've met."

"Sorry, sir," Travis said. "This is Jesse McDermitt, captain of *Ambrosia*. Jesse, meet retired Major General Leopold Earnst, former chief of the trauma center at Landstuhl Regional Medical Center in Germany. Jesse's a retired enlisted jarhead, General, but we don't hold it against him."

He shook my hand. "Colonel Stockwell may well owe his life to your dog, Captain."

"I'll see that Finn gets checked out by a vet at our next port of call."

He chuckled and nodded. "A wise idea, I'm sure. Did you retire as a sergeant major?"

"No, sir. Gunnery Sergeant."

His eyes sparkled with mirth. "And now captain of Jack's infamous pirate ship, eh?"

CHAPTER TWENTY-FOUR

G eneral Earnst was a bewildering man. At times, he had a gentle manner about him, taking great care with his patient. And at other times, he'd seemed more like an infantry officer, exchanging profanity-laced barbs with Travis's team.

It was obvious that there was history with all of them. As he worked, setting up an IV drip, I studied each member of the security team a little closer.

Duster seemed the youngest, but even he was in his thirties. He reminded me of a bird of prey, perched high on a limb overhanging a gorge, body unmoving, sharp eyes not missing a thing.

Meachum was a few years older, I figured. He was taller and heavier, but that wasn't what separated the two men. Duster looked up to Meachum, admired him in a way that told me they'd been through a shitstorm together.

But the other two, Gerald and Oswald, were both more

than a decade older, probably late forties. They both had a look about them that told me they had been career soldiers.

These were men who'd all served together, comfortable in whatever bond that held them. Meachum and Duster had probably been in high school on 9/11, Oswald and Gerald already staff NCOs. Stockwell was still an active-duty officer until he was tapped by Homeland Security in early 2007.

My guess was that Stockwell had met and worked with each man while in the Army, sometime between 2002 and 2007. Knowing his background and observing the casual way they all interacted, I assumed it was probably some covert operation.

Somalia, Syria, Lebanon, and Yemen were all hotbeds of clandestine military operations during that time. Iraq and Afghanistan had been more overt, but it might have been one of those just as easily.

The retired general was the wild card. He appeared to be in his early seventies and, being a doctor, had probably never served in a war zone. At least not this latest, long war. But that fact also might have allowed him to serve beyond mandatory retirement. On 9/11, when the two younger men were likely still in school, Earnst probably had the first star on his shoulder board, a brigadier general.

But in the medical field? How would their paths cross?

Earnst had given Stockwell a unit of blood and another of a saline solution loaded with antibiotics to ward off infection.

As Meachum and Duster loaded the doctor's gear into the boat, he picked up the briefcase and nodded toward the far side of the deck. I followed him.

He handed me the briefcase, then a slip of paper. "Here's the combination."

"What's in it?" I asked.

General Earnst went on to tell me a few things he thought Tank might have overlooked in his estate planning and said there was documentation in the briefcase that would not only allow us to take his body back home, but would also smooth things over in the future.

I knew the documents would have to be all phonied up. Tank had died in Brazil, and since we'd not cleared into the country, he'd died on foreign soil after illegally entering the country.

"That could pose problems," Earnst said.

"He should have died at home."

"Nobody chooses when or where that happens," he told me, as we moved toward his boat.

"He did," I countered. "His oncologist had told him it was a matter of days just before he decided to come down here."

General Earnst stopped at the side of the boat and looked at Stockwell and his men, then turned to me. "If a man leads a good life, he might be able to choose *who* he wants with him when the time comes. Isn't that more important than when or where?"

Without waiting for a reply, he swung his legs over the

gunwale and Meachum untied the line. In seconds, the boat was up on plane and heading back toward the mainland.

"How do you know him?" I asked Travis, as we climbed the steps to the cockpit.

He stopped and faced me, his men proceeding on into the salon. Oswald went up the spiral staircase to the bridge and the others went down to the lower deck.

"It was in 2012," Stockwell said. "A small task force was sent to Jordan, in case Syria lost control of its chemical weapons during their civil war. General Earnst headed the task force, because of his background in chemical and biological weapons. I went as part of Homeland Security's specialists in the region. Meachum took a bullet protecting Duster during a night incursion across the border. Duster dragged him back and the general saved his life."

Stockwell turned and went inside, leaving me with a few answers to questions my mind had formed, as well as more questions. Travis was a man of few words. What he'd said might be the mechanics of how he'd met Earnst and the two younger men, but it didn't explain the deep bond I could sense among all six of them.

I stepped over to the maneuvering console and pushed the button for the ship's intercom. "Captain McDermitt to all hands. Secure from restricted movement. We're anchored in the Bay of São Marcos but will be getting underway shortly."

Then I carried the briefcase up to the bridge deck and entered the op center. Chyrel and David were smiling at one another. I walked over to stand beside Flo.

"What's going on?" I whispered.

"They got in and got the information you wanted," she replied. "Now they just have to get out, which Chyrel said was harder. David came up with a way that might make it easier."

I stepped closer and watched the two monitors as lines of code were fed from one to the other. That went on for several seconds, then suddenly, both screens went blank and an image appeared—a plain white shield with a sixteen-point star in the center, and an eagle's head in profile above it. The logo of the CIA.

"And we're out!" Chyrel said, rolling back and giving David a double high-five. "That was brilliant!"

"Thanks," David said. "I always wanted to try that."

Chyrel looked up, then stood. "You have the makings of a first-rate analyst here, Jesse."

"What did you find out?"

Chyrel took a stack of papers from a printer between her monitor and David's. "Let's go somewhere."

I led the way down the inside passageway and unlocked a hatch just before my quarters. After the three followed me inside, I closed the hatch to my private office, placed the briefcase beside my desk and sat down in my chair. Chyrel took a seat next to my desk and the kids sat on a small sofa.

"Okay," I said. "Give it to me. Santiago first."

She told me how, in October 1976, Marcos Santiago, who was then only fourteen years old and a resident of the border town, Bôca da Mata, had escaped almost certain capture by right-wing extremists, with the help of an unidentified American spy. Even at that young age, he'd been a leader among the guerilla freedom fighters, and had been smuggled across the border into Venezuela.

"During that same month," Chyrel continued, "Bud Ferguson was also in Bôca da Mata, investigating guerilla activity. The following month, he was suddenly sent back to Langley. He became a paper pusher, Jesse, finally retiring in 1996 as a GS-10."

General Service pay grades were assigned to federal civilian workers. Bud's was a mid-level, non-management position.

That had to be why Marcos had reacted the way he did when the two met. Bud had somehow helped the younger man get across the border, either taking him to Maracaibo himself, or arranging transportation.

"Anything to tie them together for certain?" I asked.

"Just this entry on Ferguson's record book," Chyrel replied, taking the stack of papers, and flipping through them. "Here, read this."

I took the sheet she handed me and looked at it.

"The entry for the fourth of November," David said.

The entry read simply: *Accused of transporting a suspected guerilla fighter from Bôca da Mata to Maracaibo. No corroborating evidence or witnesses. Detained in Maracaibo by Venezuelan authorities and expelled from the country. Secret clearance revoked.*

What had Marcos done or said to make Bud take such a risk? A GS-10 civilian employee was barely higher than his rank of captain in Vietnam. Yet, he'd said he'd retired as a lieutenant colonel.

"Anything on his military service?" I asked.

Chyrel flipped through the papers again, then handed me one. "This is from his SRB," she said. "Retired from the Marine Corps Reserves as a lieutenant colonel in '95."

It was still a mystery why he'd even stayed with the CIA after being stripped of his clearance and passed over for numerous advancements.

"I guess some spooks do retire," I said offhandedly.

"Lots do," Chyrel said. "It's the ones who have been out in the field a long time that never retire. They know too much."

"Anything on the ship and its crew?" I asked.

"Here's everything on the freighter *Canopus*," David said, handing me another short stack of papers. "A full accounting of all present crew members, as well as past crew going back three years, and all their current addresses."

"Sorry," Chyrel said. "We couldn't find any information on where they like to drink in such a short time."

"Good work," I said, then turned to David and Flo. "Will y'all give us a minute?"

The weight of what had happened on the beach suddenly dropped on them like a ton of bricks. I could see it in their faces. They'd no more set foot on shore when we started loading Tank's body in the chopper.

"What is it, Jesse?" Chyrel asked, as my daughter and possible future son-in-law left the room.

I picked up the briefcase and put it on my desk, then fished the slip of paper with the combination from my pocket. Once I had the case open, I lifted out the first sheet of paper and handed it to her.

"These documents were left by the doctor who treated Stockwell," I said. "They should allow us to get you and Tank home."

She looked at the paper in her hands. "It's a death certificate," she said. "But it says Owen had a heart attack right here on the boat."

"I don't know how the doctor could have known anything about Tank," I said. "But he seemed to know a great deal about your relationship. He explained that Tank's having refused treatment might somehow stall survivor's benefits."

"How could he possib—"

"He was sent by Jack Armstrong," I interrupted. "That's probably how General Earnst knew your situation. That's who the doctor was. He served with Stockwell and his team. And knowing government bureaucracy, I wouldn't doubt it if the VA denied the survivor pension, saying if Tank had undergone treatment, he wouldn't have died."

"Not for another year, maybe," she said. "Would they really do that?"

"I don't try to figure out what goes on in the Puzzle Palace,"

I replied.

We went through the rest of the documents, all signed by General Leopold Earnst, along with a sworn statement that he was visiting *Ambrosia* in international waters when the death occurred. It had a blank spot at the bottom for the captain's signature.

I took out a pen and signed it, becoming complicit in fraud against the federal government.

"When will you want to leave?" I asked.

"Right away, I suppose. But I don't want to put the others out."

"There's room for all four of you in Charity's helo. They'll understand. I'll gather everyone in the mess hall." I reached over and pushed the intercom button. "Captain to crew. Will Mr. Ferguson, Mr. Stone, Mr. Santiago, Miss Styles, and Miss McDermitt please report to the mess deck?"

I stood and held out a hand. "Are you ready? With these documents, you can be in Grenada by this time tomorrow, and home in Marathon before nightfall."

She took my hand and rose. "What then?"

"Life goes on," I told her. "It's what he wanted."

When I opened the hatch, Savannah, Flo, and David were standing in the passageway by the exterior door.

"Good," I said to them. "Charity and Bud should be below. It's time to take Tank home."

"We're not going," Flo said.

"What do you mean, you're not going? Classes start in

just—"

"I mean we're not going," Flo said, a firmness in her tone and manner I'd never seen. "David and I are going to take a break from school, Dad. He wants to learn more here, and I want to be close to my new little brother."

I started to open my mouth, but Savannah silenced me with a finger to my lips, as she often did. "Hush, now. It's decided. Besides, they both took classes through the summer and are miles ahead."

I knew what they were up to. David hadn't had his "moment alone" with me yet. A smart man knew when he was beaten, and Mam and Pap hadn't raised a fool.

"Let's go down and see Charity and Bud," I said.

We exited the passageway and went down to the main deck. Bud was standing outside, and I could see through the glass doors that Charity and Marcos were at a table, talking.

"Go on inside," I told my family.

Once the door was closed, Bud turned toward me. "You know, don't you?"

"About you and Marcos?" I asked. "Yeah, I know you had him smuggled out of Brazil a long time ago."

"How did you find out?"

I nodded toward the group inside. "Tank's widow is the best computer analyst to ever work at Langley. And she thinks quite highly of young David's skills."

He looked inside at the others, then down at the deck.

"It's okay, Bud," I told the old spook. "We're no longer

fighting the Cold War or the Banana Wars. But I am curious as to why you did it."

"You don't know?"

"Motives are often the last thing to come out. The only entry in your record book with the Agency is that you were a suspect, but there were no witnesses or evidence."

"My handler told me he knew all about what I did," Bud said. "He said I had to remain in Langley until they figured out what to do."

"Did *you* tell him anything?" I asked, wondering why there was nothing in Bud's record if they knew.

"Never," he replied. "It would have meant Marcos's death. I didn't ever say anything or admit anything, all those years."

"So, why'd you do it?" I asked. "Don't get me wrong; I think what the U.S. government was doing back then was horrible. But why'd you risk your life and career on a fifteen-year-old border-town street kid?"

"You don't see it?" Bud asked.

"See what?"

"The resemblance," he said and looked inside. "Marcos is my son."

CHAPTER TWENTY-FIVE

Bud's revelation startled me. He quickly explained that he had been to Rio in 1962, vacationing with his family the summer before he went off to college. He'd met a girl there. They'd stayed in touch for years, a love affair through airmail. He'd had girlfriends, but he'd never been serious with anyone. Except in his letters to Estella.

He told me about the short letter he'd received from Estella in the spring of 1964, in which she'd told him of a coming military coup, and the news that her father was taking his family out of the city. Bud didn't hear from her again for a long time since they were in hiding. The coup toppled the government and put the military in control until 1985.

"I only got one letter after that," Bud said. "It was when I was in my third year of college. She told me I had a son and she and her family had settled near the border of Venezuela under assumed names. The letter said she was worried it would be read by the wrong people, but she had to tell me about our son. She didn't mention the name she was going by, nor my son's name.

"When the opportunity came," Bud continued. "When I was asked to fly for the CIA in Brazil, I jumped on it. I knew what I had to do. Marcos had found my letters in his mother's things and wrote to me, telling me that his family had all been killed, and he was living on the street, organizing other street kids."

"And you found him," I said, looking in at the others.

"Yes, I found him," Bud said. "I took him to Maracaibo. Set him up with a place to live, money to last a few years, and put him in school."

I followed his gaze to where Marco sat, talking to Charity. "Maybe it's time you got to know your son," I said. "The secret's safe. Besides, I don't think it matters much anymore. Nearly everyone involved is dead."

As I started to open the hatch, I saw Val appear at the inside staircase. She showed Charity something on her Metis, then Charity nodded toward me, and Val came out to the cockpit.

"Can't this wait?" I asked her.

"It will only take a second, Captain."

She showed me a communication from Jack, ordering Charity to escort Chyrel from Grenada to the U.S. Virgin Islands, where they would be met by a Marine honor detachment who would escort Chyrel and Tank's body back to the States in one of his corporate jets.

"Very well," I said.

We went inside and Val continued up the steps to the bridge. Marcos tried to avert his eyes from me. He was fidgeting in his chair, nervous.

"He knows," Bud told him.

Marcos's face looked confused, panicked, as if he might bolt from the room and jump overboard.

"*Todo está bien*," I said to him. "It was long ago, Marcos, and forgotten by most. You don't have to hide anything."

He looked from me to Bud. "Is this true?"

"It is," Bud said. "There is no mention in my record. You and I, and now Captain McDermitt here, are the only ones who know."

Marcos's eyes darted from Bud to me. For a moment, he looked like a frightened child, which was probably how seeing his father again after more than forty years had made him feel.

"Does this mean I can tell my family?" Marcos asked.

I was astonished. "They don't know?"

"No, *Capitan*. I thought it might put them in danger."

I motioned Marcos to join me at the intercom console. "Enter your cabin number and push the *Call* button, then have your family join us here."

He did and a moment later, Mayra's voice said hello.

"*Mayra, este es Marcos,*' he said. "*Por favor, traiga a la familia al restaurante, inmediato.*"

Savannah left her seat and joined me, speaking quietly.

"What's going on?"

"You'll see in a minute," I replied, moving to the seat at the head of the table.

She sat next to me, and Bud sat down across from her. When Mayra appeared at the glass door, Marcos quickly went to open it for her. Any trepidation he'd felt earlier seemed to be gone.

The Santiago family filed in, standing in a half circle around the far end of the table, all looking bewildered.

"What is this, Marcos?" Mayra asked.

He went and stood beside her, then extended a hand to Bud, who rose and approached his son.

"This is my wife, Mayra," Marcos began, his voice halting, but not because of his poor English. "And our daughters, Crystal, Kassandra, and Giselle. And this is Giselle's husband, Ricardo Lopez, and their son, Fernando." He paused and picked the boy up, though he was at an age when boys usually didn't like that. "*Fernando, este es mi padre, tu bisabuelo, Señor* Bud Ferguson."

"*Su padre?*" Mayra asked, her eyes moistening with tears. "This man is your father, Marcos? The one who took you out of Brazil?"

The whole Santiago clan gathered around Bud, all talking over one another in excited Spanish. I couldn't keep up, but I sensed that they all knew about Marcos's past.

I rose and walked toward them. Bud turned to face me, a hand on Fernando's shoulder.

"We're heading back toward Grenada," I told him. "Tomorrow, as soon as we're within range, Charity is going to take Tank's body to a waiting jet to be returned to Florida."

"Tomorrow?" Bud said. "But I've only just met my great-grandson."

"You're a retired Marine officer, Bud. And a retired government employee with a clean record. You should have no trouble at all getting green cards for your family."

Marcos looked at me, shocked. "America?" he said with a sigh. "We can go to America?"

I nodded. "I don't know much about the legalities," I admitted. "You and Bud might have to get a paternity test to prove the relationship. But the child of an American citizen, born abroad, can usually claim dual citizenship."

Marcos's mouth hung open for a moment. "Do you mean that I might be a citizen of America?"

"You'll have to check with the authorities, and maybe get a lawyer," I said. "But if you're granted dual citizenship, I'd bet you can all live in America."

"Come," Marcos said to Bud. "We must go to my room and talk. All of us."

As they filed out, I tried to visualize all eight of them in one tiny cabin. It wasn't a hard image to conjure, as close a family as they were, but Bud would likely be uncomfortable. For a while.

I turned back to Chyrel. "Flo and David are going to stay aboard," I told her. "Charity will fly you and Bud back to

Grenada tomorrow around zero-nine-hundred." I looked over at Charity. "Jack will have a jet standing by. He wants you to escort them to St. Thomas, U.S. soil, where a Marine officer will meet you to escort Tank's body back to the states. Full honors."

By early afternoon, we were making fifty knots, heading back in the direction of Grenada, and far from land. I knew there were a lot of conversations going on below, but I needed to be on the bridge.

I would have loved to be the one to escort Tank, but I had a job to do, and a lot of people depended on me. I only hoped I could be there for the funeral.

So, I sent Matt to get some rest. He would relieve me at 2100 and we'd rotate every three hours through the night, along with the bridge crew.

As the sun slipped toward the horizon off to port, Giselle entered the bridge wearing her uniform. She and Val exchanged a few words, Val smiled, handed Giselle the Metis, then left the bridge.

"I didn't expect you to continue," I said quietly to Giselle.

She smiled warmly. "*Capitan*, you have no idea how overjoyed my family is this day. But as my father would always tell us, a promise made is a promise kept, and a person is measured not only by their work but by their word."

I knew a thing or two about promises kept and a strong work ethic. I lived it as a kid under my grandparents' roof. And I'd promised Jack Armstrong I would take care of his ship and crew.

"*Tu padre es muy inteligente*," I said. "I was raised by my grandparents and Pap often told me the same thing."

"With your permission, *Capitan*. My father would like to speak to you. He is just below, in the dining room."

Though only certain people were permitted on the bridge, I didn't see the harm. I also didn't see the need for his wanting to thank me in person. All I did was force the reality.

"Have him come up," I said.

"*Si, Capitan.*"

She returned a moment later with Marcos. He wore his apron and chef's hat, cocked slightly to one side. He marveled at the instruments and controls, then at the sea ahead, rushing toward us at highway speed.

I nodded toward the rear, and we receded to the shadows at the back of the bridge deck. Giselle went to stand between Axel and Ross as she scrolled through Val's notes on the Metis.

"*Capitan*," Marcos began, whipping his hat off, and holding it in both hands in front of him. His face was a mix of joy and humility. "I would like to ask a favor."

"What is it, Marcos?"

"I have discussed this with Mayra and our family, including my father, because I know you would have me do so before making my decision."

"Your decision?"

"*Si, Capitan*. My family and I would like to remain part of the crew *por favor*."

"I thought you wanted to go to America?"

"One day, perhaps," he said, turning the hat in his hands. "But for now, we all have jobs. My father said there is no guarantee of that in America."

Bud was right. Sort of. It was true that unemployment was at record levels, but businesses were clamoring for employees.

"All of you want to stay on?" I asked.

"*Si*," he replied. "My father will return to America to make... *preparativos*...for us to join him later."

I was happy for them, of course, but I also had a responsibility to my ship and crew. Heitor and Grady were both quite happy with the new arrangement. Matt had told me that Giselle was going to make an excellent yeoman.

"How much later?" I asked.

He shrugged. "A year perhaps. Father said he could come to Bimini sometime, or we could go to his home to visit, whenever we are not needed here."

"A year, huh?"

"*Si, Capitan*," he replied, extending his right hand. "One year before the mast, is what Ricardo called it."

I grinned at his use of the old maritime phrase used to describe the service of an ordinary seaman, who were quartered in the forward part of the ship, forward of the mast.

I shook his hand, sealing the deal in the manner I preferred. "*Es un contrato, Señor Santiago.*"

"*Si, Capitan.* It is a contract."

CHAPTER TWENTY-SIX

When I relieved Matt at 0600 the following morning, we were off the coast of Guyana, but still almost five hundred miles from Grenada. It would be another three hours before we'd be within fuel range of Charity's helo.

Ambrosia's two Lycoming TF40 turboshaft engines were basically the same as those used in aircraft but were designed for marine use. Every hour, they used about as much fuel as a big chopper would use in a whole day.

When we slowed for launch, we'd top the bird's tank. *Ambrosia* kept jet fuel onboard just for that reason. Then we'd need to find fuel ourselves. Using just the slow-turning, high-torque diesel engines, we could cross the Atlantic, but the turbines sucked it up at a much higher rate.

The morning went by quickly. People came and went on the bridge, including Savannah and Alberto. They brought me a breakfast biscuit, which, although quite good, I wasn't much interested in.

"You think you should go with him," Savannah said. "That

it should be you escorting Tank's body home."

I put my arm around her waist and pulled her close to my side. "You think you have me all figured out, huh?"

"Tank would understand," she whispered. "You've done your part—you got him halfway home. It's time to let others do theirs."

"I know," I said, though we both knew she was right. "We all have our jobs to do."

Charity came up the stairs along with the deck hands, Jocko and Al. The two men continued up to the flybridge.

Charity stepped over to the chart plotter and zoomed it out until the Lesser Antilles appeared.

The final way point, just south of the airport, displayed 367 nautical miles in the *Distance to Destination* field.

"I can go anywhere inside three-fifty," Charity said.

"We'll slow and turn to windward when we're 330 miles out," I said. "You'll need some reserve." I nodded for her to accompany me.

Leaving Savannah, Charity followed me down the passageway to my office. I opened the hatch, allowed her to go ahead of me, and then closed it behind us.

"I know what you're going to say," she said. "I'll see that he's taken care of every step. Colonel Stockwell and his men are getting him prepared. Marcos and Ricardo are helping them."

"What are they doing?"

"They're cutting up their boat to make a casket."

I was speechless for a moment.

"What I wanted to talk to you about," I said, "was the assignment you're going on. Jack has people right there on St. Thomas. Why you?"

"Snyder and Martin?" She shook her head. "They wouldn't look good tending a bar in a short skirt and heels."

I arched an eyebrow in question.

"It's just a fact-gathering mission," she said. "I'll be posing as a bartender on a rented mega yacht. The guy leasing it is an insanely wealthy businessman from the west coast, not far from my hometown. He has ties with a man suspected in underage sex trafficking and that man and a bunch of his sicko buddies are meeting 'Ritchie Rich' on his rental boat. I used to tend bar in college and the guy specifically requested an attractive female bartender from a local employment agency. Besides, the odd couple are already on an unrelated assignment."

She was referring to the way DJ Martin and Jerry Snyder had started out with Armstrong. Most operatives worked alone, like Charity. But DJ Martin's quick temper had nearly blown a couple of solo assignments and Jerry Snyder's steadfast, plodding methods had allowed one suspect to disappear before he made his move. Everyone in the know thought they were both on their way out when Stockwell suggested that they be put together with him as their handler. They were an unlikely pair, to say the least. It was like partnering Yosemite Sam with Dudley Do-Right. One wanted to "blast 'im to smithereens" and the other was strictly by the book, following the rules all the way. The jury was out about whether the two would ever work out their differences, but they'd been successful on several assignments.

"Fact-finding only, huh?" I said.

"Yeah," she replied, sounding a bit huffy.

"Not your thing, is it?"

"Some of the players are way up there in the business and political world, Jesse. Men with power in high places. Armstrong wants to get names, dates, times, locations—anything he can hand over to the FBI when the time comes. Personally, I'd just as soon pull the plug on the tub and let it take them all to the darkest depths of hell."

"That's what worries me," I said. "You'll be on your own with a lot of people who have a lot to lose, on a ship with no means of egress."

She stepped a little closer and smiled up at me. "You do care about me, don't you?"

Charity had changed over the years. Not in looks, she was still a beautiful specimen of womanhood. But in the last couple of years, she'd become more evocative. I'd grown accustomed to her new, often suggestive behavior. The woman standing in front of me—the new Charity— was flirty and wildly abandoned. Someone meeting her would never suspect she'd been a dangerous covert assassin, someone who'd endured the worst of human depravity and not only survived it but gave back a whole lot more punishment than she'd endured.

When we'd first met, she'd been coolly professional, even analytical, completely open about what had happened to her in Afghanistan. But after getting to know her better, I'd learned that openness had just been a con, a way of concealing the real person behind the mask.

Inside both personas, she was a dark, moody, and mysterious woman, conflicted by the hand she'd been dealt.

The new Charity was sort of a morph between the con of openness and the woman she *should* have become, had fate not altered her course—a fun-loving California girl. Maybe even someone's wife and mother. I couldn't say which Charity I preferred.

"Yes, I do," I said, pulling myself from my reflections to look deep into her eyes. "I know the real Charity Styleski, and what she's capable of."

The mask melted. Her face dissolved into that of the young college girl she'd once been, trying out for the Olympic swim team over twenty years earlier. For an instant, I saw Flo's eyes looking back at me.

"Be careful, kiddo."

And just like that, the mask returned. "And if I'm not?" she asked, with a coquettish grin.

"You will be," I said. "Keep in touch?"

"Who knows?" she replied, with a wink. "I might show up in Florida one day—right outside your shower window."

I felt my face flush as she turned and left the office, closing the door behind her.

I shook my head as I reached for the latch, muttering, "You're gettin' too old for this shit, McDermitt."

When I reached the bridge, Matt was already there. "I have the conn, Cap'n. They'll be bringin' him out soon. The others went topside."

I nodded. "Slow her down and turn us into the wind at idle speed, Matt."

"Aye, Cap'n."

I headed toward the spiral stairs, but instead of going up, I went down—all the way to the lower deck, where the galley was located.

With the sound of the big turbines slowly winding down, I heard voices, and through the round portholes, saw a flag-draped casket with seven men standing around it.

When I stepped inside, all activity stopped.

"Give the captain some privacy," Travis said, moving past me and holding one of the double doors open for the others.

The men left, leaving me alone with Tank. All around the galley were scraps of wood, boat parts, tools, and sawdust. I stood at the head of the casket and gently folded back the flag to reveal a crude wooden box.

"It ain't pine, Master Guns. But I guess for a simple Montana boy, it's appropriate, huh?"

I pulled the flag back down, straightening it, then flicking away an errant piece of sawdust. I placed my hand on the blue field of stars. "I know how the events of an instant can change and shape our lives, brother. Had it not been for your one moment, you might have done your tour of duty and gone home to be a farmer with a houseful of kids and grandkids, and we'd never have met. Had it not been for my moment, who knows? Maybe I'd be the guy who served five decades. Then I wouldn't have the family I have now."

I stepped back and looked at the box and flag. "I guess in your own way, Tank, even though you never had one of your own, you created a lot of families."

I knew the world was a lesser place without Owen Tankersley in it. He'd always insisted that he was no different than anyone else and that it was the circumstances of those moments that defined us. He'd said that everyone had the potential to rise to meet those defining moments and others would one day stand to take all our places.

I turned, saw Travis through the little window and nodded. He came back in, the others following him, Marcos and Ricardo last.

"Thank you both," I said to them. "It's just what a farm boy from Montana would have wanted."

I turned to Travis. "How are you going to do this?"

"You're gonna be pissed," he said. "The aft ladders are too steep. So, we enlarged the deck hatch at the forward end of the passageway."

"You what?"

"I'd told Jack several times there was a need for it," he said. "Provisions can be directly loaded from the foredeck straight back to the galley. Same with heavy things to or from the engine room. Once we get a watertight hatch installed, it'll be fine."

"You did this while we were underway?"

"Heitor did most of it," Travis said. "We were just the muscle. He has the original plans and there were actually supposed to be two hatches in that part of the foredeck. Nothing structural or functional was ever at risk."

The second deck hatch to the passageway would have been covered by the large sun pad, which was probably an afterthought.

"Easier to ask Jack's forgiveness for cutting up his boat?" I asked rhetorically. "Rather than to ask his permission?"

"Something like that," Travis replied. "We have a high-lift from the engine room in position. Then we just have to carry him up three flights of stairs and the forward ones are plenty wide enough."

I looked at Travis's team. "Can the four of you handle it?"

"If not, *Capitan*," Marcos said, "Ricardo and I can help."

I turned to the two men. "Thank you, Marcos. But these men are military. It's nothing personal."

"All six of us," Travis said. "You and I will be at his feet."

"Then we'd better get a move on," I said. "I can feel the boat starting to turn to windward."

With great care, we carried Tank's casket forward. The opening in the overhead nearly spanned the whole passageway and was six feet in length. We placed the casket on the lift and got it centered under the opening.

"You go ahead up," Ricardo said to me. "Marcos and I will operate the lift, then join the others on the flybridge."

One by one, we climbed the rungs mounted to the bulkhead, until the six of us were standing on the foredeck. Slowly, the casket came up, fitting easily through the opening.

The six of us stood three on a side, looking down as the lift stopped with the bottom of the casket just above the deck.

"We didn't have time for handles," Travis said, looking at each of us.

"That leaves only one option," Oswald added. "A shoulder carry will be easier on the steps, anyway."

Travis nodded. "Take over, Sergeant Major Oswald."

"At the ready," Oswald said, keeping his voice low.

Each of us bent and put our hands under the casket.

"Prepare to lift," he ordered. "Lift!"

As one, the six of us raised the casket to head level.

"Aft...face!"

Turning toward the rear of the boat, we rested the casket on our inboard shoulders.

"At slow time," Oswald ordered, "mark time, march!"

I could pick out the sound of my feet from the others. They wore boots and I wore deck shoes. But I kept time with the sounds of their footfalls.

"Forward...march!" Oswald ordered loudly. "Guide on!"

Oswald counted a slow cadence as he guided us as one toward the side deck.

I heard the crackle of the PA speaker, then a bosun's

whistle first sounded attention, then all hands on deck. When he finished, Peter Jarvis, who headed the deck crew as bosun, announced solemnly, "All hands, attention to the foredeck."

Oswald and Duster, being shorter, were at the head, with Travis and I at the foot. Being taller, it would make the steps easier. We moved along the starboard side deck, Oswald's slow, mournful cadence keeping us steady.

Reaching the first set of steps, Travis and I raised the foot of the casket, so that it remained level as we went up. We did the same for the next two sets of steps, until we arrived on the helipad. Axel, Ross, Matt, and Val stood as side boys, waiting to help load the casket into the helo.

Bosun Jarvis stood off to the side, as we approached the chopper and piped the high-low-high-low call honoring a shipmate leaving for the last time. "Attention on deck! Master Gunnery Sergeant Owen 'Tank' Tankersley, United States Marine Corps. Departing."

The entire crew had gathered along the port steps, on the flybridge, and even on the forward edge of the helipad. Charity, Chyrel, and Bud were already beside the bird. We loaded the casket in, making sure it was secure.

Then we stepped away from the bird, forming a line.

"Ha-and salute!" Stockwell commanded.

We rendered honors, then I escorted Chyrel to the backseat. Bud and Charity climbed in, and as she began to spool up the helo's turbine, we joined the rest of the crew around the flybridge.

A moment later, the turbine ignited, and the rotors spun faster as Al and Jocko quickly released the tie downs and moved away.

Charity stared at me, waiting. I nodded my head and she returned the gesture. The beating of the rotors got heavier, then the bird rose slowly from the deck, and *Ambrosia* slipped out from under it. Charity held it in place a moment, hovering over our churning wake, then slowly turned the bird in place, pointing the nose toward the west. The helo rose gently and steadily into the sky.

CHAPTER TWENTY-SEVEN

"**A**re you okay?" Flo asked, stepping up beside me. I glanced at her, then looked around at the crew. "We have work to do," I said. "Val, where's the closest gas station?"

"Grenada," she replied. "I can make a call and arrange delivery to the dock."

"Mr. Troutman," I said, turning toward Axel. "Resume course toward Grenada at cruising speed."

"Aye, Captain," he said, then hurried off.

"Dad?"

"I'm okay," I said, turning back to my daughter.

Savannah and Alberto were beside her. "Did you arrange that?" Savannah asked, her eyes moist.

"Arrange what?" I asked.

"The flag and all that military precision."

I looked around at my crew. Stockwell and his guys were

filing down the steps, returning the way we'd come, along the side deck. They probably weren't even aware of it, but they were all in step. The others were breaking apart and going down the other side, a few taking the ladder down to the cockpit. Each had a job to do, and all were headed there in an orderly manner.

I shook my head. "There wasn't anything to arrange," I replied. "Though he didn't like being thought of as one, Tank was a hero. It's what a hero deserves. This was just people doing what they're supposed to do. Why don't you take the kids and go on down to our quarters? I'll join you there in a few minutes."

When I reached the bridge, Axel was already accelerating westward, running the diesel engines. Val stepped up beside me and handed me the Metis, which was open to the tankage app. Our supply of low-sulfur diesel was down to just twenty percent, meaning we'd need 12,000 gallons.

"Can we get that much fuel there?" I asked her.

"Already ordered," she replied. "It will take two deliveries, but yes, it's available. They just need to know when to deliver."

I had no idea what the fuel cost, but our little overnight run along the northern coast of South America had probably cost Jack a lot of money. And money was the one thing he'd forbidden me to talk to him about when I took command.

"Let's plan on staying a few nights," I said, catching Ross looking over at Axel with a grin. "The crew needs a rest. Arrange the first delivery for later in the morning, after everyone goes ashore."

"Aye, Captain," Val said. "I'll pass the word to the crew and message Mr. Armstrong. He can arrange for customs officials to check passports at the dock."

"You have the conn," I said. "But I'll be back in a few minutes."

"I have the conn," she replied.

I went back to our quarters, wondering why Flo suddenly wanted to stay. We hadn't really had time to discuss it. Was she having trouble in school? On the swim team? Did David crave the excitement of working full-time and she just wanted to be with him?

When I opened the hatch, Savannah and Flo were in the little galley with their backs to me. They were shoulder to shoulder, working on something, instinctively knowing what the other was doing, needed, or wanted.

"They're making brownies," David said.

He and Alberto were at the table in the living room, a chessboard between them. The dogs sat at opposite ends, seemingly intent on the game.

I sat down beside David. "They do that a lot," I told him.

"Make brownies?"

"It's not about the brownies," I said. "It doesn't matter what they're making or doing. They're working something out between them."

"They've barely said ten words," he said, looking toward the galley.

"Flo spent nearly her entire life alone with Savannah on *Sea Biscuit*," I said, my voice low. "And before that, she was in Savannah's womb, while she was alone on the boat. Savannah told me once that she talked to Flo all the time then. Every word that could ever be said by either of them, has been. Now it's a deeper form of communication. An occasional word to direct them, but it's mostly about body language and expressions, as they do something together, like make brownies."

David looked bewildered. "Is this normal for moms and daughters? I never saw my sister help mom in the kitchen—ever."

"Normal behavior?" I began. "Wouldn't that be the behavior between normal people? Do you think Flo is normal?"

"Far from it," he said, still staring. "She's the smartest, funniest, and prettiest girl I've ever met. And she does it without even trying."

"That's the way I feel about her mom," I said. "And everything that Flo is and will ever be is on account of her."

He looked at me seriously. "I don't think that's exactly right."

I lifted an eyebrow. "Oh?"

"Flo told me she didn't know who her real dad was for most of her life, but she'd always been sure it wasn't the man her mom had divorced, Derrick Coleman. That's why she changed her name to McDermitt. She didn't want to be associated with him. I heard he was a bad person."

"He was," I said, remembering how Savannah's ex had died on Norman Island.

"I know there's a lot of you in her DNA," David continued. "Like when your eyebrow went up just now. She does that, but Mrs. McD doesn't."

"Still," I said, "there's far more of Savannah's influence in Flo. They're having a discussion right now, barely saying a word, and it's probably about either you or me. Maybe both of us."

"Oh, you're here," Savannah said, looking back, then sliding a ceramic baking dish into the oven. She came and sat next to me.

Flo sat on the floor beside Alberto, putting an arm around Woden's neck. "Who's winning?"

"Nobody," Alberto said. "They're just talking about you and mom."

"Oh?" Flo's left eyebrow came up as she looked at David.

I couldn't stop myself and sat back, laughing.

"What are you laughing at?" Flo said, looking back and forth between me and David.

David explained that we'd been talking about how he sometimes saw certain mannerisms in Flo that he could tell came from me, not Savannah.

"We're going to arrive in Grenada later tonight," I said, changing the subject. "We'll be there a few days, refueling and resting up. I'm giving the crew shore leave."

"Ugh, customs lines," Savannah said.

"No, Val's contacting Jack to arrange for the customs man to come to the dock."

"Flo has decided to go back to Florida," Savannah said.

David looked at Flo, shocked. "But you said—"

"I changed my mind," Flo replied, cutting him off. "It's a woman's prerogative. But you're going to stay here."

"Wait...what? That's not what we talked about."

Flo sat up straight, her hands in her lap. "It's decided. I'll fly home from Grenada, while you continue your work here. You promised Mr. Armstrong, remember? The first intra-squad competition is in six weeks, and our first SEC meet is against the Bulldogs four weeks after that. I'll be able to train more and there are...arrangements to make."

"I'll be flying home with her," Savannah said.

"What?" I was ready for them to conspire against David, but this was a surprise.

She ignored me, looking past me at David. "Isn't there something you want to ask Jesse?"

All eyes—even the dogs'—turned toward him. David sat back, his own eyes wide. "Well...I...um...well, I wanted to ask him alone."

"You like Flo and she likes you," Alberto said. "And you want to ask Dad if you can marry her. I've only been in this family a little while, but I already know everything is done together. You gotta get used to that, David."

He stared at Alberto for a moment, then his eyes flicked to

Flo. He even looked at the dogs for guidance, though Woden's expression was passive-aggressive at best. Then he looked at Savannah, and finally me.

David's eyes became calm. He sat up straight.

"Alberto's right, sir," he began. "I want to ask Florence to be my wife. And I would like to have your blessing."

I tried hard to appear the menacing father, but I liked David and he was good to Flo. As long as he continued to do right by her, who was I to stand in their way? She'd told me that she'd made him read the *Rules for Dating a Marine's Daughter*. At first, he'd thought it funny. But he'd been informed, in writing, that if he ever hurt her, there would be the consequences of Rule Six.

I looked at Flo and smiled. "As an engagement gift, I'm giving *you*, and you alone, Rule Nine."

"Rule Nine?" David asked.

Flo smiled. "Never lie to me," she stated flatly.

David nodded and continued. "On issues relating to you, he is the all-knowing, merciless god of my universe?"

"Now *she* is," I said, nodding to Flo. "Yes, you have our blessing."

"I think I'll change that to Rule One," Flo announced, putting a finger to her cheek, as if in thought. "And of course, 'merciless *god*' will have to be changed to merciless goddess."

"Does that mean you're going to ask her?" Alberto asked.

David yanked his backpack up off the floor, digging through its contents. Finally, he stopped and pulled a small box out. He glanced at Savannah and me, then rose and walked around the table, finally kneeling beside Flo.

He opened the box and Flo and Savannah both gasped.

"Flo," he said. "If you grant me just one wish, I promise, I'll never ever lie to you. Will you be my wife?"

She jumped like a coiled spring, grabbing David by the neck, and rising up with him. Then she kissed him all over his face and neck.

Alberto looked over at Finn. "I think that means yes."

"Yes!" Flo cried. "Yes, I will marry you, David."

He slowly pushed her back and took the ring from the box. Flo was practically bouncing as he knelt again and slid it onto her finger.

I pulled Savannah closer. "You're leaving?"

"Sorry we didn't have time to discuss it," she said. "I'll be back in two days. We're going shopping for a dress."

CHAPTER TWENTY-EIGHT

Back during the Golden Age of Sail, what happened with David might have been referred to as being shanghaied.

Ships often lost crew during a voyage, and able-bodied seamen were hard to find. Some died and others simply jumped ship while in some exotic port. Shanghai was one of the busiest ports of the Orient and enticed many sailors to miss their scheduled ships' departures. As a result, quite a few able seamen could be found there.

If a ship were short-handed, the captain might send a bunch of burly men out with the bosun's mate in what was called a "press gang." Sailors tended to congregate in the many bars along the Bund, the city's waterfront on the Huangpu River, so that was where the press gangs would go, entering a bar at random, where the mate would smack a sailor or two in the head with a leather sap, and they'd be carried back to the ship. It was called an impressment. Whether they were already conscripted to another vessel anchored in the harbor or had stayed when their ship left didn't matter much. They were pressed into service and often didn't wake up from their sap nap until the ship was underway.

Of course, I didn't know the whole story. I figured David must have been dragging his feet. Maybe he thought if they were both aboard *Ambrosia* for a few weeks, he'd eventually find the right time. Savannah or Flo had seen through it and had plotted against him, simply hurrying the process along a little.

While Flo and Savannah got busy making reservations and plans, I went back to the bridge with Alberto and the dogs.

David stopped me just before going into the op center. "That wasn't the way it was supposed to happen."

"Of course, it wasn't," I replied. "You got shanghaied, son. Those two will do that to you a lot. You'll get used to it."

"They've done something like that to you?"

"More than a few times," I replied.

"I was totally blindsided. I was just playing chess with Alberto, and really thought they were just making brownies. I did want to ask you properly."

"I like you, David," I said. "You and I both *love* the same girl. Just don't forget that, okay?"

He disappeared into the tech-bowels of the ship, and Alberto headed straight to the sonar station.

Ross handed him a headset. "Not much going on, buddy. I

did hear a blue whale a couple of hours ago, though."

Val handed me the Metis. "Everything's arranged. We'll arrive at 2100 and the customs officer will be waiting. He assured me the inspection would take less than an hour."

"An hour? To process forty-one people?"

"I mentioned that," Val said. "He said no more than an hour."

"Interesting," I said, with a slight shrug of one shoulder. "Would you arrange a late dinner ashore for ten? Somewhere nice and not too loud. And invite Mr. and Mrs. Santiago and Mr. and Mrs. Lopez to join us."

"Us, Captain?"

"My daughter just became engaged, Val." I looked back at David, working at his station. "Savannah and I would like it if you and Matt could join us to celebrate?"

"Thank you," she said with a warm smile. "I'd love to. I'll go ask the others right now."

"I have the conn."

"Aye, sir," she replied. "This will be fun."

After she hurried off, I stepped up between Axel and Ross. "I want you two on the bridge tonight," I said. "Along with two of Travis's men."

"Are you expecting trouble?" Axel asked.

"Expecting? No. What happened yesterday was a fluke, an accidental crossing of paths. Tank's death just compounded it. But these things usually come in threes."

"Old mariner's superstition?" Axel asked.

"Something becomes a superstition due to repeated cause and effect," I said. "If you wrecked your car three times in a month and all three times, a different brown dog sat on the sidewalk watching you go by, what would you think?"

"I think I'd avoid brown dogs," he replied.

"The dog didn't cause the accident, but the effect of its presence makes you want to avoid them. The crash and the dog are just examples. A superstition is created when one thing seems to cause another, but there's no earthly explanation for it. Is water turning to ice in the freezer a superstition? Not now. But a long time ago, some guy in a cave noticed it and he probably became superstitious about cold and went south."

"We'll keep an eye out," Ross said with a chuckle. "For brown dogs or icebergs. You can count on us."

"I'll make it up to you tomorrow night," I promised.

"New contact," Ross said. "First new one in three hours."

Alberto turned his head quickly toward me, smiling broadly.

"Contact bearing one-seven-eight degrees," Ross said, looking at the chart plotter.

He zoomed it way out, to show all of the Caribbean and most of the Atlantic. He typed on his keyboard and thousands of little wedges appeared, each representing a ship.

"Overlaying data from Marine Traffic and coastal AIS relays."

He zoomed out even more, until an icon appeared on the line in the direction he'd said. The coast of all of Africa and part of Europe was on the screen and there was only one green icon on the bearing line.

Ross typed a few more strokes and the dual oscillators appeared on the left half. The sound waves matching perfectly.

"It's the super-tanker *Excel*," Ross said. "Off the coast of Angola, almost five thousand nautical miles astern."

"Is that the farthest you've ever heard something?" Alberto asked.

"By a long shot," Ross said. "Until now, I'd never been able to pick up anything farther than two thousand miles. Which is still a really long way."

The day wore on with only a handful of new contacts. Although we were going to be taking a well-deserved break, we would continue the ship's assignment all the way into port.

I was off duty, a couple of hours after sunset, when we approached St. George's Inner Harbor and the approach to Port Louis Marina.

The steady hum of the engines diminished as I entered the bridge at 2045. We were right on time.

"Ha, Cap'n," Matt said. "Port Louis has four dock hands standing by, two forward and two aft."

Port Louis was owned by Camper and Nicholsons, a large, luxury marina operator with facilities all over the world. They specialized in catering to the largest yachts and wealthiest owners.

"Go ahead and take us in, Matt," I suggested.

"Aye, Cap'n," he replied, then turned to Axel. "Ready the

thrusters for maneuvering."

Axel activated the controls. "Thrusters ready," he said. "Helm controls are switched to the joystick."

Matt moved over next to Axel, where the joystick control, similar to the ones on either side of the stern, was located. Using thruster controls only, he turned *Ambrosia* into the marina, moving at no more than two knots.

Bright lights came on all along either side of the first slip, illuminating the piers and the water between them.

Using the dual sticks, Matt stopped and began turning *Ambrosia* and backing her stern-first toward the slip.

Reaching up, Matt switched on the three upper monitors, showing a livestream from cameras mounted on either side of the bridge roof, as well as from the aft edge of the helipad. The three cameras provided a view aft, along both sides of the ship, like the rearview and sideview mirrors on a car.

Deckhands stood on the work platform, ready to throw dock lines, and men stood on the pier, waiting to catch them. Two other men, both in uniform, stood ready to board.

With a finger pier length of two hundred feet, it was the shortest slip of the twelve they had for larger yachts. The longest one, at the far end, could accommodate two ships twice *Ambrosia's* size.

The other half of our slip was empty, so Matt had no trouble. Even if another boat of equal size had been there, he wouldn't have come anywhere close to it. There was at least eighty feet between the two piers, and *Ambrosia's* beam was only thirty-two.

"Good job," I said, as the dock lines were thrown.

"Thanks, Cap'n. The new thrusters 'll take some gettin' used to. A lot more power over the old ones."

"That they have," I said. "Makes the job considerably easier when there's a current. Let's go down and meet the customs men."

When we reached the bottom of the steps descending from the cockpit, I made for the hydraulic controls and lowered the work platform from its fully raised position five feet above the water down to dock level, and then stepped out to greet the two men.

"I heard dere was a new Cap'n," the older of the two uniformed black men said. "Welcome to Greens. I am Inspector Claude Whyte. Permission to come aboard."

"Please come aboard, Inspector," I said, extending my hand. "I am Captain Jesse McDermitt."

He stepped over and shook my hand with a broad smile. "Yes, I know. How is Captain Hansen enjoying his retirement?"

I smiled, liking the man. "Last I heard, Inspector, he and his wife were sailing the Med."

Whyte laughed. "Yes, yes. He and I talked about dat many times."

I glanced over at Matt, then back to the customs man. "I wasn't aware *Ambrosia* was a regular visitor here. I'm sorry. This is *Ambrosia's* first mate, Matt Brand."

"Pleasure," Matt said. "But *Ambrosia* ain't been here as long as I've been aboard."

The two shook hands, then Whyte turned back toward me. "Before I settled here in Grenada—de locals call it Greens—I was one of de navigators aboard a cruise ship in de Mediterranean. Nils was my captain. We often talked of sailing dere wid our wives when we retire."

Val appeared at the top of the starboard steps with Savannah and Alberto. "Everything is ready, Captain."

As we went up the steps, Whyte said in a low voice, "Unofficially, de country of Grenada is aware of and appreciates all Mr. Armstrong does."

I introduced him to Val, Savannah, and Alberto, and Whyte went through the clearing process quickly and efficiently at a table set up in the cockpit. All the crew's passports were stamped or scanned using a portable unit, and Whyte asked only for a cursory look at the bridge deck and salon area before I escorted him back to the work deck.

Whyte's assistant stepped over to the dock, but Whyte turned to shake my hand again. "I see dere is a problem on de foredeck."

"We had to enlarge the forward hatch," I said, glancing that way. "It wasn't a planned change."

"If you would like, I can have a friend take a look. He is a retired ship builder."

"That's not really necessary," I said, knowing how things worked on island time. "We're scheduled for maintenance on Bimini in about a week."

"A lot can happen," Whyte said. "I wouldn't be surprised if my friend couldn't have it completed before you sail."

"We're only here for three or four days," I said.

"Luis Bishop will be here at dawn," Whyte said. "If he takes more dan two days, I will eat my hat."

"Thank you."

"Anything Greens can do to help Armstrong Research, Cap'n."

"Please, just call me Jesse," I said.

"Den, Jesse, you will call me Claude."

"It's been a pleasure meeting you, Claude."

When he stepped over to the dock, I looked at my watch. It had only taken thirty-five minutes.

Savannah waited at the top of the steps. "Alberto and Fernando are staying with Crystal and Kassandra for the night."

"Really? I assumed the sisters would want to go ashore."

"Because they're single?" she asked. "Or because they're pretty?"

She played this game with me often, and I was getting good at avoiding the trick questions.

I nodded toward the port side, where several of the crew, all young, adventurous, and enthusiastic, were headed down to the dock. "Because they're young."

She smiled. "Remember when we were young? Life was one big adventure, and everyone was in a hurry to see what was around the corner or over the horizon."

"Exactly," I said.

"You forget the dynamics of family," she said. "You invited their parents and married sister. They felt obliged to watch their nephew."

"I should have invited them, too?"

"Not for this," Savannah said. "You did right. Who else is staying aboard?"

"Axel and Ross. I told them I'd make up for it tomorrow. Plus, two from the security team. Aside from them, everyone is permitted ashore."

She gave me a slightly mischievous look. "You should also make it up to the Santiago sisters tomorrow."

"You mean Ross and Axel and the sisters all together?" I asked. "Are you playing matchmaker again?"

"So, what if I am?" she asked, sliding the door open to the salon. "Let's get dressed."

CHAPTER TWENTY-NINE

Just before 2200, we returned to the work deck, dressed for dinner ashore. Savannah wore a lightweight, sleeveless blue dress with matching sandals, and I wore a white guayabera, khaki pants, and Docksiders. The others were dressed similarly.

"Giselle will be here shortly," Ricardo said. "She stopped to check on Fernando."

"The restaurant is called Patrick's," Val said. "Reputed to be the best local fare on the island. It's a short walk, about five hundred meters, just across Lagoon Road at the end of the dock."

When Giselle arrived, we started walking along the dock. There were only two other boats in this part of the marina, a massive barquentine as big as *Ambrosia*, and a sleek super-yacht at least three hundred feet long.

"You're a long way from the boat bum I met twenty years

ago," Savannah said, strolling along beside me. "Remember when we first met? You were climbing out of the bilge, all dirty."

"It was the engine room," I argued. "And it was spotless, so I wasn't dirty." I looked down at her stylish dress and sandals and those long, perfect legs. "And you've come a long way from bare feet and cutoff jeans."

"You do remember," she said with a smile. "I was mad enough to tear your head off for scaring Char the way you did."

I pulled her closer. "I was hoping you'd try."

We rounded the marina office and continued south along the wide boardwalk to the end, then crossed the street and we were there.

A lattice fence surrounded the front yard, which, instead of a lawn, contained tables and chairs arranged on a concrete patio. The restaurant itself looked like a simple West Indian home, bright blue paint, corrugated metal roof, and supported on short brick piers, with a crawlspace under the structure, just big enough for a dog to get out of the weather. There were two concrete steps up to a low porch, with tables set to either side. Most of the seating seemed to be outdoors.

I introduced myself to a very buxom black woman with long, reddish-blond hair. "Pleased to have you with us, Captain," she said with a bright smile. "I am de owner, Karen. Please follow me."

She led us all inside to a large table in the corner. Not several tables pushed together, but a massive slab of mahogany with room around it for at least a dozen people.

"I assumed the owner would be someone named Patrick," I said to Karen, as I pulled a chair out for my wife.

"Patrick was my dear friend. He passed away...oh...eleven years ago." Two waitresses joined her. "Sit, everyone," Karen said. "Welcome to Greens. This is Paula and Janet. If you have any questions on anything, they will be happy to help you. Enjoy your meal."

Paula and Janet handed out menus and took drink orders. I was still a little jumpy and just ordered coffee. I couldn't quite put my finger on what it was that had me on edge, but it was there, way down in the dark part of the reptilian brain we all have.

Most people tend to ignore those warnings or instincts, but I'd learned to trust them. It'd saved my ass many times. Nine times out of ten, I'd sensed some threat, and nothing had happened. But when nothing happened, it didn't always mean the threat wasn't real. Whoever the threatening person or thing might have been could have gotten the same feeling and passed on by.

"I have an announcement to make," I said, once the waitresses left with our drink orders. The others looked my way. "You've all met our daughter, Flo, and her boyfriend, David," I began, gesturing toward them. "Earlier this evening, they became engaged."

There was a flurry of congratulations from the others at the table. Giselle reached over and took Flo's hand, admiring the ring David had put there. The men stood and shook his hand, clapping him on the shoulder.

"When is the wedding?" Val asked. "Or have you set a date yet?"

"No date yet," Flo replied, her face flushed.

"Next spring?" David asked her. "After classes?"

She nodded excitedly.

"So, this sabbatical isn't permanent?" I asked.

"No, sir," David said. "I would like to stay on and learn for a few months, though. I'll still finish my junior year on time this May, after the spring semester."

"And if I take classes again next summer," Flo added, "I'll start next fall as a senior and we'll graduate together."

"Aren't classes supposed to start tomorrow?" I asked.

"Yeah," Flo replied. "But I don't have any in-person classes until next week."

"How's that going to work?" I asked her. "David here and you back in Gainesville for the fall term?"

"I'll have a three-day weekend for Labor Day and *Ambrosia* will be in Bimini that week, so David can come home. I'll have another one in October for Homecoming. And I don't have any classes on Friday before Veterans Day, and I'll have five days off for Thanksgiving. It's not like we'll be apart for a super long time."

"And classes end before Christmas," David said. "Where is *Ambrosia* going after Bimini?"

"That's always the question," Val said. "We didn't know we

were coming here until we were on the way."

"You'll just have to play it by ear," Savannah said.

From where I sat, I could see the three masts of the barquentine that was docked near *Ambrosia*. They were awash in lights from the deck. A little to the left of it, above the roofline of the houses lining the adjacent street, I could just make out the back part of *Ambrosia's* salon and bridge deck, including the balcony of our quarters.

"What are you looking at?" Savannah asked.

"*Ambrosia*," I replied. "At least part of her, anyway."

Conversation flowed, drinks were delivered, and dinner orders taken. When the food arrived, I kept glancing toward the boat.

Val was beside Matt, who was seated to my left. He noticed me looking out toward *Ambrosia* and followed my gaze.

Then he leaned in close. "Awright air 'e, Cap'n?"

"I just can't help feeling something's amiss," I replied, keeping my voice low. "But I have no idea what it might be."

"Ross and Axel are good men," he said. "Plus, Gerald and Oswald stayed back. There ain't goin' to be no trouble, I'lltellywot."

"You're right," I replied. "Maybe it's just being ashore for the first time in several weeks."

"We were just ashore yester—" He stopped, remembering the events of the previous day. "Sorry, Cap'n."

I gave him a grin. "We'll sort it," I said, doing a poor British accent as I glanced over at my daughter. "Life's for the livin, innit?"

"Oye, Cap'n."

"We're off the boat, Matt," I reminded him. "I wish you'd just call me by my name."

He winked and grinned. "Oye, Jesse."

"How is everytin'?" Karen asked, suddenly appearing beside me.

"Sensational," I replied, then nodded toward Marcos at the far end of the table. "Mr. Santiago is the chef aboard *Ambrosia*. I imagine he'd like to steal some of your recipes."

She turned toward one of the waitresses. "Run get me a copy of my cookbook."

"You don't have—"

"Nonsense, Captain," she interrupted with a big smile. "In Greens, we share what we have. Now," she said briskly, rubbing her hands together and looking up and down the table, "did you save room for dessert? Our coconut drops will knock your head right offa your shoulders."

"I was nearly hit in the grape by a falling coconut once," I said. "It nearly broke my collarbone."

Savannah looked at me, shocked. "Jesse!"

"What?"

She leaned in. "That's a bit vulgar—talking about getting hit in the testicles at the dinner table."

I burst out laughing, then quickly apologized. "Sorry. In boot camp, our drill instructors referred to a recruit's *head* as a grape."

Then I leaned toward Savannah. "How does a falling coconut almost hit me there and end up breaking a collarbone?"

"Dese are a bit different," Karen said, laughing. "Sweet pastries made with grated coconut."

"Sounds perfect," I said. "Coconut drops on everyone."

After dessert, I paid the bill with my own credit card, over-tipped, as is my nature when the service is excellent, and then we started back to the boat.

Marcos and Mayra led the way, and Savannah and I brought up the rear.

"What about those two?" Savannah whispered.

"Those two what?"

"Matt and Val."

Ahead, Mayra held onto Marcos's arm, behind them Ricardo had a hand around his wife's shoulder and her arm was around his waist. Just in front of us, Flo and David walked hand in hand. Matt and Val were in the middle, chatting and laughing, but not in contact.

"You need to rein that in," I whispered. "You can't go around creating couples out of shipmates."

"But they're so perfect for each other," she said, hanging on my arm.

"He's ten years older than her and barely speaks the same language."

"You're ten years older than me. At least in the spring."

"It's not the same," I said, kissing the side of her head.

"They're young."

"Are you calling me old, Jesse McDermitt?" she said in a scolding manner.

"The thought never crossed my mind," I said. "It's just different when a couple is in their fifties, versus being in their twenties and thirties."

"It better not cross your mind," she said. "Because Alberto is spending the night with Fernando and the sisters."

"He is?"

"They insisted," she replied. dropping her right hand to my waist. "And the dogs too."

I grinned at her. "You thought of everything, huh?"

"Flo and I aren't leaving until noon, the first fuel truck won't arrive until ten, and Mayra will have the boys in school all morning."

"School?"

"She asked me about it yesterday morning," Savannah said. "Public schools have already started back home. She already has lessons planned through our arrival in Bimini."

"So, we have the cabin all to ourselves until mid-morning?"

She lowered her hand and pinched me on the butt. "I'll show *you* who's old."

CHAPTER THIRTY

F ar to the southeast, twenty miles off the coast of French Guiana, *Canopus* was making eighteen knots. Her AIS was turned off, relying on radar and great visibility to stay clear of other vessels as she moved through the darkness. It wasn't uncommon for ships in this area to not be equipped with the automated identification systems that made the ship's radar more reliable.

It was early morning, a couple of hours after midnight, and just off the port bow, the full moon shone down from a vantage point well above the horizon. It and the stars provided plenty of light on the vast waters ahead of the ship. It was more than enough.

After the incident with the rich yacht owner, Captain Mauricio Gonzales had made an unscheduled stop in Porto do Itaqui, anchoring far from shore in the late evening. Mauricio had gone ashore himself, with four of his best crewmen rowing the lifeboat. It hadn't taken them long to find a few ill-tempered sailors who would do anything for a peso.

On the way back to the ship, they'd rowed into a nearby marina and stolen a matched set of outboards from two newer looking rental boats. Once they'd returned to the ship, Paulo Sousa, the ship's engineer, took the outboards to his engine room to check them over and make any repairs they might need. They'd quickly gotten back underway, running the freighter at full speed through the night, the following day and into the next night.

"The *Americano's* boat is fast," Paulo said, standing on the bridge next to the captain.

"Yes," Mauricio agreed. "However, he is stopped now."

"But for how long, *Capitão*?"

"It does not matter, Paulo. As long as he leaves his AIS turned on and continues to broadcast it to the satellites, I will chase him down."

"But what of our scheduled stops?"

Mauricio glared at the engineer. "Make no mistake, Paulo. I *will* take the rich *Americano's* boat. *And* his women. Then I will use his boat to take his women to be sold in the Middle East."

Under the red glow of the instruments' lights, an evil smile crossed his features. "I will have my way with his women, right in front of him. And as I defile each one in that way, I will know which means the most to him. Then the crew will have her, and afterward, I will hang her body from his boat's bow as a figurehead to ensure good weather."

Mauricio knew his engineer had a sadistic side and saw him grin at the thought. "But a boat like that would cost a lot of money to cross the ocean. Even if we sold the whole crew, it wouldn't be enough. And what about Juan and the cartel? Cutting them out would be dangerous."

"Leave Juan to me," Mauricio said. "The *Americano* had to stop for fuel after such a long run at high speed. When we take the boat, the tanks will hold enough to reach Syria."

"He will leave once his tanks are full."

"I do not think so, Paulo," Mauricio countered, switching on the AIS, and looking at the icon on the chart plotter, still sitting on the south side of Grenada. "They went to *Parque Nacional dos Lençóis Maranhenses* for a reason."

"To explore?" Paulo asked.

"To have fun on the beach, Paulo," Mauricio said. "These are wealthy people. They do not work. They go around in that big boat and play. They will stay in Grenada, I think. There is fun to be had there."

Paulo gazed at the green icon on the screen. "They will have called the authorities."

"We've received no call from anyone," Mauricio countered. "That means the rich *Americano* didn't report the incident. How could he? After all, did he not have his men kill ours? Just because they were having a little fun? We are working people, Paulo. We are not *permitted* to have fun. Not in the way he and his friends do. They lie on the beaches in the sun, drinking expensive wine and liquor. They will stay. They came here to lie on a beach and the women won't care which beach it is. They are lazy. We will find them on one of the more popular beaches close to the boat."

"Grand Anse Beach," Paulo said. "Or maybe Morne Rouge Bay."

"We will arrive about this time in two days and anchor beyond the reef off St. George's Bay. If the Port Authority asks, we will say we are awaiting a shipment coming to the cruise ship dock—something to make repairs to our engine. Grand Anse is two kilometers away. The lazy Americans will be there."

"You wish to take them on the beach? During the day? What about the yacht?"

"I want to *watch* them on the beach," Mauricio said with a lecherous grin. "See if we can pick out who is the owner and which woman he is closest to. Then, after midnight, our men will go ashore and scout their boat. It may prove to be easier to take it while at the dock than out at sea, where he can outrun us."

"I may know someone who can help," Paulo said. "Two men who will do anything for money. They are there—on Grenada—right now."

CHAPTER THIRTY-ONE

I woke late, feeling stiff and sore, just as Savannah had promised. Or was it what she'd *threatened*? Either way, we'd taken advantage of having the cabin all to ourselves.

We'd made love under the stars on the patio. The flybridge and helipad, which were above and forward of the patio, were off limits after sunset. We'd spent most of the night on the patio, wrapped together in a blanket on a double lounge chair, retreating to our bedroom after sunrise to make love again. We'd both fallen asleep, and I'd only been awakened by my alarm, at 0900. I'd set it as a reminder that the fuel truck was coming.

Savannah stirred and sat up, the sheets tangled around her legs and waist. Her hair was disheveled and hung over one side of her face.

"Timezit?"

"Your flight leaves in three hours."

"Huh? I haven't packed. Why'd you let me sleep so late?"

"*Let* you?" I questioned with a grin. "That was you last night, right? The nympho contortionist?"

She threw a pillow at me as I was pulling on my boxers and nearly knocked me over.

"Be very careful, Jesse. You've yet to meet my dominatrix side."

"Oh, really?" I said, feigning fear. "Should I be scared?"

"If you're smart," she said, tossing the sheets off and heading toward the shower. "I'll be ready in ten minutes."

"I'll get the coffee and bacon on."

I went into the galley and made coffee, then started breakfast. When she came out, she took the tongs from me, and I went back into our bedroom to get dressed.

We ate quickly. The fuel truck would be arriving soon, and she had to pack. After breakfast, I headed up to the bridge, while Savannah got her stuff ready for her trip.

"Good morning, Captain," Val said cheerily when I walked in.

"Good morning, Val. What's the status on our fuel delivery?"

"The first truck should be here any minute."

Matt was leaning against the dash on the port side. "*Myttin da*, Cap'n. Thanks again for denner lass night."

"You're welcome. Thanks for joining us." I glanced from one to the other. "Where'd you two disappear to on the walk back?"

"'eard music back behind the marina office," Matt said. "Me feet just sorta shuffled that way."

"He asked if I danced," Val added. "So, since we had nothing to do until now, we went dancing."

"I see," I said, taking the tablet from her and looking over the night's communications log.

There was one from Charity that had an attachment.

"Have you checked the file Charity sent?" I asked Val.

"No, sir. It was addressed to you personally."

The message said they'd arrived on St. Thomas and Tank's body had been transferred to the care of a Marine captain by the name of Ray Megginson.

I tapped the attached file and a video opened. The image shook and moved around for a moment, then a Marine Corps honor detail appeared, marching toward a plane.

"Jesse," I heard Charity's voice say. "It's amazing how fast they pulled this together. Tank and Chyrel will be taken directly to another waiting Armstrong jet for the last leg, straight to Marathon, with Captain Megginson escorting them."

The honor detail came to a halt beside the Gulfstream. Two of the Marines entered the plane and a moment later, the flag-draped casket appeared near the door. The Marines climbed out and took their places by the steps. With help from someone inside, the two men pulled it out until all six Marines were holding the casket.

They sidestepped away from the door, holding the casket

at shoulder level, then executed a facing movement and supported it on their shoulders.

"At slow time," I heard a man's voice command, as Val and Matt joined me, looking down at the screen. "Mark time...yarch!"

The six Marines, all staff NCOs in dress blue uniforms, began marking time. I didn't hear a command, but they all stepped off at once, marching at slow time toward a building. Chyrel joined the procession, along with a Marine officer whom I assumed was the man Charity mentioned, Captain Ray Megginson.

When they entered the building, the image shook and turned, then Charity's face appeared. Her eyes were puffy and glistening. "I gotta go now," she said. "Tank and Chyrel have to clear customs, then they're headed home. Take care, my friend."

The video went blank. I looked at the email and saw that it was time- stamped just a couple of hours earlier, at 0724.

From the shadows on the video, I could tell it was recorded not long before or after noon. My guess was it was early afternoon the day before and she'd only sent the email this morning.

"A right proper job, that," Matt said. "Bleddy dress blues and all."

"Yes," Val agreed. "It was nice of her to record that for you, too. You and she go back a ways?"

I nodded. "We worked together for DHS a long time ago."

"How long?"

"First met her in twenty-oh-six."

"There's the truck," Matt said, looking out the starboard hatch. "I'd best get down there. Will you be takin' the missus to the airport, Cap'n?"

"Yeah," I replied. "Then I think I'll go and visit an old friend."

"You know someone here in Grenada?" Val asked.

"Not exactly," I replied. "But if you're not busy, you're welcome to come along. Both of you if you like."

"Thanks, Cap'n," Matt said. "But no tellin' 'ow long the bunkerin'll take, and you'll need to get to the airport an hour ahead of the flight."

"I'd be happy to accompany you," Val said. "I'll arrange for a van."

Matt left the bridge, and I went aft to see how Savannah was making out. She was just pulling a suitcase through the hatch when I reached our quarters.

"All set," she said with a smile. "I see the fuel truck is here. I just talked to Flo and they're heading for the dock now."

"Matt's going to handle the refueling," I said. "So, Val and I can take you to the airport."

"Val?"

"We're going sightseeing after we drop you off."

"Any sights in particular?"

"LZ Fuel," I replied. "It's a long story."

"All your stories are long," she said with a smile, as I

pushed the outer hatch open.

I carried her suitcase down to the work platform. A moment later, Val, Flo, and David joined us, just as a white Toyota van pulled up. The driver opened the back and loaded the suitcases, then opened the passenger door.

Alberto came running across the work platform and jumped up to the dock. "I thought I was going to miss you," he said, hugging Savannah tightly.

"I'll just be gone a couple of days," she said, holding him to her side. "You be good and do everything Mayra tells you to, okay?"

"I will," he promised, then turned to hug Flo. "Will you be coming back in two days too?"

She laughed and hugged him tightly. "No, I have to go to school, just like you. But we'll see each other again real soon."

"When?"

"Next week," I said. "We'll all meet up at home for a few days while *Ambrosia* is getting some work done."

Alberto ran back over to the boat as we got in the van. I climbed into the front seat, noting the driver's name on the business license displayed on the dash—Turi Joseph.

An hour later, David and Val stood with me at one of the airport terminal's windows, watching the plane take off with Savannah and Flo. They'd fly straight into Miami, then on to Orlando.

When we got back outside to the van, I asked David if he'd like to join us for a ride up to Grand Mal Bay.

"Sure," he replied. "What's up there?"

"Just some old fuel tanks," I replied.

We got in and I told the driver to take us to Grand Mal Playing Field.

He was an older man, with mostly white hair under his cap. He looked over at me, his wizened dark eyes studying my features. When he looked down at the tattoo on my forearm, his mouth broke into a smile, showing two missing teeth.

"Welcome back to Greens," he said.

"I've never been here before," I replied. "But some friends have."

"Why are we going to a playing field?" David asked. "What's there?"

The driver looked at my two young friends in the backseat. "Nuttin' now," he said. "But when I was about your age, dere was a bunch of tanks and liberators dere."

"Liberators?" Val asked. Then realization appeared in her eyes. "The liberation of Grenada by U.S. and coalition forces in 1983."

"Yes, Miss," the man said, as he started to drive. "I was de governor general's driver at de time."

"Why'd you stop?" David asked.

"I am retired now," Turi said. "I drive dis van a couple of days a week. Tings was difficult den. On de day of liberation, we had to go into hiding until de liberators come. De People's Revolutionary Army held Mr. Scoon's mansion. He was de governor general back den. De PRA had some Cuban men in suits with dem. I was dere, along with nine of Mr. Scoon's aides, and his wife, Esmai McNeilly Scoon, a fine lady. I work for her father before dat. A beautiful woman she was."

David sat forward in the backseat. "How long were you held?"

"Not very long," Turi replied. "It was very late at night, close to midnight, if I remember right, on de twenty-fift of October when de liberators come."

"I was in Lebanon," I said. "The Marine barracks bombing was just two days before. We didn't hear about the invasion for over a week."

"What happened?" David asked.

I stared through the windshield. "A friend of mine, Sergeant Ramon Garcia, was a squad leader for Gulf Company, Second Battalion, Eighth Marines. He and I had gone through NCO school together. Gulf Company made a helo insertion south of Pearls Airport on the east side of the island earlier in the morning. Once Fox Company was on the ground there, Gulf saddled up and flew to the *Manitowoc*, a Newport class tank-landing ship. Their mission was to support Army Rangers, who'd taken the new airport, south of St. George's."

Turi nodded. "De airport and mansion was under control of Cuban military, who was posing as construction workers."

"Gulf Company made the initial assault on the beach at Grand Mal in four amphibious assault vehicles. Ramon was in the lead AAV, which included his recon team. Later that night, they moved overland to secure the governor general's house, which was occupied by Navy SEALS, who were trapped by the Cubans."

"Wait," Val said. "They captured an airport at one end of the island in the morning by air, made a shore landing in the evening, then marched on to take the mansion?"

I looked back at her and grinned. "It's in the first sentence of the Marines' Hymn—in the air, on land, and sea."

"But all in one day?"

"Sometimes, all before breakfast," I said. "Anyway, just after dark, Ramon's AAV reached the beach without resistance. They set up a perimeter and waited for Fox to join them, with four M-60 Patton tanks."

"Earlier dat day," Turi said, "U.S. Navy men, de SEALs, come to evacuate Mr. Scoon and his people. But de Cubans came through de gate and we was confined to de mansion. I don't tink dey knew de SEALs was inside wid us."

"Ramon and his recon squad headed out on point," I continued. "They encountered little resistance at first. Near the mansion, just about sunrise, they surprised a Cuban patrol. The firefight only lasted a few minutes, but Ramon was killed in action."

Turi turned off the road into a small parking lot. Ahead was a soccer field. There was a game going on; boys dressed in blue and white jerseys kicked the ball back and forth across a verdant playing field. Beyond the field, I could see large fuel tanks painted a bright white, the reason the landing zone had been named LZ Fuel. To the left, the sparkling turquoise waters of the Caribbean met a white, sandy beach, with palm trees waving along the dune. It was hard to imagine tanks, AAVs, and 250 Marines hunkered down there.

"I am sorry," Turi said, his head bowed for a moment. "It was a time of great strife here on Greens. Many people died and some just disappeared."

"Here?" David asked. "This doesn't look like a battlefield."

"Socialism is a bad ting," Turi said. "It develop slowly and can only be applied by force. My family was simple people. We grow spices in de hills and fished de sea, but we was happy. Maybe more happy dan de rich peoples, down in de city, wit deir busy schedules. Socialists say dat everyone must be de same. So, dey take from de rich. But while Bishop was in power, de poor wasn't happy either. It become worse when Coard take over."

"What happened to the governor general?" David asked as we got out of the van.

"By mid-morning," Turi continued, turning to face me, "de men wit your friend got to de mansion. Dey blow up an armored car protecting de gate and shoot some of de PRA guards. De rest drop dere guns and run away."

Turi helped Val out of the back and then turned to David. "Mr. Scoon and de rest of us was evacuated and he serve as governor general for nine more years. We welcome de liberators with open arms, let dem use our cars and trucks, and we show dem where de Cubans had guns and men hidden."

Turi smiled with admiration. "Sir Scoon was knighted by de Queen, and dough he was a nobleman, he talk to me and ask me questions like I was de same as him. De people was happy again."

We stood and looked out over the tranquil sea for a moment. Today's Grenada was a far cry from what it was like in the early 1980s. It probably didn't look a lot different, but people can be trampled and made unhappy, even in paradise.

"I hear de gunshots before dawn," Turi said to me. "Dey come from Grand Anse, just up de road from de mansion. I can take you dere if you like."

I turned my head and looked down at the slight, old man, imagining him forty years younger, helping to protect his leader. "Yes, Turi, I would."

"And I will be honored."

We climbed back into the van, and he started driving, trying to lighten the mood by describing the places we passed during the twenty-minute drive along the coast.

Finally, just after a traffic circle, he pulled to the shoulder.

"Dat is Grand Anse Beach," Turi said, looking off to the right at a long, beautiful beach. Then he pointed to an opulent stone structure ahead, sitting on a hill, overlooking the beautiful beach. "And dere is de governor general's residence."

"This is where the firefight happened?" I asked, getting out.

Turi climbed out and joined me on the side of the road.

"Yes," he replied. "When we hear de shooting, we could see

it from de windows on de top floor—flashes from de guns." He pointed behind the van. "Dat roundabout was built on de very spot."

I started walking back toward the traffic circle, not sure exactly why. The others followed behind me. There was little traffic and no reason for the circle. A simple stop sign would have sufficed for the Y-shaped intersection.

Continuing across the road, I walked out to the middle of the small, well-manicured lawn. The others stopped at the edge of the grass.

When I reached the center, I found a bronze plaque fixed on a concrete pedestal just a few inches above the ground. The inscription was simple, done in raised gold letters on a field of blue.

VIVE LA LIBERTÉ
25 OCTOBRE 1983

CHAPTER THIRTY-TWO

When we returned to *Ambrosia*, it was mid-afternoon, and Matt reported that the tanks were all full, and that Heitor had run diagnostics on all systems, including the fuel polishing system, and everything was good to go.

"Where're Axel and Ross?" I asked.

"I saw them a few minutes ago in the dining room," Val said, as Travis Stockwell came through the hatch.

"How's the shoulder, Colonel?" I asked.

"A little stiff," he replied. "But give your wife my thanks. I sometimes have to be reminded that I'm not as invincible as I once was."

"Will do."

"A man named Luis Bishop came by a few hours ago," Travis said. "He took some measurements of the opening in the foredeck and now he and two of his workers are installing a new hatch."

I moved toward the front of the bridge and looked out over the long foredeck. A high-lift was parked on the end of the dock, its arm extending out over the bow, where a large, smoked glass hatch was being lowered.

"He had one in stock," Travis said. "Said it could support three hundred pounds. It's a few inches longer than the hole we made, but they adjusted it."

"I didn't think he'd even *be* here until about now," I said.

"Walt and Duster will be up here soon," Travis said. "The three of us will stand watch through the night."

"You haven't been ashore?"

His left eyebrow moved almost imperceptibly. "Been here a few times before. Fun place for younger folks."

Without another word, he turned and strode into the op center, where he sat at a terminal and put on a headset.

"Does he even *have* an off switch?" Val asked.

"Not that I'm aware of," I replied. "Where is everyone?"

"Most of the crew went to Grand Anse Beach," Matt said. "We're going to join 'em in a few minutes, do all the proper emmet stuff."

I tried to picture Matt as a beach tourist. He was broad-shouldered and very fit—not a bad-looking man—but he had the typical pale complexion of his countrymen.

"Take some sunscreen," I advised him. "I don't want you ending up in sick bay."

Then I turned to Val. "Would you mind contacting the two

younger Santiago sisters and asking them if they'd meet me in the mess hall?"

"Right away," Val replied, thankfully without asking why.

I went down the spiral staircase to the mess deck and found Ross and Axel there, eating burgers and fries.

"Late lunch?" I asked, taking a seat at their table.

"Late night," Axel said.

"How'd you guys like to hit the town?" I asked, as Kassandra and Crystal Santiago entered. "My treat."

Both men's eyes cut to the sisters as they moved toward us.

"Sure, Captain," Ross said. "Sounds like fun."

"You wished to see us, *Capitan*?" Crystal asked.

The three of us stood and I waved a hand to two empty chairs, inviting them to sit.

Crystal was the younger and smaller of the three sisters, the one who Marcos had said was an expert in stick fighting. She had hair as dark as night but light brown eyes. That and her sister's auburn hair spoke to Marcos's mixed ancestry. Crystal was slim to the point of being skinny, but she moved with the sultry grace of a feline.

"I wanted to thank you for taking care of Alberto and the dogs last night. I know that couldn't have been easy."

Kassandra smiled. "It was nothing," she said. "Alberto is a very bright young man." She paused. "But your dogs snore."

I grinned at her. "That was what I meant. But wherever Alberto goes, they go."

"It was no trouble," Crystal said. "We played games and the

dogs mostly slept."

"I'd like to make it up to you," I said. "I'm taking Axel and Ross here out for dinner and drinks later. Would you care to join us?"

Kassandra, who was a couple of inches taller than her sister, glanced at the two men, then smiled. "We would be honored, *Capitan*. Will there be dancing?"

I looked at the two men, who both nodded quickly.

"Yeah," I replied. "Dinner, drinks, and dancing. Matt and Val told me about a place just down the dock. About nineteen—er—seven o'clock?"

The sisters rose, followed quickly by the three of us.

Crystal smiled. "We will be ready."

The three of us sat back down slowly as the two women left.

"Did you just—" Axel started to say.

I raised a hand to stop him. "No," I said. "First night in a new port and the four of you had duty. I'm just making it up to you. Nothing more."

Both men grinned as I stood.

"Just doing our jobs," Ross said.

I wondered what I'd gotten myself into as I went out the aft hatch of the mess hall.

Taking two young crewmen out for a pub crawl was one thing. I'm not big on social drinking, though no stranger to the custom. But Savannah had been right; I owed the sisters something also. It was the fact that all four were young and single that was the problem. Not for them. I was neither and would feel like a fifth wheel all evening. Of that, I was certain.

I went up the side steps to the passageway's exterior hatch. I didn't want to field the questions Val and Matt would have.

Sitting on the sofa in my quarters, I stretched my legs and kicked my shoes off, thinking about it. Four young people, drinking and dancing, while the salty old captain sat alone at a table.

The chessboard was still set up where David and Alberto had been playing just the night before, as if waiting for them to return. I studied the positions of the various pieces. David had been winning.

They'd played a few games during the day, and David won them all, except for one stalemate. He'd mentioned to me that Alberto seemed more intelligent than a lot of his college classmates.

It seemed that Alberto had met his match with David.

As I started to lie back on the sofa, something caught my eye. I leaned forward and studied the pieces some more. A slow grin came as I realized that David was in trouble.

Depending on whose move it was, Alberto would win in either two or four moves. If it were David's turn and he moved the right piece, it would be the latter. If he made the wrong move, or if it were Alberto's turn, the game would be over in two.

Just then, Alberto came in, Finn and Woden preceding him.

"Hey, little man. How's it going?"

Woden stopped and did a couple of circles before settling onto the deck in front of the hatch. Finn came over and sat on my foot, leaning his head against me as his thick tail thumped the carpet.

"I finished my lessons," he said. "Ms. Santiago is very smart."

"She is, huh? What were you studying?"

"Nothing really," he said with a shrug. He sat on the floor and looked at the chess set. "She just wanted to find out where I was on a bunch of things."

"And what was her conclusion?"

"She said I could move into middle grade math and science."

"Middle grade?" I asked. "What's that? Like twelve-year-olds?"

"Eleven," he replied. "A year ahead of me. Want to finish David's game?"

I grinned at him. "No, I think David needs to finish this one out, himself. What about reading and writing?"

He shrugged again. "I don't know."

"Oh? She was able to assess your math and science level and she told you where she thought you were. But she couldn't do that for reading and writing?"

The shrug again.

"Look, son, being good at something is great," I told him. "But never let your greater ability make you think you're somehow better than others. Being behind on something else isn't the end of the world. You can catch up easy enough. Just like any skill, it just takes a lot of practice."

"What are you not good at?"

"Me? We're not talking about me."

"I'm just curious," he said.

"Women," I replied. "I'm definitely no good at understanding women."

"I kinda noticed that."

"What do you mean?" I asked.

"Sometimes when she says something, you look confused," he replied.

I grinned. "Guilty as charged. Women are confusing."

"But Mom seems to know what you think all the time."

I thought about that a moment. He was right. Savannah was very intuitive to what I wanted or needed. I'd have to make a concerted effort to not just listen but understand.

"I guess I oughta try harder, huh?"

Alberto nodded. "What's for supper?"

"I'm taking Ross and Axel out to eat," I said. "You'll stay with Fernando again, I'm afraid. In the Santiago's cabin."

"Aw, man."

"What's the matter?" I asked.

"Can they just come here to babysit? The rooms down there are small. Woden farted in my face last night."

I threw myself back on the sofa, laughing.

"It wasn't funny, Dad. You shoulda been there."

"In that case, I probably owe a dinner to the sisters, too."

"Yeah, you do," he replied. "I think Kassandra likes Ross. She was asking me a lot of questions about him."

"Is that right?" I said, as a knock came at the door. "Excuse me."

When I opened it, Mayra was standing in the passageway.

"Please, come in," I offered.

"*Graçias, Capitan*," she said, and entered the room. "I suppose Alberto told you of my testing?"

"He did," I replied. "Middle grade math and science."

She sat on the sofa and smiled at Alberto. "It is not often that a teacher has such a bright pupil. I have been blessed with two. Both Fernando and Alberto are highly intelligent. They can become anything they want to be."

"But I need to learn to write better," Alberto said.

"And by doing more, you will." She turned and looked up at me. "My daughters told me you have asked them out for dinner."

"In gratitude for last night," I said. "Two other crewmen who had to stay aboard will be joining us. I hope it's okay with you and Marcos."

"You will be chaperoning the whole evening?"

Chaperone? I thought. It wasn't like I was setting them up on a date or anything.

"Kassandra and Crystal are very young," Mayra continued. "And they sometimes attract the wrong type of men. It makes me nervous when they are not with me."

"Rest assured," I said, "I'll be with them at all times. Nothing will happen to your daughters."

She stood. "Very well, then. Will you bring Alberto to our cabin for the night?"

I glanced down at him, sitting on the floor. "Would it be possible for you and Marcos to come here? Two boys and two dogs will make your cabin very crowded."

"*Si, Capitan*," she replied with a smile.

"About seven o'clock, then?"

"We will be here," she replied.

"And Mayra," I said with a grin. "Please tell Marcos to make himself at home. The Diplomatico is on the top shelf."

CHAPTER THIRTY-THREE

Once more dressed for a night on the town, I headed down to the cockpit. Axel and Ross were waiting on the work deck, both wearing comfortable, tropical-casual clothing, the same as me. Nothing flashy but dressed up by our standards.

Social engagements and all the niceties that go with them were a little foreign to me. For me, a really good evening was a blackened fish sandwich, a beautiful sunset, two fingers of good rum, and maybe a fish tugging on the line. Even in my younger days, I wasn't one of those guys who cruised around looking for girls or who hung around shooting pool all night. Most weekends as a teenager, I'd spent sleeping under the stars.

"Did your wife and daughter get home safely?" Ross asked, as I joined them on the work deck.

"Savannah called about an hour ago," I replied. "They're at

a hotel in Orlando and hitting the dress shops in the morning."

"You have two other daughters, right?" Axel asked.

I nodded. "Eve's thirty-seven and Kim just turned thirty-two."

"Grandkids?" Ross asked.

"One grandson," I replied. "He's almost fourteen."

"And now you've adopted a son, half your grandson's age?" Axel asked. "That takes some nerve, Captain."

"You guys call me Jesse when we're off duty, okay? Alberto's nine—he's just small for his age. The thing is, I never had much of a hand in raising my own children and I regret that sometimes."

"Uh-oh," Ross said, looking past me and Axel toward the top of the steps.

I looked over my shoulder and saw the Santiago sisters starting down the steps, both smiling radiantly. Crystal wore a white dress with an angled hemline that showed a lot of leg. Her long, jet-black hair hung down in front of her shoulders, contrasting sharply against the white fabric. Kassandra had her thick, auburn hair done up on one side. She wore a tight-fitting red dress with a deep neckline that accentuated her natural curves. They were both barefoot and carried matching high-heeled shoes in their hands.

"*Buenas noches*," Kassandra said, stepping off the last step.

"Good evening," I replied. "The place we're going to is just a short walk down the dock."

"I must apologize," Axel said. "It looks like Ross and I are a little underdressed."

"*Disparates*," Crystal said. "You look very handsome."

Axel's face flushed.

"We came aboard with very little," Kassandra said. "Val bought us these dresses and shoes last night as a gift." She smiled. "So, it was this or the same clothes we were wearing earlier."

"Shall we go?" I said, waving a hand toward the side of the boat.

Once more, I'd failed to grasp women's needs. While Marcos and Ricardo would be fine in whatever they had, even Mayra to an extent, the younger Santiago women needed a wardrobe. I made a mental note to have Val take them shopping on Jack's dime, knowing he would have grasped the need.

I helped the girls up to the dock, noting how nervous my crewmen were in their presence.

Yeah, this is going to be a lot of fun, McDermitt.

Axel and Ross were twenty-nine and thirty-one, each seven years older than Crystal and Kassandra, yet they acted more like schoolboys on prom night than former military men and experienced world travelers.

Once on the dock, the sisters slipped their heels on, each leaning on one of the men to do so. They'd obviously discussed the pairing arrangement before meeting us.

I could hear the music as we walked toward Victory Bar

and Restaurant; a driving bass sound accompanied by steel drums emanated from behind the building. Once inside, only the heavy bass filtered through the thick wood walls.

"Captain McDermitt?" a young man dressed all in black asked.

"Yes," I replied.

"We have your table all set up, sir," the young man said. "Please follow me."

He led us to a large table by a window, which provided a magnificent view of the harbor, steeped in the warm glow of the sun's aftermath. The hour of sunset is a magical time when colors take on a different hue and everything looks inviting.

A waiter appeared and took our drink requests. I noticed that the sisters ordered non-alcoholic drinks, while Axel and Ross opted for West Indies pale ales. I stuck with water.

"So, how do you like *Ambrosia*, so far?" I asked the women.

"It is a beautiful ship," Kassandra replied. "And working with father and *Señor* Grady is fun. He makes father laugh."

"What about you, Crystal? I know working in the laundry can't be overly exciting."

Her smile seemed to light up the room. "It is good work," she replied. "And doesn't require a lot of time. When I am not working, I love being on deck, feeling the wind. Besides, I love the smell of clean linens."

The waiter returned and took our dinner orders. Unlike Patrick's, Victory catered to a wealthy, international clientele, offering a wide array of Mediterranean fare, as well as American beef, which I took advantage of.

"I feel bad for Mother and Father," Crystal said, a devious smile on her face. She leaned toward Axel. "The captain's dog has terrible gas."

"Ew!" Ross said, laughing. "I used to have a black Lab with that problem. He could peel the paint off the walls."

With the ice broken, and the four of them having common interests in the ship, they talked mostly among themselves as we ate. Axel and Ross relaxed a little as the girls proved to be more than just pretty faces. They were bright and engaging and apparently, well-traveled.

Before we finished, I already had the fifth wheel feeling, but I'd promised Mayra I'd make sure nothing happened to her daughters.

"Will there be anything else?" the waiter asked.

I handed him my AmEx Black card and told him we'd be moving out to the patio to listen to the music.

He offered my card back. "I'll take your bill out to the bartender and you can enjoy yourselves out there."

A good idea on his part, I thought. In most cases, more booze meant more tip.

When I led the way out to the patio, the dance music hit me, full force. Several couples were gyrating in front of the stage, where a band was playing. It seemed to be a cross between Bahamian junkaroo band, playing Jamaican jump up with an American techno-music feel.

As we passed the bar, I noticed the eyes of more than one man following the girls. One man got his arm punched by his wife or girlfriend for looking too long.

I led the way to a table against the wall, which was two tables away from the stage. As usual, I took the chair nearest the wall.

A waitress appeared and took our drink orders. She was back before we'd fully settled into place.

"Thank you for the dinner," Crystal said. "The lobster was delicious."

"You're very welcome," I replied, noticing that of the two of them, Crystal, although she was younger, seemed to be the one in charge.

I wondered if she was the same with their oldest sibling, Giselle.

"I want to dance," Crystal said. "The band is very good."

"Then let's cut a rug," Axel said.

"Cut the rug?"

"That's what Cajuns call dancing," Ross explained.

"I'm from Mississippi," Axel said, standing, and offering a hand to Crystal. "Not Louisiana."

"And where are you from, Ross?" Kassandra asked.

"Where the corn grows tall and the cattle are fat," he replied. "The great state of Oklahoma."

"Do they cut rugs in Oklahoma?"

Ross smiled and took her hand, leading her onto the dance floor. I noticed that both sisters had left their shoes under the table.

Sitting back in my chair, I let my eyes drift around the patio and bar area, stopping for a moment at each face I could see. It wasn't packed, but it was a good-sized crowd. Men outnumbered women almost two to one, which was typical for a bar near a marina, even if it was a high-end marina.

Two of the men I'd noticed earlier staring at the sisters were in a deep conversation, both taking occasional glances toward the girls on the dance floor. One looked like a surfer type, blond hair to his shoulders, clean shaven, with a square jaw. His friend was a black man, muscular, with a shaved head. Both looked to be in their prime, no more than twenty-five, and were dressed nicely. But they had a predatory look about them.

After two songs, the others returned to the table, out of breath and laughing. I couldn't help but notice a sheen of perspiration on Kassandra's ample cleavage. Crystal, on the other hand, barely showed any sign of exertion. My guess was she was the more athletic of the two.

We ordered more drinks and talked for a moment, then the band started a song with a sultry island beat. Crystal grabbed Axel's hand and the two were off again.

"My sister can dance all night," Kassandra said to Ross, as if apologizing. "I have to take a break to catch my breath."

"Same here," Ross said with a smile.

The black man from the bar moved toward the dance floor and I saw the surfer headed our way. I shifted my chair around slightly, making it easier to get to my feet if need be.

"Would you like to dance?" the surfer asked Kassandra, totally ignoring me and Ross.

She looked up at him and smiled. "Thank you, no."

"Aw, come on," he said. "Just one dance. That's not going to hurt anyone."

Ross rose slowly to his feet. "The lady said no. So, why don't you just go on back to the bar? We don't want any trouble."

The two men were matched in height, but the surfer looked like he probably had a few pounds on Ross, mostly in his bulging upper arms. In grappling, he would have a slight advantage. But I'd read each crewman's bio and knew that Ross could hold his own if he had to.

Still, I shifted my chair again.

"I wasn't asking you, man," Surfer said. "I was talking to Red here."

"Don't be rude, son," I said, just loud enough for him to hear me, but not so loud as to make a scene.

He looked over at me and grinned. "And I'm definitely not talking to you, Pops."

I rose slowly. At six-three, I'm usually the tallest person in a room. I often used that to my advantage. Surfer had to look up a couple of inches to meet my gaze, putting him in a subordinate position from the start. Especially since there were two of us.

"I'm not your pop," I said, low and menacing, as I took a

step toward him. "If I were, you'd have been raised to be more respectful to women and your elders."

"Whoa," he said, raising both hands in supplication. "I don't want a fight. Not when it's two against one."

He started to turn, but I knew from experience that he wasn't quite finished yet. The empty shot glasses on the bar where he'd been sitting with his buddy pointed to the fact that he'd loaded up on liquid courage before coming over.

When he suddenly stopped and started to spin back toward me, I was not only ready for him, but anticipating the move. His wild attack was poorly timed; I caught his fist in my left hand, stopping the punch in full swing, with my fingers wrapped solidly around his knuckles. My hands are bigger than most, and I'd spent a lifetime using them, making them stronger, harder. I could see that my block surprised him, and when I applied pressure to a nerve in the back of his hand, I knew I had his full attention.

"Strike two," I growled. "You need to take a long, hard look at your next move, boy. You're not the first and I didn't get old by rolling over."

There was a scream. I looked over and saw Surfer's buddy grabbing at Crystal. I released my grip and held my hands out wide, moving closer. Before Surfer could take another swing, I headbutted him in the face, sending him sprawling on his butt. The shape of the forehead makes it able to withstand a powerful blow. Not so much for the nose and facial bones.

"Watch him!" I ordered Ross, then headed for the dance

floor.

The crowd had separated, and the band had stopped playing. Crystal stood a few feet behind Axel, who was in a fighting stance as the bald black man stalked around them.

A deep rage rose within me when I saw that Crystal's pretty, white dress was torn at the high part of the hem, exposing her hip and the side of her panties.

Baldy had his back to me, so I simply tapped him on the shoulder.

"I'm cutting in," I announced loudly.

He whirled to face me, ready for a fight.

I wasn't in the mood.

The fight started and ended with a single right jab, which landed squarely on the man's nose. He was unconscious before he hit the deck.

"You and Ross take the girls outside," I said to Axel.

As they hurried toward the table, stepping around the inert surfer guy, I went to the bar. The patrons made an opening large enough for a truck as I fished my card from my pocket and handed it to the bartender.

"Please close out my tab," I said softly, as the pounding rage in my temples started to subside a little. I glanced at the two men sprawled on the deck. "Add theirs to mine also. Plus, three hundred East Caribbean dollars for any damages."

The bartender looked around, noting the two men, unconscious and bleeding on the deck. "I don't see any damages, Captain."

"Then call it a tip," I said with a wink. "For the trouble."

CHAPTER THIRTY-FOUR

"A headbutt?" Ross asked, as we hurried along the dock. "Why in the world would you want to get that close?"

I needlessly looked back over my shoulder before answering him. "It just seemed like the thing to do at the time."

"Are we in any trouble?" Crystal asked, trying to hold the hem of her dress together.

"No," I replied. "Those two won't be waking up any time soon. And I paid the bartender for any damages."

"I could have taken him," Axel said.

Looking over at him, I nodded. "No doubt in my mind, Axel. I've read both of your bios. But as captain, I'm responsible."

He grinned. "I don't think I could have taken him with one punch, though. You're definitely not another Captain Hansen."

"Are you okay, Crystal?" I turned to her with concern. "He must have frightened you."

She brushed away my worry with a wave of her hand. "I wasn't frightened. I can handle myself. The only thing suffering here is my dress."

I wasn't looking forward to explaining to Mayra about what had happened. In hindsight, I probably should have chosen a different place.

Although the marina and restaurant were trendy and catered to the mega-yacht crowd, it was still a marina, a stopping place for boats of all types—boats predominantly crewed by young men. And when a boat arrived in port after a lengthy time at sea, it meant a bunch of horny crewmen going ashore and heading to the nearest watering hole, tipping the balance in the male to female ratio. An unlevel balance created competition. It's as true today as it was in the 1600s.

"Your orders?" Axel asked, as we reached *Ambrosia*.

The women made their way across the work deck and were talking by the fishing tackle station.

I looked at the two men. "None," I said, slowly releasing a breath. "You're off duty still and I'm tired and going to bed." I paused and glanced over at the sisters. "But may I suggest a nightcap on the foredeck?"

Ross looked over to where Kassandra was kneeling, trying to do something with her sister's dress. Then he looked back at me. "Where'd you learn to fight?" he asked.

"I was a Marine infantryman for twenty years," I replied.

"And I picked up a few things in Israel."

"Israel?" Axel asked. "Krav Maga?"

I nodded as the women started back toward us.

"All fixed," Kassandra said, taking her sister's hand and twirling her around.

I looked down and stifled a laugh. "I hope you cut the barbs off."

Axel bent and looked closer. Kassandra had used several fishhooks and a lure to pull the torn hem back into place. The lure was a simple spoon with the treble hook removed. It covered the thin line of her panties completely and was held in place by small fishhooks bent to form loops and hooked through the separated parts of the hem.

Axel looked at Crystal and smiled. "Very fashionable."

"I'm sure it will be all the rage this fall," Crystal said, with a modest curtsy.

"Would you like to have a drink on the foredeck?" Ross asked Kassandra. "It's a beautiful night."

She nodded and they started up the steps.

"Go ahead with them," Crystal said to Axel. "I will join you in a minute. I want to speak to the captain."

When we were alone, she turned and looked up at me. "I want to thank you again for a wonderful evening."

"Are you always so proper, Crystal?"

"What do you mean?"

"I have three daughters," I said. "The middle one, Kim, is twelve years older than Flo, who you met. But sometimes, she acts just as goofy and excited as a teenager. Aboard *Ambrosia*, I'm the captain. But off the ship, like tonight, I'm just an old guy you work with."

She smiled, then glanced forward to where Axel was waiting by the starboard side deck. When she turned back to face me, she stepped up on her toes and kissed my cheek.

"Thanks, Jesse," she whispered, then gave me a heart-warming smile. "Tonight was a lot of fun. But I want to ask you a favor."

"What's that?"

"Please don't say anything to my mother and father about what happened with those two men at the bar."

"I can't lie to her," I said. "If she asks how the dress got torn."

"I'll take care of that," she said. "Thanks again."

She turned and hurried to catch up with Axel.

I shook my head as I headed up the port side. "Oh, yeah," I muttered to myself. "Take two young couples ashore in a harbor town. Have a drink or two in a wharf bar. What could possibly go wrong?"

When I reached the bridge, I found Travis there, drinking coffee with Walt Meachum and Duster. The closed circuit was on, with angles displayed on the three monitors, showing the dock area all around *Ambrosia*.

Stockwell glanced over at me as I entered. "You have a drop of blood on your collar, Captain. Yours?"

"Probably not," I replied. "There was a little skirmish at the bar."

He took a mug from the cupboard and filled it, then handed it to me.

"Thanks."

"Let me guess," he said. "Those two young women attracted the wrong kind of attention. Pretty much like I warned you they would."

"Yeah," I said, then nodded toward Walt and Duster, sitting in the helm seats. "But you actually warned me they'd be a distraction to these two knuckle-draggers."

Duster grinned. "Hey, I resemble that remark."

"You're a wise man, Colonel," I said. "I failed to extend that caution."

"Anyone hurt badly?"

"Just a couple of college boys," I said. "Once they come to, it'll be their pride that hurts the most."

He huffed. "I remember an old man whupping my ass in Germany during my first enlistment. Caught me with his daughter."

"Not an easy pill for a young man to swallow," I said with a nod.

"Get a tub of water and some soap, Duster," Travis ordered. "And some antibacterial ointment from the first aid kit." He turned to me and pointed to the chair. "Sit down. One of those college boys busted your knuckles all up with his pretty face."

"I don't need a nurse," I said, looking at the back of my right hand.

"Who's nursing?" Duster said, putting a small tub on the deck in front of me. "There's bacteria in a person's mouth that can cause severe necrotizing soft tissue infection. If that shit's not cleaned out good, it could kill a man in hours."

I bent and washed my hands. "I punched him in the nose."

"Yeah, well, that's still a tooth mark on your right ring finger."

I looked at the wound. It was small—less than half an inch—nearly flat on one side and concave on the other.

"Central incisor," Duster said, handing me a tube.

I squeezed a small drop into the wound and moved it around with my finger, working it in.

"You sound like a doctor," I said, putting the lid back on and handing it to him.

"Finished med school and was about to go into residency when the Colonel came to visit me."

I looked up at the young man. "You gave up being a doctor to go back to being a door kicker?"

He shrugged. "I wouldn't say 'gave up.' It was more like postponed."

"What made you want to do that?"

Duster was quick to answer. "To make a real difference without bullshit politics." Then he glanced over at Meachum. "Plus, the colonel said Walt was in and I figured he'd need to be looked after."

"You keep thinking that, kid," Walt said, lifting his mug in a toast.

"Think there'll be any blowback?" Travis asked.

"Not likely," I said. "They were a bit hammered. Once they sleep it off, they'll move on. Uglier for a while, but I don't think they'll come sniffing around *Ambrosia*. I only wanted to alert you before I went to bed in case they *didn't* learn from their mistake."

Stockwell glanced at his two operatives and nodded. "I'll post an extra man in the cockpit, just in case."

Duster refilled his mug and left without another word.

"Were the girls shaken up?" Travis asked in a low voice, as we moved toward the passageway hatch.

"I don't think so," I replied. "The younger one's as cool as a cucumber. Her father said she's an expert in *juego del garrote*."

"Venezuelan stick fighting? That little thing?"

"It's not the size of the warrior in the fight," I said.

He nodded and pushed the hatch open. "You're right, Jesse. It's the size of the fight in the warrior. Have a good night."

I handed him my empty mug. "Thanks, Colonel. You do the same."

When I got to my quarters, Mayra and Marcos were at the dinette, playing a card game. The dogs, lying in front of Alberto's room, lifted their heads. Soft Latin music played from the radio.

"Good evening, *Capitan*," Mayra said, laying her cards down. "We didn't expect you back so early."

"The boys asleep?"

"Probably," she replied. "They went to Alberto's room more

than an hour ago. Even the dogs slept."

"What's that you're playing?" I asked, looking at the cards on the table. They weren't American playing cards, but somewhat similar. There were two cards faceup; one had five cups and the other six swords.

"It is called truco," Marcos replied. "And she always beats me."

I glanced over at the sofa and table, noting the chess set was gone.

"Did David come by to finish his chess game with Alberto?"

Marcos grinned. "*Si, Capitan.* It did not last long. When they sat down, it was over in two moves. David seemed"—he glanced at his wife— "*sorprendida?*"

I grinned. "A surprise to him, but Alberto had him all set up."

"They played another game, which ended in a draw," Marcos said.

"Where are my daughters?" Mayra asked.

"I believe they went forward to look at the stars and say goodnight to Ross and Axel."

"It was nice of you to treat them," Marcos said. "They do not have much chance for fun."

"The dinner was great, and their company excellent."

"I am glad they enjoyed it," Mayra said. Then she looked at her husband. "Perhaps we should go look at the stars, as well?"

"You have nothing to worry about," I assured her. "Ross and Axel are fine men, and the girls will likely be back in their cabin shortly. They are excellent conversationalists. They seem well-traveled."

"We took them abroad every summer," Mayra said, smiling with pride. "When times were better. To Europe and Asia mostly. Giselle is fluent in several languages and Crystal is nearly so. Kassandra..." She shrugged her shoulders.

"Our middle daughter is more like I once was," Marcos said. "I was *impetuoso* until I met Mayra."

I got the Diplomatico and three glasses, noting that the bottle didn't look as if it'd been touched. "Let's drink to our daughters," I said, delaying their departure.

Marcos rose immediately and accepted a glass. "Mayra does not drink."

I poured a shot in each, then we clinked our glasses together, and tossed down the rum.

Marcos placed his glass on the table. "And now, *Capitan*, we must say *buenas noches*."

Mayra rose and said goodnight also. Then I was alone.

I sat down on the sofa and blew out a long breath, drawing the dogs' attention.

"I did my part," I told them. They both cocked their heads, as if expecting an explanation. "Never mind," I said, and went to bed.

CHAPTER THIRTY-FIVE

M att felt uneasy. He had ever since the helicopter left, carrying the body of the cap'n's friend home. The cap'n hadn't said much about it since, but Matt hurt for him. He knew the pain of loss and somehow sensed that his cap'n was no stranger to it, either.

Finally, he rose from his bunk and put his clothes back on. Coming from generations of hard-working Cornishmen who'd scraped out an existence on the bony peninsula at the southwest tip of England, his subconscious told him that if he were awake, he should be doing something productive.

His father, Maddern Brand, Senior, was a fisherman, as was his father before him. The men of the Brand family had earned a living pulling nets and lines from the sea for four generations. Arthek Brand, Matt's third great-grandfather, or granfer as is said in Cornwall, had been a carpenter. But before him, more fishermen.

He went up to the bridge to check on things. The two older men on Mr. Stockwell's team were there, both drinking coffee while looking out over the harbor.

"*Gorthugher da*, mates," Matt said.

"Don't you mean *nos da?*" Oswald said.

"Oye," Matt replied, nodding. "Technically it is night, but *nos da* is more of a partin' sayin'."

"Ah," Oswald said, grinning. "That makes sense."

"All's well, is it?"

"Nothing at all moving around on the water," Gerald said, then pointed up at the screens. "And the docks have been clear for over an hour. I guess all the bars closed up."

"The cap'n and 'is party get back in one piece?"

"He had a dustup with two tourists," Gerald replied. "The colonel had us post an extra man in the cockpit."

"Dustup?"

"A fight," Oswald added.

"Giss on!" Matt scoffed. "Cap'n McDermitt? Takin' on a coupla young emmets?"

"Apparently, he's more than a laid-back Florida Keys boat skipper," Gerald said. "From what the colonel told us about him, he's had quite a past."

"Was anyone 'urt?"

"According to Mr. Mosely," Oswald said, "the captain waded through both men like a tornado and left them unconscious and bleeding on the floor."

"Bleddy hell, you say!"

"Headbutted one," Oswald added. "And dropped the other with a single punch. All he got was a little scratch on his knuckles."

"Ye never bleddy know," Matt said, grinning. "A right proper brawler, the cap'n, yeah?"

"Apparently so," Oswald said. "But to look at him, you might guess he'd been in a scrape or two, a big guy like that."

Matt picked up the binoculars and scanned the inner harbor. "Ross and Axel I can see it 'appnin' to. But not the cap'n. 'E's as even-keeled a man as I ever met."

The digital night optics pierced the dark, turning night into day, and Matt could see into the shadows with little problem. Then he went over to the port side hatch and looked out the window, raising the binoculars to scan the outer harbor and approach. He slowly moved the glasses over the rooftops and trees, looking out into St. George's Bay and Grand Mal Bay, farther to the north.

A light caught his eye as he scanned past it. When he brought the binos to bear on the light, he could see that it was a cargo ship, lying at anchor.

"When did that ship arrive?" he asked, turning to Oswald.

The man checked his watch. "Less than an hour ago. No AIS, but that's normal for tramp cargo ships."

Matt trained the optics on the ship again. It was at least two miles away and barely visible above the taller rooftops in that direction.

"I think I'll be goin' topside for a better look, mind."

From what he saw of the ship, it looked a lot like the one that'd nearly swamped them in the tenders. Going out, Matt moved aft and went up the steps to the flybridge.

"Something troubling you?" Gerald asked, following him.

"Not sure," Matt replied. "But it's a fine night for lookin' around, innit?"

Standing on the highest deck of the ship and feeling exposed to the wind reminded Matt of going to sea with his father and granfer. As a boy, he'd wanted to be a fisherman like them. As a man, he'd seen some of the world beyond the rugged coast of the North Atlantic between Port Isaac and Port Quinn and wanted to see more.

Matt looked through the binoculars in the direction of the freighter. It wasn't a big ship, as cargo ships went, but it was bigger than *Ambrosia*. Aft the bow, lumber was stacked on the foredeck, behind that were a number of twenty-foot cargo containers, then the bridge and ship's house, more containers, and stacks of what looked like large bags, probably produce.

But it was what was going on at the stern that interested Matt. Several men were working to lower a lifeboat into the water. A lifeboat with two outboard engines.

"I think we'd best wake the cap'n, mate."

CHAPTER THIRTY-SIX

I t felt like I'd only been asleep for a couple of minutes when
the intercom beside my bed buzzed.

"Bridge to Cap'n McDermitt." It was Matt, and his voice was
tinged with urgency.

I sat up and looked at the clock before pushing the talk
button. "On my way."

"Up to the flybridge, Cap'n."

"Roger that."

I'd been asleep for a couple of hours. Had the surfer and
the bald black guy come looking for payback? I doubted that.
Stockwell's team would have made quick work of moving
them along. They wouldn't need me, except to read the report
about it the next day.

I dressed quickly, then went out into the passageway,
through the exterior hatch, and was up on the flybridge less
than two minutes after Matt's call.

I found him looking through a pair of night vision binos toward the northwest. Gerald, who was with him, also had a pair, trained to the west.

"What's going on?" I asked calmly.

Matt handed me his binos. "It's the *Canopus*," he said. "I'm certain of it. She's anchored two miles out at three 'undred five degrees."

I looked through the night vision binos, moving them until the little compass at the bottom found the bearing. An island freighter lay a couple of miles off Grand Mal Beach, its anchor light and a couple of deck lights the only ones on.

"The boat's gone out of sight," Gerald said. "Five men aboard. Headed toward shore, southwest of here."

"What boat?" I asked.

"A lifeboat," Matt said. "Like the one that attacked us. They just launched it from that ship."

"And you're sure it's *Canopus*?"

"Nothin' on the AIS," Matt said. "But that lifeboat 'ad two engines and the one you blew up 'ad three. Who puts more 'n one bleddy motor on a lifeboat?"

I turned to Gerald. "There were five men on the lifeboat?"

"Yes, sir," Gerald replied. "I couldn't make out much, but they looked like trouble. Five big men. Dark features. Maybe Hispanic."

"Wake the colonel," I said. "Rally the troops. If that is *Canopus*, they may think they have a score to settle."

I trained the binos in the direction Gerald had been

looking, while he got on a small UHF radio, identical to the ones all the security team carried. Though it didn't have the range of a VHF radio, ultra-high frequencies penetrated better and were more suited for communications inside a building or ship.

I couldn't see anything close to shore—trees and rooftops blocked everything.

Suddenly, a boat appeared. It had twin engines and there were five people aboard.

"The lifeboat's headed back out," I said.

There were five people on it, but not five big men. Two were obviously women. The women were struggling but being held tightly by two of the men, while a third man worked the tiller. I couldn't see either of the women clearly, as the two men had them wrapped in their arms and bent over. One of the men looked up, his long blond hair whipping over his face. It was the surfer guy from the bar.

"The five men you saw, Gerald?" I asked, still watching the boat as it sped away. "Was one black, with a shaved head and another, white with long blond hair?"

"No," Gerald replied. "They were all dark-haired. None were bald."

"Have a look now," I said, handing him the binos.

He scanned the water and found the boat. "They have two women!"

"The two men holding the women. Were they on the boat when you saw it?"

"No, Captain," Gerald replied. "Definitely not."

Stockwell appeared at the top of the stairs. "What is it?"

"*Canopus* has followed us," I said. "They sent a lifeboat ashore and now it's returning, along with two female captives *and* the two men who attacked us in the bar tonight. They left four men behind. A possible raiding party."

"How long has *Canopus* been here?"

I handed him my binos. "A little over an hour is what Gerald said."

Stockwell looked through the binos in the direction I'd been looking, then moved them on out toward Grand Mal Bay.

"Probably not a raiding party, then," he said. "More likely a scout team."

Stockwell removed his own UHF radio and spoke into it. "Walt, you and Duster move south, set up near the road and the dock, just past the marina office. Those are the only two ways in here. Oswald, continue past where they stop and set up a listening post between the road and dock."

"What are you thinking?" I asked, once the three security men confirmed their orders.

"Those two might not have been frat boys," Stockwell said. "Maybe they work for the *Canopus* crew and were pissed you intervened in their first kidnapping attempt, so they grabbed two others. Are all hands aboard?"

I moved over to the console and pushed the ship-wide intercom button. "All hands, all hands, this is the captain. Everyone is to report immediately to the mess deck. Yeoman

McLarin, give me a head count as soon as possible."

The seconds ticked by like hours as I watched the lifeboat speeding away toward the freighter in the distance.

"Cap'n," Matt said, "there's activity on *Canopus's* foredeck."

I moved my binos out toward the ship. A crane was lifting a container out of the forward hold. The stacks in front of it and behind it were taller than they'd been before. As I watched, the crane moved a container and stacked it precariously on the others. After a moment, the cables were moved back down into the hold.

"They're moving the containers," I said, "Making room at the bottom of the hold."

"Or providin' access to it," Matt said.

"McLarin to bridge," Val's voice came over the comm.

I pushed the button. "Is everyone aboard, Val?"

"No, sir," she replied. "We have three not back aboard yet; Jocko Landris, Emma Hall, and Nancy Graves. Al said that Jocko had taken them shopping earlier in the evening."

Nancy Graves was a new crew member. She'd been hired in the States and had been flown to Bimini just before we'd set sail a month before. She helped Emma in the mess hall.

"Thanks, Val. Tell the others to go back to their quarters."

A moment later, I heard the distinct sound of dog's claws on the steps. Woden appeared first, materializing out of the darkness like some kind of apparition. Then Finn joined him.

"I'm sorry, Captain," Val said, as she and the boys appeared at the top of the steps. "Alberto insisted."

I knelt in front of the two boys. "You can't be up here right now, Alberto. You know that."

"I was worried about you."

"I'm fine," I told him. "I just have some work to do. You need to go back down and get to bed."

"Okay," he said. "But Woden needs to stay here."

I didn't have time to argue with him. "That's fine. He'll be a great help. Now, you and Fernando take Finn back to our quarters."

I stood and faced Val. "Would you mind staying with them?"

"What's going on?" she asked.

I leaned in close and whispered. "*Canopus* is out there."

She nodded her understanding, then herded the two boys and my dog back down the steps. Finn was reluctant until I told him to watch Alberto.

When they were gone, I trained my binos on the ship again. The lifeboat was alongside, and the men were lifting the two women up to the deck. I still couldn't see either one and at two miles away, wouldn't be able to identify them for sure anyway. But it was obvious they were being put aboard against their will.

"We should call the authorities," I said, as the captives were shoved forward along the ship's deck toward the hold.

"Wait one," Matt said. "What's that they're liftin out of the 'old now?"

When I trained my binos on the forward part of the ship,

the crane was lifting what looked like a steel deck plate. The women were forced down a ladder and a few minutes later, the plate was lowered back into the hold.

"Oswald to base," came a voice over Stockwell's radio. "I have one of our crew members out here. He's hurrying back toward the ship."

"Is it Jocko Landris?" Stockwell asked.

"Yes, sir. He's not walking very steady. Looks like he took a beating."

"Have Duster escort him back here," Stockwell said. "Bring him to the flybridge."

I pulled my satellite phone from my pocket and used the internet to find the number for the Grenadian Coast Guard. When a man answered, I identified myself and explained what had happened and everything we'd seen. He replied that he would have a patrol boat go out to inspect.

"You'll probably find them in the bilge area," I told him. "Beneath a removable steel panel in the bottom of the hold."

A few minutes later, Duster helped Jocko up the steps to where we were watching *Canopus*.

"I'm sorry, Captain," Jocko said. "But there was two of 'em."

Jocko was a mess. His left eye was nearly swollen shut and he had a good deal of blood on his shirt. He was a big man, powerfully built, but as gentle as they came.

"A muscular black man with a shaved head?" I asked. "And a white guy with long blond hair?"

"Yes, sir. They jumped us down on Lagoon Road as we were

heading back. Maybe an hour ago. I don't know what happened to Emma and Nancy. They were gone when I woke up. Did they make it back okay?"

"They might have been kidnapped," I told him. "Go below and get cleaned up."

As we continued to watch helplessly, the crane started to move the containers back into place one by one.

"What the bleddy hell is keepin' 'em?" Matt whispered, as if to himself.

"There!" Stockwell said. "Headed out from the cruise ship pier."

"That's where the Port Authority is," Matt said. "The Grenadian Coast Guard keeps a patrol boat there, mind."

Sure enough, a small patrol boat headed away from shore just beyond Fort George. It turned to the north and increased speed with three armed men aboard. I hoped it would be enough.

Two quick clicks came from Travis's radio. He picked it up and spoke into it. "Hear that, Walt?"

"It was Oswald," Meachum said, his voice a whisper. "Three men on the road just passed his position. There's another on the dock."

"I'm close," Duster said. "I'll get the guy on the dock."

Two more clicks acknowledged him.

They were too far away to hear anything short of gunfire, but a moment later, Oswald's voice came over the radio. "One tango down, three in custody."

"Bring them here," Stockwell said. "I'll meet you on the work deck."

I started to go with him, but Travis stopped me. "Your job's here, Captain. I'll handle the interrogation. You need to find out what the authorities will do with the crew."

CHAPTER THIRTY-SEVEN

Matt and I went down to the command bridge. As we descended the steps, I heard the hydraulics activate and saw the large hatch open to the garage below the cockpit.

"Looks like the cops have taken the ship without incident," Gerald said as we entered the command bridge. "The ship's all lit up now."

Even without the binoculars, I could see *Canopus* out on the bay, the lights outlining the familiar shape of the ship that had paralleled our course several nights earlier. Raising the binos, I saw the Grenadian Police had the crew kneeling on the deck, covered with two rifles. Surfer and Baldy were with them.

Another patrol boat was approaching from the north. When it arrived, more police officers swarmed the ship.

"The crane's movin' again," Matt said.

As we watched, the crane began moving containers,

stacking them haphazardly on top of the lumber. Finally, the steel plate came up and then two officers escorted the two women out of the hold, leading them aft. With the decks awash in bright lights, I could see it was Emma and Nancy. They were helped into one of the patrol boats, where one of the cops stayed with them.

I punched the button for my quarters. "Bridge to Val."

"What's going on?" she asked immediately.

"Emma and Nancy are safe," I said. "Let Jocko know."

"I will," she said. "Thanks."

"And can you tell David to report to the bridge?"

"Right away," she replied.

I looked back into the op center. Chip McAllister was the only one there. I went back and tapped him on the shoulder. He jumped, then removed his headset.

"Captain McDermitt? Sorry, I'm working with one of the field ops and didn't hear you."

"That's okay, son. Finish up and then clear the op center."

"Clear the—"

"David's on his way up here and I need him to do something illegal."

Chip looked confused. "But just about everything we do is technically illegal, sir."

"This time, we'll be doing something illegal to a friendly government."

"Oh…uh…just give me a second to finish up with DJ."

"Tell him I said hi."

I returned to the bridge to wait for David. Chip left a few minutes later. When David arrived, I nodded toward the empty op center and he followed me.

"I need you to get into the Grenada Police Department's network," I said. "They'll be bringing in several men soon, and I want to know everything there is to know about them."

He glanced forward, to where Gerald and Matt continued to monitor the situation on *Canopus*. "What's going on?"

"Remember the boat that attacked our launches, just after Tank died? It came from that ship out there. I think they're part of the human trafficking operation we've been looking for."

"Do the authorities know that?"

"No," I replied. "And we don't want them to know. At least not yet."

"Okay," he said, moving toward his usual console on the port side. "Do you know where these men are being taken?"

"Not for certain," I replied. "One boat came from the Port Authority pier just across the inner harbor. The other came from up north somewhere."

"I'll get started," he said. "The main police station is near the Port Authority. That's probably where they'll take them."

I grabbed his elbow as he turned. "What I'm asking you to do, hack into a friendly government's computer, is not just illegal, it could get the ship and crew expelled from the country. Permanently."

"I understand," he said. "No tracks."

I returned to the bridge to watch the activity on *Canopus*. A third, larger boat was moving toward the ship and the first one with our crew aboard was about to leave.

The ship's phone rang on the bulkhead. I picked it up. "*Research Vessel Ambrosia.*"

"Is dis de cap'n?" a man with an island accent asked.

"Yes, this is Captain McDermitt."

"Dis is Inspector Whyte. Do you remember me?"

The customs inspector?

"Hello, Claude. Yes, what can I do for you?"

"I am on my way out to a ship anchored in St. George's Bay, Jesse. I am told you provided de tip about what was happening out dere."

"The two women being kidnapped are part of my crew," I said.

"I was told dat, as well," Claude said. "I just wasn't aware dat you knew who dey were."

"I wasn't until I saw the police removing them from the ship."

"*Ambrosia* will still be here for a day or two?"

"Yes," I replied.

"Den I will have de police bring your crew to your ship," he said. "De officer I spoke wit said dey appear to be unhurt. I will come by in de morning to question dem."

"Thank you, Claude."

We ended the call and I looked toward *Canopus* again. The patrol boat with Emma and Nancy aboard was already headed our way.

I pushed the button for the intercom to the equipment area below the cockpit. "Bridge to security."

"Stockwell," came the quick reply.

"The police are bringing Emma and Nancy straight here, Travis."

"Roger that," he said. "We already closed the garage door. I'll move our guests to the engine room."

"Keep the noise down," I said with a grin. "They'll be here in less than five minutes. I'll come down when they're gone."

I turned to Matt. "Head down to meet the police boat. I'll join you in a minute."

He left the binos on the nav desk and exited the bridge. I picked them up and studied the ship for a moment, then turned to go down and join him. I paused by the hatch and looked back at David.

"I'm in," he said. "So far only preliminary dispatch reports on the event have been submitted."

I nodded and started to open the hatch but paused. "Just out of curiosity. Would it be possible for a report to be changed without anyone knowing it?"

He looked at me questioningly. "An arrest report? Something like that?"

"Yeah. Is it possible?"

"I can change it or make it all disappear permanently from their files," he stated. "And get out without anyone knowing. It would be like they'd never been there."

I nodded and left the bridge to join Matt. A couple of minutes later, the patrol boat came alongside and turned around, maneuvering stern toward the dock beside the work deck.

We helped Emma and Nancy over the boat's low gunwale and onto the work platform.

"Are you all right?" I asked them both.

"Yes," Emma said. "It all happened so fast. Has Jocko been found?"

"He's safe aboard," I said. "Probably on the mess deck."

"They beat him terribly," Nancy added. "No telling what would have happened to us if the police hadn't gotten there in time."

"Go find Jocko," I said. "He could use a little good news."

When they left, one of the officers leaned against the gunwale. "I heard de tip about de attempted kidnapping came from you."

"Lucky I was on the flybridge, stargazing," I lied.

"Did you happen to see another boat leave de ship? Dere are davits for three lifeboats and only two are dere. Questioning de crew, we found dat de captain was not aboard."

"No," I replied, knowing they'd never find the third boat. "I saw the boat leave the ship with three men aboard and a little while later, it returned with the same three men and two of my crew members. I didn't know it was Emma and Nancy at the time but could easily tell they were being taken against their will. That's why I called you guys."

"Tank you, Captain," he said. "Inspector Whyte will be in touch tomorrow."

The driver put the small patrol boat into gear, and it idled away,

"That's not exactly 'ow it 'appened, Cap'n," Matt said. "Wasson?"

For a long time, I'd wondered why Jack Armstrong wanted me to command *Ambrosia*, and suddenly it became quite clear. Nils Hansen had been a great skipper. He knew the sea better than most and ran his ship in the traditional way. But he was a civilian and likely lacked tactical skills and battle instincts. Which was probably why Jack had insisted that his head of security be stationed aboard *Ambrosia*, rather than at the company's headquarters in New York or the logistics command center in Bimini.

"We're about to commit a few crimes, Matt."

CHAPTER THIRTY-EIGHT

I sent Matt back up to the bridge, telling him I'd join him there as soon as I checked on things with Stockwell. Rather than open the garage door again, where there was a watertight access hatch to the engine room, I went up to the salon and down the spiral stairs to the crew's deck and then down to the engine room.

One man lay prone on the deck, not moving. Woden sniffed at him a second then followed me.

"Sorry, Captain, that one's dead," Duster said. "He came at me with a knife and left me no choice."

I didn't care. These men had chosen their path in life. Few ever went that route who didn't end up meeting a violent end. I'd been the instrument to that end a few times in the past and likely would be again.

The other three men were seated on the floor, hands bound behind them. Each had busted lips or open cuts on their faces, with blood on their shirts.

"Which one of you is Mauricio Gonzales?" I asked.

"Fuck you!" the man on the left said.

I kicked him in the groin and he rolled on his side, curling into a fetal position, moaning loudly.

In my experience, the first to speak was never the one you sought. They spoke out of allegiance to the one you wanted. That left two.

"The police have your ship," I said to the remaining two men. "The women you took are back aboard my ship. So, I'll ask one more time. Which one of you is the captain?"

"He is," the man in the middle said, nodding toward the other.

"He's lying!" the last man exclaimed. "He is captain!"

I studied the two men carefully. Then, without warning, I pulled my Sig from under my shirt and pointed it at the man I'd kicked.

I shot him in the head, and he stopped his whining.

Putting the barrel against the last man's head, I bent closer, looking into his eyes. "*You* are the captain of *Canopus*."

He nodded.

"I would have gotten them to talk," Travis said. "Eventually."

I turned toward Oswald. "Move the other three over by the garage access hatch."

Duster and Walt dragged the two dead men and Oswald forced the third man to follow.

"Who do you work for?" I snarled at Gonzales.

"I don't know what you mean," he replied in broken English.

"You kidnap innocent people, mostly women and girls. Who do you take them to?"

"I have never—"

The back of Stockwell's hand knocked the rest of the man's words right out of his mouth.

"Not cooperating means you'll end up like those two men back there," I said. "If you want to live to see dawn, you'll tell me everything I want to know."

"Who are you people?" Mauricio asked with a gasp.

Travis grabbed him by the shirt front and lifted him to his knees, bending to sneer in his face. "I'm your worst damned nightmare," he growled menacingly. "Your thugs shot me the other day. I don't like being shot." Then, he nodded toward me. "And he's the devil himself. He dispatched your men straight to hell for shooting me. You picked the wrong damned boat to mess with."

Gonzales looked from Travis to me, then back at him. "They will find me and kill me if I talk."

"Maybe they will," I said. "At some point in the future. But I will kill you right here, right now, if you don't talk. Then I'll go to bed and sleep soundly."

He didn't say anything.

"Woden, make him talk," I ordered.

The big dog lumbered toward the man, his lips pulled back

in a menacing snarl, as a low rumble eliminated from deep in his chest. "*Cartel de los Soles!*"

"*Bleib stehen,*" I ordered, and Woden stopped his advance.

"Cartel of the Suns?" Travis asked.

He nodded.

Travis turned toward me. "That organization is run by top-level officials and high-ranking officers in Venezuela's military."

I nodded, then bent down to Gonzales. "Where do you take them?"

"To a man in Puerto Borburata," he said.

Once the dam is opened, most will continue talking.

"What's his name?" I demanded.

"What does it matter?" Gonzales pleaded. "You cannot possibly take on *Los Soles.*"

"Then telling me who you took your captives to shouldn't make any difference," I said. "What's his name?"

He was silent for a moment, then his shoulders slumped. "I only know him as Juan. He puts the cargo into vans and leaves the port."

Cargo? To this man, the people he kidnapped and sold into slavery were nothing but a commodity—cargo to be transported to market.

Moving them by van didn't make sense. Sure, there were a lot of nasty characters in South America—murder and rape are considered a pastime in some of the more lawless regions. But they just took what they wanted; they didn't have to buy slaves. And many of the people reported captured had been grown men, which were far easier to force into labor locally.

"Where does Juan take the captives?" I asked.

"I do not know," Gonzales replied, fear evident in his eyes.

I brought the Sig up and pointed the barrel at his groin. "I can shoot you many times without killing you."

"I swear it!" he shouted. "There are rumors of a ghost ship—a ship that cannot be seen on the ocean. That is all I know."

"Are you sure that's all you know?"

He looked over at Travis, who was now leaning against the bulkhead, examining his fingernails.

"Don't look at me for help," Travis said. "I warned you that he was the devil."

"Juan sometimes keeps a girl for himself," Gonzales said. "He told me one time that the sultans in Damascus should not get all the fun."

"When was the last time you took people to Juan?"

"On Monday," he replied. "Nine days ago."

I looked over at Travis and he nodded aft. We went back to where Oswald and the others waited with the one remaining prisoner, who was now gagged.

"I think he's telling the truth," Travis said. "He said it himself, he's just a freight hauler. All we have to do is check ships bound for Syria that left Puerto Borburata nine days ago. It couldn't have crossed the Atlantic and run the length of the Med in that time."

"What do we do with these?"

He shrugged. "Leave that to me. I overheard you outside, talking to the policeman on the boat. You know they're going to continue to search for the captain."

I grinned at him. "I've got an idea about that."

I went up to the op center. David glanced at me as I entered.

"They're being booked," he said, pointing to the screen. "Half have already been processed."

I looked at several mug shots on his monitor, each with a name below. One was the surfer guy from the bar, a man named Brad Thomas.

"Make it so that blond guy is the captain of *Canopus*. When a black man with a shaved head gets booked, make him the first mate."

"What if they check licensing?"

"It wouldn't be the first time someone without a license commanded a ship. Besides, who are they going to believe?" I pointed to Thomas's picture. "That guy or their own report?"

EPILOGUE

*A*mbrosia lay against the dock at the Armstrong shipyard in Bimini. Most of the crew had been given a week off, but Heitor and Ricardo, plus a handful of others, had stayed aboard, including the rest of the Santiago family.

I was planning to fly *Island Hopper* back to the Keys the following morning with Savannah and Alberto. But first, Jack wanted to see me.

"He didn't say what he wanted?" Savannah asked.

"Just that he had something to show me over at the dry dock."

"Well, you'd better get moving," she said. "You don't keep a man like Jack Armstrong waiting. I'll get everything packed and have Jocko take it over to the hangar."

As I walked down the gangway, Matt and Val were coming toward me on the dock.

"I thought the two of you were going down to Freeport," I

said.

"The bleddy mailboat won't be 'ere until morn," Matt replied.

"So, we're just going to hang out with Giselle and Ricardo," Val added. "We could fly Bahamas Air, but we're in no hurry."

"Any word yet on that container ship, *Canadian Gold*?" Matt asked.

We'd pulled up shipping records and found that only one ship left Puerto Borburata bound for Syria during that whole week. It had made one stop, in Miami, where, overnight, cocaine busts on the streets were on the rise. We knew we'd found the right ship.

"*Canadian Gold* was raided yesterday by UN forces," I replied. "Just as it docked in Latakia, Syria. They had an underground facility there to unload some sort of container which was attached to the belly of the ship."

"Did they say how many people were in it?" Val asked.

"Thirty-seven victims were rescued," I replied. "Mostly from Guyana and Brazil, but there were also four American women. And there were also two bodies."

Matt shuddered. "I wonder 'ow many times she took 'em poor people across the ocean."

"Early interrogations revealed who Gonzales's contact was," I said. "A man named Juan Espinoza, a colonel in the Venezuelan Army. An American spec-ops team, flown in by none other than Bud Ferguson, raided Espinoza's compound."

"Giss on!" Matt exclaimed. "Once a birdwatcher, always a

birdwatcher. Ain't that what I said?"

"They found a young Guyanese girl in the basement of his house, barely alive," I said. "Along with a mass grave behind the house. They're still counting the bodies of the girls he took there to torture and kill."

"Sick pervert," Val said. "There's a special place in hell for men like him."

"I have to go meet Jack," I said. "But I'll see you again before we take off in the morning."

"Aight," Matt said, and the two headed up the gangway.

When I got to the dry dock, I could see that it was empty. Well, not entirely empty. Workers were busy in many places, moving things around. A couple of men were busy in the middle, welding two giant aluminum plates to a crossmember.

"Ah, there you are," Jack said, stepping out of the main office. "Right on time. Come in, come in."

"What's going on in the dry dock?" I asked, following him into the office.

"I'll show you in just a moment," he replied.

There was another man in the office, wearing a coat and tie. He had a lined face and wore a mustache with the ends waxed to extend straight out.

"Jesse, I'd like you to meet William Marshal. Will, this is Captain Jesse McDermitt."

I shook hands with the man, noting a strong grip.

"Pleased to meet you, Captain. Jack's told me a lot about

you."

"Will is a naval architect," Jack said. "We're building a new vessel."

"What kind of new vessel?" I asked.

"Purely research," Will said with a wink. "She'll be three hundred feet and have a full-time crew of forty, with four laboratories, and room for twenty visiting scientists and engineers."

"Was that the keel being laid?" I asked, jerking a thumb toward the dry dock.

"Yes," Jack said. "That's one of the reasons I wanted to see you before you left."

"All I do is drive boats," I said. "I don't know much at all about building them."

"We'll get to that part later," he said. "And before we go any further, I just wanted to say thank you. Through your efforts and that of *Ambrosia's* crew, a huge portion of *Cartel de los Soles* has been dismantled, putting a massive hit in their pocketbook."

"Just doing our job," I said.

"Nevertheless, several dozen people owe you their lives. DJ sent word that the man who'd contacted him weeks ago about the abduction of his mother, sisters, brother, and fiancée, contacted him again, and they have all been reunited."

"What's this new ship going to be called?" I asked, glancing out the window.

"We don't have a name yet," Will said.

"That's something I'd like your input on," Jack added. "I want you in command of this new ship when it launches next year."

"Me?"

"Yes, you. As Will said, it will be a full-blown research vessel, but it will also fill other needs, just as *Ambrosia* does today."

I nodded my head in understanding. "I see. And it will be built in a year?"

"This shipyard is about to be overrun," Jack said. "Once the keel is laid, dozens of shipwrights will be flown in from all over the world. They'll be working around the clock to launch before the end of 2022."

"Do you have a keepsake coin?" Will asked.

"Huh?"

"In the old sailing days, the mast was stepped on coins, usually provided by the ship owner and captain."

"Yes," I said. "I know of the tradition of stepping the mast."

Jack reached into his pocket, then slapped his hand on the table, revealing a challenge coin with the seal of the President of the United States.

"I understand that you once took the man who gave me this fishing."

How did he know that? It happened fifteen years ago.

"I have one just like it," I said. "Given to me by that same man."

"Call your wife," Jack said. "Have her and Alberto bring

your coin to be put with mine."

I did. It took Savannah a minute to find it, but then she and Alberto hurried down to the dry dock.

A high-lift was in position and the five of us stepped onto its platform. A moment later, we were at the bottom of the dry dock, thirty feet below sea level. Giant steel doors at one end held back the sea. But the concrete deck was still wet in places.

Will led the way to the middle of the work area. Several men stood next to a large aluminum cross member. The other one, ten feet from it, had already been welded to two large aluminum panels. I could see that the hull would be an inch thick in this spot.

"What's going on, Dad?" Alberto asked, looking up at the burly workers.

"This ship won't have a mast, son," Will said. "But the tradition we're following is still important today. So, the coins will be placed under the mounts that will hold the power plant. In the early Roman days, the coins placed under the mast were payment to Charon, who was the ferryman to Hades in Roman mythology. The Romans believed the money would allow the ship to cross the River Styx into the afterlife, should an unfortunate event take place."

Jack pointed to the hull plates where the cross brace was going to be welded. "See the two holes cut into the aluminum?"

Moving closer, I could see them, Two round depressions, no deeper than the thickness of the coin in my hand, and exactly the same size.

"Here," I said, handing my coin to Alberto. "You place it in the hole."

Jack bent and put his coin in place, turning the red, white, and blue presidential shield so that the top was facing forward. Alberto put my coin in place, and I bent down and adjusted it.

I felt something when I touched the cold aluminum plate. Almost like a spark, as if the plate warmed to my touch, becoming a smoldering ember, on the verge of catching fire.

One of the workers signaled the crane operator and the cross member was lifted a few inches. They guided it into place, aligning the edges with lines scribed in the two plates. Welders hit it with several spot welds, and it was done.

When the high-lift put us back above sea level, I kissed Savannah and told her I'd be along shortly.

Then I turned and looked at Jack. "Those engine mounts were only ten feet apart. What's this ship going to have for power?"

We arrived in Marathon the next morning before noon and I put the *Hopper* down just off the beach behind the Rusty Anchor. Rusty was expecting us and there were several people with him at the boat ramp to watch the *Hopper* waddle up out of the water.

Later, as Rusty, his wife Sidney, and Jimmy Saunders all sat

371

with me over a couple of beers on the back deck, he asked about Tank's funeral arrangements.

"He wanted to be cremated," I said. "The service will be this Saturday, up on Grassy Key."

"At their home?" Sid asked.

"It's what Tank wanted," I replied.

"You're doing the eulogy?" Rusty asked.

"Chyrel said that was another thing he wanted," I replied.

Though it'd been over a week since he'd passed peacefully while sitting on the beach in Brazil, it wasn't easy to accept the fact that he was gone.

"How's she doing?" Rusty asked.

"Day to day, I guess. She's staying busy with work. She decided not to put the house up for sale."

"Huh? That's a lot of house for one person."

"She's not going to be alone for long, man," Jimmy said. "She's going to open it up to some of the kids from the Lodge."

The Alex DuBois McDermitt Fly-Fishing Lodge on Grassy Key had been in business for over a decade now. Fly fishermen from all over the world came there to spend time out on the water. They paid exorbitant fees, knowing that the Lodge was a place for troubled kids from all over South Florida and the Keys, many of them fosters.

They weren't ordinary fly-fishing aficionados, but people of wealth and power. I'd met a few and some had come from humble or tragic beginnings themselves. The kids sent there learned fly-fishing from some of the best guides in the Middle

Keys, and also got to talk to successful people who'd started in similar situations in a much more relaxed atmosphere—sitting in a boat, rod in hand. It was sort of an Outward Bound kind of school, which my late wife had envisioned before she was killed. Locally, it was just called the Lodge, and Jimmy was one of the guides.

"Tank woulda loved that idea," Rusty said. "And with the Lodge doing so well, I hear it's been sorta crowded there."

Jimmy nodded. "Yeah, man. And the housing isn't exactly set up like a co-ed dorm."

"They've made do," I said. "But going forward, any girls enrolled there will be staying with Chyrel."

"That's so sweet of her," Sid said. "Do they have many girls, though?"

"Sometimes," Jimmy replied. "But now we might get more. Chyrel can be a good influencer."

"So, what's this you said about Armstrong building a new boat?" Rusty asked.

I went on to tell them about Jack's plan to build a new research vessel, bigger and more advanced than *Ambrosia*.

"Three hundred feet?" he asked shaking his head. "You gonna be able to drive it without hitting something?"

"He doesn't drive it," Alberto said, coming out the door with Savannah and the dogs. "The helmsman does."

"Well, I hope you got a real good helmsman," Rusty said with a chuckle.

"Mr. Axel's the best," Alberto replied.

"That big a boat's gonna suck up a lot of fuel, dude," Jimmy commented. "Will it have turbines like *Ambrosia*, that'll melt your credit card, or just regular diesel power?"

"Neither," I replied, taking a long pull from my bottle. "It'll have a near-zero carbon footprint."

Rusty's eyes widened. "A three-hundred-foot sailing vessel?"

I grinned and shook my head.

"*Phoenix* will be powered by a miniature nuclear reactor producing fifty megawatts of power."

THE END

But really just a pause. Jesse has a whole new adventure ahead of him in the next book in the series, All Ahead Full.

AFTERWORD

This book was huge fun to write. Bringing in new characters to an existing storyline isn't always easy. And I thought surrounding Jesse with so many new characters would be doubly so. But Matt, Val, Marcos, Mayra, and the others made it simple, mixing new crew with what already existed before Jesse took command. In a way, they were all still getting to know one another and for Stockwell's part, getting to know the new role and relationship. I think Savannah made that quite clear on the deck of the tender.

Not to worry, we're not abandoning our friends back in the Keys. *Ambrosia* is a big yacht and visitors will come and go, and Jesse will go home often. And next year, *Phoenix* will be even bigger. Plenty of room for visiting guests.

Oh, and while I'm on the subject of *Ambrosia*, and because like many of you, I tend to doubt some of the things I read, here's the skinny on this amazing yacht. *Ambrosia* is sort of real. She's based on a Millennium Yachts 149 called *The World Is Not Enough*, which reached seventy knots during sea trials. I made *Ambrosia* fifty feet longer and not quite as fast. Check out *The World Is Not Enough* on YouTube.

And a nuclear powered private research vessel, you scoff? While you're over there on YouTube (which I can get lost in for days), have a look at *Earth 300*, a 300-meter superyacht/research vessel, currently being designed. None other than Bill Gates is involved in this project through a company he's chairman of the board, called TerraPower. They intend to build miniature molten salt nuclear reactors that are hermetically sealed and transportable, to be used to provide electricity to small, remote communities. And ships.

As I write these closing remarks, it is now the first day of summer, Monday, June 21, and still almost two months before this book will be published. Unlike many people, I love the summer heat. The heavy, humid, oppressive air that drives most people indoors is what I relish. If there ever is an apocalyptic, long-term interruption in the power grid, I don't think half the population will survive the first week.

I'd been anticipating writing this book for a long time. I had a vague idea what it would be about more than a year ago, when I was still debating writing a twenty-first novel in the Jesse series and tying the number with John D. MacDonald's twenty-one Travis McGee books. So, the storyline literally fell off my fingertips. By the fourth week, I was more than a week ahead of schedule. By the eighth week, I was almost two weeks ahead, and by the end of the eleventh week of writing, I'd already passed the goal I set for all my books of 65,000 words. But the story wasn't finished. When the thirteenth and final week started, I was 10,000 words over my goal, the equivalent of two full weeks of writing. I hope all y'all enjoyed reading it as much as I did writing it.

As always, I owe a great deal of thanks to my family for their encouragement, as well as an apology for all the hours I spent at the Down Island Press office. Our youngest daughter, Jordan, manages the Down Island Press "Ship's Store" online, where you can buy my books directly, either in paperback or ebook format, as well as T-shirts, coffee mugs, tote bags, and many other items relating to my books. She is also the producer of my monthly livestream on YouTube, Talk Write Podcast, where my audiobook narrator, Nick Sullivan and I discuss writing and narrating with author and narrator guests. It streams live at 6:30 PM Eastern, on the first Monday of every month. If you're interested in a behind-the-scenes look, go to the link below and subscribe, then click the Notification bell to be updated when we go live.

www.gaspars-revenge.com
www.youtube.com/waynestinnett

"Beta readers" isn't quite the right term for the first group of people who see my manuscripts. They're definitely the A-Team. Some are friends from my days at Eau Gallie High

School, a few are experts in fields that are covered in my books, some are prior military, and some are lawyers, doctors, and law enforcement officers. All are very important in bringing the best, most accurate portrayal to you, the reader.

On this project, I had help from Kim DeWitt, Debbie Kocol, Glenn Hibbert, Rick Iossi, Dana Vihlen, Katy McKnight, Alan Fader, Jason Hebert, Drew Mutch, Tom Crisp, John Trainer, Chuck Höfbauer, David Parsons, and Deg Priest. Without their help and advice, this story wouldn't have been nearly as accurate and entertaining as I hope you found it.

I do want to point out one thing though, that several of the above folks mentioned to me. There are no airplane hangars nor a large shipyard on North Bimini; just an old, abandoned seaplane base. But given the wealth and contacts that Jack Armstrong has, one could be built there in a matter of months. So, I've taken a little artistic license with that, just as I have with the Rusty Anchor Bar and Grill. Neither place exists in reality.

A special thanks to author Chelle Bliss for allowing me to include a mention of her latest novel, *Singe*, in a bedroom scene. At first, I had Savannah reading *Fifty Shades of Grey*, but a couple of my beta readers pointed out that she wouldn't likely be reading that, and she couldn't possibly "show" Jesse what it was about without having whips and chains.

Thanks also, to my friend and editor, Marsha Zinberg, for all the help in turning my sometimes-rambling thoughts into a story worthy of you, the reader. She was followed by Donna

Rich, who has had the final critical eye on all my works since *Fallen Out*. And many thanks to my good friend and narrator, Nick Sullivan, who is also the co-host of my monthly livestream on YouTube, the Talk Write Podcast.

Finally, I owe a great deal of thanks to Samantha Williams, Ashley Lobocki, and the whole team at Aurora Publicity. Aurora takes care of all my advertising, formatting, cover designs, and provides technical support. Last year, Samantha mentioned that she would one day like to own a small publishing house to help authors realize their dreams, which has also been a vision of mine, as well as the next step in the evolution of my helping other storytellers become published authors. As of August 1, our goals have started to become a reality. Samantha is now the Chief Operating Officer and part owner of Down Island Press, the company I founded seven years ago to publish my own books. As of this writing, the announcement hasn't even been made public, and I have no idea if we'll have accepted any submissions by the time you read this, but I have a strong feeling that we will have.

Lastly, I want to again thank all of you readers. Some of you have stuck with me from the start. As I write this, that was eight years ago last week. You've provided feedback, ideas, and even guidance about what you like and dislike. I hope I've listened.

If you'd like to receive my newsletter, please sign up on my website.

WWW.WAYNESTINNETT.COM.

Once a month, I'll bring you insights into my private life and writing habits, with updates on what I'm working on, special deals I hear about, and new books by other authors that I'm reading.

The Charity Styles Caribbean Thriller Series

Merciless Charity	*Enduring Charity*
Ruthless Charity	*Vigilant Charity*
Reckless Charity	*Lost Charity*

The Jesse McDermitt Caribbean Adventure Series

Fallen Out	*Rising Fury*
Fallen Palm	*Rising Force*
Fallen Hunter	*Rising Charity*
Fallen Pride	*Rising Water*
Fallen Mangrove	*Rising Spirit*
Fallen King	*Rising Thunder*
Fallen Honor	*Rising Warrior*
Fallen Tide	*Rising Moon*
Fallen Angel	*Rising Tide*
Fallen Hero	*Steady As She Goes*
Rising Storm	*All Ahead Full*

THE GASPAR'S REVENGE SHIP'S STORE IS OPEN.

There, you can purchase all kinds of swag related to my books. You can find it at

WWW.GASPARS-REVENGE.COM

Made in the USA
Las Vegas, NV
06 August 2023

75744827R00214